Bronze
and
Sunflower

Cao Wenxuan

translated from the Chinese by Helen Wang

illustrated by Meilo So

CANDLEWICK PRESS

This book received financial assistance from English PEN's PEN Translates program, supported by Arts Council England. English PEN exists to promote literature and our understanding of it, to uphold writers' freedoms around the world, to campaign against the persecution and imprisonment of writers for stating their views, and to promote the friendly cooperation of writers and the free exchange of ideas.

This is a work of fiction. Names, characters, places, and incidents are either products of the author's imagination or, if real, are used fictitiously.

Published by arrangement with Phoenix Juvenile and Children's Publishing Ltd. First published in English by Walker Books UK Ltd.

First U.S. paperback edition 2019

Library of Congress Catalog Card Number 2017931375
ISBN 978-0-7636-8816-5 (hardcover)
ISBN 978-1-5362-0637-1 (paperback)

19 20 21 22 23 24 BVG 10 9 8 7 6 5 4 3 2 1

Printed in Berryville, VA, U.S.A.

This book was typeset in Berkeley Oldstyle.
The illustrations were done in watercolor.

Candlewick Press
99 Dover Street
Somerville, Massachusetts 02144

visit us at www.candlewick.com

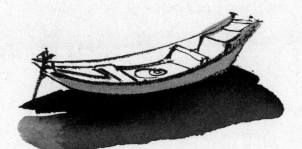

A Little Wooden Boat

Sunflower was on her way to the river. The rainy season was over, and the sky, which had hung so low and so dark, had lifted. Now it was big and bright, and the sun, which hadn't been seen for days, seeped across it like fresh water.

Everything was wet: the grass, the flowers, the windmills, the buildings, the water buffaloes, the birds, the air. Soon Sunflower was drenched too. Her hair clung to her scalp, making her look thinner than usual. But her little face, which was naturally pale, was full of life.

Along the path, beads of water hung from the grass. Soon her trouser legs were soaked through. The path was muddy, and once her shoes had gotten stuck a few times, she took them off, held one in each hand, and walked barefoot through the cool slime. As she passed under a maple tree, a gentle breeze blew, shaking off droplets of water. A few of them ran down her neck. Sunflower flinched, hunching her shoulders instinctively, and looked up. The branches above were covered in glistening leaves, washed clean by the many days of rain.

She could hear the river calling her, the sound of flowing water, and she ran toward it. She went to the river almost every day, because on the other side there was a village. A village with a lovely name: Damaidi, which means "the barley lands."

On this side of the river, there were no other children but Sunflower. She was alone, like a solitary bird in a vast blue sky with nothing for company but the sound of its own beating wings. In a sky that stretches on forever, broken occasionally by a cloud or two, but otherwise huge and unblemished, like a perfect turquoise gemstone. At moments of extreme loneliness, the bird cries out, but its cry only makes the sky seem even emptier.

On this side of the river, the reeds spread endlessly and peacefully as far as the eye could see, as they had for centuries. That spring a group of egrets, startled from their nests, had taken flight with a great commotion. They had circled above the reeds, then flown over to Damaidi, croaking noisily as though eager to share the news of their misfortune. They didn't come back; their old home in the reed marsh was now full of people. Unfamiliar people, quite different from the villagers of Damaidi.

These were city people, and they had come to build houses, to transform the wilderness, to plant crops and dig fishponds. They sang city people's songs, in the city people's way. Their singing was loud and vigorous, unlike anything the villagers had heard before.

A few months later, seven or eight rows of brick houses with red roofs arose out of the reeds. Soon after that, a very tall flagpole was put up, and early one morning, a red flag appeared in the sky, where it flickered like a ball of fire above the reeds.

The city people were like a flock of birds that had flown in. They looked at the villagers with curiosity, and the villagers looked back in the same way. They felt connected, yet at the same time utterly unconnected. As though they were a different species.

The city people did their own thing. They had their own language, their own activities, and their own ways of doing things. In the daytime they worked, and in the evenings they held meetings. Deep into the night, the villagers could see their lights shining in the distance, twinkling like fishermen's lights on the river, full of mystery.

The city people lived in a world of their own. The people of Damaidi soon came to know the name of this "world": the May Seventh Cadre School, which they then shortened to "the Cadre School."

"Your ducks swam over to the Cadre School."

"Your buffalo ate the Cadre School's crops, so they're keeping it."

"The fish in the Cadre School fishpond already weigh a full *jin*." This was about a pound.

"This evening they're showing a film at the Cadre School."

And so on.

This was not the only May Seventh Cadre School in the area. There were many more spread across the reed lands. The people who lived in them came from several big cities, some very far away. And they didn't all work in offices; there were writers and artists too. They had come to do physical labor.

The villagers had a vague idea of what Cadre Schools were, but they weren't sufficiently interested to try to find out more. These people didn't seem to cause any trouble—in fact, they made life more interesting. When they occasionally came over to Damaidi for a stroll, the village children would run after them. They'd stop and stare, or follow them, darting behind a tree or a haystack if the Cadre School people looked back and smiled. The Cadre School people thought the village children enchanting and beckoned them to come closer. The braver ones would step forward, and the Cadre School people would reach out and pat their heads. Sometimes they'd pull candy from their pockets. The children ate the city candy and treasured the pretty wrappers, smoothing them out and tucking them between the pages of their schoolbooks. The

Cadre School people sometimes bought things in Damaidi to take back with them: melons, vegetables, duck eggs.

The villagers also took walks on the other side of the river. They liked to see how the Cadre School people farmed fish. Damaidi was surrounded by water, and where there was water there were fish — it had never occurred to the villagers to try to control them. But these educated city people knew what they were doing. They gave the fish injections that made them leap with excitement, the males and females weaving around one another, whipping up waves. Then they waited for the fish to calm down and caught them in nets. The females were now swollen with roe. Gently, the Cadre School people stroked their sides, massaging their bulging bellies. The fish seemed to enjoy this, and, gently, the eggs were squeezed out. They splashed into a big bucket and swirled about. The countless shiny white dots soon became countless shiny black dots, and after a few days, the black dots became the tails of tiny fish. The villagers, young and old, stared in wonder: the Cadre School people could perform magic!

There was another reason the village children were curious about the Cadre School. There was a little girl there: a city girl who had a country girl's name.

Sunflower was a quiet, gentle little girl who had been brought up to be neat and tidy. She had come with her father to the Cadre School. Her mother had died of an illness two years earlier. Both of her parents had been only children, so her father was her only relative. Wherever he went, he took her with him. When he was sent to the Cadre School, Sunflower came too. She was only seven.

They had arrived in the early summer, and at first Sunflower had found everything new and exciting. The reed lands were enormous; they seemed to go on forever. She was too small to see very far, so she held out her arms for her father to pick her up.

"Can you see where they end?" he asked, holding her up high.

The young reed leaves pointed up at the sky like swords, and as they swayed in the reed marsh, they reminded Sunflower of the ocean she had seen with her father. Here, in front of her, was another vast ocean, rippling with green waves and giving out a fresh fragrance. She recognized the smell from the *zongzi*, the parcels of sticky rice wrapped in reed leaves that she had eaten in the city. But here it was more intense, heavy with moisture. It enveloped her. She sniffed the air.

"Is there an end?" her father asked. She shook her head.

A sudden gust of wind turned the reed marsh into a battlefield. The long swords slashed the air. A group of frightened waterbirds rose up and took to the sky. Sunflower wrapped her arms around her father's neck. She was drawn to the reed marsh, but it filled her with a mysterious terror.

After that, she didn't stray from her father's side, afraid that the marsh would swallow her up, especially on windy days when turbulent waves of reeds surged one way and then the other. And when they surged toward the Cadre School, she would grab her father's hand or a corner of his jacket, her dark eyes filled with worry.

Her father had come here to work; he couldn't be with her all the time. He was part of a team whose job it was to cut down the reeds and transform the marshes into crop fields and fishponds. In the dawn haze, when the wake-up call rang through the reed lands, Sunflower would still be asleep. Her father knew that when she woke and saw that he was gone, she'd be scared and would cry. But he couldn't bring himself to wake her from her dreams. With hands that were rough and hard from physical labor, he would stroke her soft, warm cheeks, then pick up his tools with a sigh and close the door quietly behind him; and in the pale mist of early morning, he would walk with all the others to the work site. He would think about her all day long. By the time they packed up their tools in the evening, moonlight would be spilling over the marshes.

Sunflower would spend the whole day by herself. She would go to the fishpond to watch the fish, to the kitchens to see the cooks making food, and then wander from one row of buildings to the next. Most of the doors were locked, but every now and then one would be open — perhaps because someone was ill or because they were assigned to work at the Cadre School itself. She would walk up to the open door and peer inside. Sometimes a frail but friendly voice would call out, "Come in, Sunflower!"

But she would shake her head and stand for a while in the doorway before running off in another direction. She preferred to talk to a golden chrysanthemum flower, to a crow perched on a branch, to pretty ladybugs on a leaf.

In the evenings, in the dusky lamplight, her father's heart would fill with sadness. Often, after eating with Sunflower, he would have to leave her again to go to a meeting. He was always going to meetings. Sunflower couldn't understand why, after a full day's work, he had to go out again. She'd already spent the whole day by herself. She wished he didn't have to go, leaving her on her own with the sound of silence or the rustling of the reeds in the wind. She wanted him to let her rest her head on his arm and tell her a story. She would cling to him and he would hug her so close, so tight. But she would have to wait. Later, when the lights were out, they would talk—it was the warmest, happiest time of the whole day.

It was not long before her father was staggering home exhausted. He would begin to tell her a story but would only manage to slur a couple of sentences before nodding off. Sunflower would be left waiting for the next part of the story, but she wouldn't get irritated; she would just look around her, quietly resting her head on his arm, taking in the smell of him, waiting for sleep to come. She would reach out her little hand and gently stroke her father's unshaven face as he snored. In the distance she would hear the faint sound of dogs barking, perhaps from Damaidi across the river, or from farther away: Youmadi, or even Daoxiangdu.

And so the days passed, one flowing into the next.

The river soon became Sunflower's favorite place. She would spend most of the day there, gazing across at Damaidi, which was a large village surrounded by reeds. The cooking smoke, the sound of buffaloes, dogs, and happy voices . . . all of this drew her to the riverbank. Most of all, she was fascinated by the children and their joyful laughter. It seemed such a happy world.

Between Sunflower and the village was the river, a big river with no beginning or end in sight, flowing all day and all night, never ending. The reeds on either side stood guard over its journey from west to east. The river and reeds whispered and chuckled like best friends, teasing and twitching. Day after day, month after month, year after year, they played together tirelessly.

How Sunflower loved this river! She watched it flow; she followed the ripples and waves, watched it carry off wild ducks and fallen leaves, watched boats of different sizes move upstream and down, watched the midday sun paint it gold and the setting sun stain it red, watched the raindrops splash up silver-specked spray, watched fish leap from its green waves, tracing beautiful arcs in the blue sky, then falling back into the water. . . .

Sunflower sat under an old elm tree, quietly gazing across the water. If people on passing boats scanned the long riverbank, they would spot her tiny figure. They would feel the vastness of the sky and the vastness of the earth, a vastness that seemed to go on forever.

One day, Sunflower was down by the river. Damaidi looked like a huge boat moored in the reeds on the other side. She saw two haystacks as high as mountains, one on the left, one on the right. She saw a melia tree in blossom, clouds of pale lilac dusting the treetops. She saw plumes of milky-white cooking smoke curling up into the sky, then meeting and drifting as one over the reeds. Dogs were running through the streets. A rooster had flown up into a mulberry tree and was crowing. There was children's laughter everywhere.

Sunflower longed to go there. She turned to look at the little boat that was tied to the old elm tree. She had seen it when she arrived, bobbing about on the water as though trying to attract her attention. A seed of an idea began to form in her mind. It grew like a shoot of grass pushing its way through the wet earth. As the grass fluttered in the spring wind, the idea took shape: I'm going to get into that boat and go to Damaidi.

But did she dare? She looked back at the Cadre School, then nervously inched toward the boat. There was no landing, just a grassy embankment, quite steep. She didn't know whether to climb down facing the river or facing the embankment. She hesitated a while, then eventually chose to face the embankment. She grabbed hold of the grass with both hands and tried to find a good place to put her feet. Slowly and steadily, she began to climb down to the water's edge.

Boats passed in the distance, helped along by the breeze. If anyone on board had looked her way, they might have been alarmed by what they saw but would have been unable to do anything about it. As she lowered herself down, drenched in sweat, Sunflower could hear the water gurgling below her feet. Her small hands clung to the grass, holding on for dear life.

A sailing boat came along. Seeing a little girl clinging to the embankment like a gecko, the man at the helm started to call out to her. Then, afraid that he might startle her, he stopped—although he worried about her long after he had passed by.

Across the river a buffalo was making a strange huffing noise like the whistle of a factory. Sunflower tried to concentrate, but suddenly the earth under her feet loosened. She clutched at the grass, but the roots came away in her hands. There was nothing to hold on to, nothing to stop her from slipping down. Filled with terror, she closed her eyes.

Then she felt herself come to a stop; her foot was resting against a small tree. She pressed herself against the embankment, not daring to move. She could hear the water flowing below. She raised her head to look at the bank, high above her. She didn't know whether to climb back up or keep going down. All she wanted was for someone to come, and more than anything for her father to come. She buried her face in the grass and clung on.

The sun was high in the sky and she could feel its warmth on her back. A gentle breeze blew past her, like softly flowing water. Sunflower began to sing. Not a city song, but one she had learned from the village girls. She had been sitting on the bank one day, listening to them singing in the reeds on the opposite bank. She couldn't see them well through the reeds, but now and then she caught a glimpse of their red and green clothes as they moved. They seemed to be cutting the leaves from the reeds. She soon learned the song by heart, and when they sang on their side of the river, she sang on hers. It was a beautiful song. Sunflower started to sing it now, her voice trembling:

> *"The rice cakes smell sweet,*
> *Their scent fills the kitchen.*
> *The leaves smell so sweet,*
> *Their scent fills the house. . . ."*

Her voice was muffled, the sound absorbed by the wet earth.

As she sang, she felt more determined than ever to get to the boat and go to Damaidi. She began to feel her way down the slope again, and in no time her feet were touching the soft shore of the river. She turned around, took a couple of steps forward, and let the water roll over her feet. It sent a cold rush through her body that made her gasp.

The little boat rocked gently back and forth. She

climbed on board. There was no hurry. She sat in the boat, swaying as it swayed, her heart filled with joy.

But when she was ready to set off, she realized there was no pole or paddle to steer the boat across the river. She looked up at the mooring rope, still tied securely around the old elm, and breathed a sigh of relief. If she had untied it earlier, the boat might have drifted downstream. She couldn't go to Damaidi that day after all, she thought sadly. Without a pole or a paddle, she could only sit in the boat and gaze across the river.

Sunflower sensed that the little boat was drifting. She looked up and saw that the rope had come loose. It was trailing behind the boat, like a long, thin tail. Hurriedly, she tried to pull it in. Then, realizing this was useless, she let go and the rope fell back into the water. That was when she saw the boy standing on the bank above her. He was eleven or twelve and was laughing hard at her. A few days later, she would learn his name: Gayu. He was from Damaidi, and his family had raised ducks there for generations.

Sunflower watched as a flock of ducks emerged

from the reeds. Out they came, hundreds of them, flowing like water, spilling as far as Gayu's feet, flapping their wings and quacking. She wanted to ask why he had untied the rope. But she didn't; she just looked at him helplessly. He laughed even louder, which sent the hundreds of ducks waddling and jostling down the embankment toward the river. A few clever ones flapped their wings and flew, landing on the water with a splash.

After all the rain, the river was full and fast. The little boat drifted sideways. Sunflower looked at the boy. Her eyes filled with tears. He stood there with his arms and legs crossed, leaning on the long handle of a shovel he used for driving the ducks, resting his chin on the back of his hands. His tongue was moving from side to side as he watched her, unmoved by her tears.

But the ducks had more heart. They headed over to the little boat as fast as they could. When Gayu saw this, he dug up a lump of mud with his shovel, then grabbed the handle with both hands, raised it high above him, thrust his shoulders back and his chest forward, and hurled the mud into the air.

It landed with a *splat!* right in front of the furthest duck. Startled, the duck turned, flapping its wings and quacking angrily before swimming off in the opposite direction. The other ducks made a similar fuss and followed it. Sunflower looked around her. She couldn't see another soul and began to cry.

Gayu turned and went into the reeds. He pulled out a long bamboo pole, which the boat's owner had probably hidden, afraid that someone might make off with his boat. Then, walking along the bank, he gestured that he was going to throw the pole to Sunflower. Her eyes were teary with gratitude.

When he was directly above the little boat, Gayu slid down the embankment to the shore. He stepped into the river, laid the bamboo pole on the water, and gave it a light push so that the end was almost touching the boat. Sunflower leaned over and reached for it. Just as she was about to grasp the pole, he laughed and slowly pulled it back. She looked at him, her hands empty, drops of water falling from her fingertips into the river.

Gayu waded through the shallows and pushed the pole toward her again. He did the same thing over and over, pushing the pole as close as he could, then pulling it away just as she reached for it. Sunflower struggled to hold back her tears.

Finally, Gayu gestured that this time he would give her the pole. She believed him. As it came toward her, she leaned over as far as she could, but Gayu jerked it back and she almost fell in. He roared with laughter. Sunflower sat back in the boat and sobbed.

Seeing that the ducks had swum quite a long way off, Gayu pushed one end of the pole into the shore and used it to climb up the embankment. With two or three strides he was back on the bank again. He glanced at Sunflower one last time, pulled the pole out of the mud, tossed it into the reeds, and, without looking back, went hurrying after his flock.

The little boat, angled sideways so it was facing the bank, was drifting downstream. The old elm became smaller and smaller. The red-tiled roofs of the Cadre School gradually disappeared behind the thousands of reeds. Sunflower was numb with fear. She sat in the boat, tears streaming silently down her face. The green haze before her seemed to spill out of the sky and grow ever wider and mistier. She wondered how much farther she would drift.

Occasionally another boat passed by, but Sunflower barely moved. She didn't stand up and wave her arms or shout. At most she gave a little wave. The people in the boats assumed she was a child having fun on the river and didn't pay too much attention. If any of them did wonder, they still went on their way.

As Sunflower cried, she quietly called for her father. A solitary white bird flew out from the reeds. It seemed to sense something and hovered above the water, low and calm, not far from the little boat. Sunflower looked at its long wings and the fine feathers on its breast that ruffled in the breeze, its slim neck, yellow beak, and bright-red feet. From time to time, it cocked its head to one side and peered at her with brown eyes.

The boat drifted on the water; the bird flew in the sky. Between heaven and earth all was peaceful and quiet.

Then, unexpectedly, the bird landed on the boat. It was a big bird, and it looked proud and haughty. Sunflower watched it calmly, as though she had known it for a long time. They looked at each other, at ease. Neither made a sound. There was just the gurgling of the river.

But the bird couldn't stay with her. It had to be on its way. It nodded gracefully, flapped its wings, leaned forward, and flew off toward the south. Sunflower watched it disappear into the distance, then turned to look downstream. The water stretched as far as the horizon. Tears filled her eyes again.

Not far away, on the grassy shore, a boy was grazing his buffalo, cutting grass while the beast ate. He noticed the little boat adrift on the river and stopped what he was doing. He stood there quietly, his scythe in his hand, watching it.

Sunflower had noticed the boy and his buffalo too. Although she couldn't see his face clearly, suddenly she felt a sense of relief, and hope welled up in her heart. She stood up and looked at him.

The river breeze ruffled the boy's scruffy black hair, which kept falling over his face. His eyes were sparkling, and as the little boat came closer, his heart beat faster. The buffalo, which had a fine pair of long horns, stopped grazing and stood with its master, gazing at the little girl in the little boat.

The boy could see right away what had happened. As the boat came closer, he picked the buffalo's rope from the ground and walked it slowly to the water's edge, keeping even with the boat.

Sunflower had stopped crying. The tear tracks running down her face had dried in the wind and felt tight on her skin.

The boy grabbed the long hair on the buffalo's back and swung himself up. Astride the animal, he looked down at the river, the boat, and the girl. Sunflower had to raise her head to see him: he was framed by blue sky and soft white clouds. She couldn't see his eyes clearly, but they seemed to be especially bright, like the stars at night.

Sunflower knew in her heart that this boy would rescue her. She hadn't called out to him. She hadn't made any gestures asking for help. She had just stood in the boat, watching him. The look in her eyes was enough.

The boy gave the buffalo a hard slap on the rump, and it walked obediently into the river. Sunflower watched the boy and buffalo sink lower into the water with every step the buffalo took. Soon the beast was submerged, save for its ears, nose, eyes, and the ridge of its spine, which were just visible above the water. The boy kept the rope tight. His trousers were soaked.

The boat and the buffalo, and the boy and the girl, drew closer.

The boy's eyes were so big and so bright — Sunflower would remember them for the rest of her life. As the buffalo neared the little boat, it flapped its ears, splashing water over Sunflower. She squeezed her eyes shut and put her hands up to shield her face. When she removed them and opened her eyes again, the boy and the buffalo were already at the back of the boat. He leaned over and deftly grabbed the rope that was floating in the water. There was a slight jolt, and the little boat stopped drifting.

The boy tied the rope around the buffalo's horns and motioned for Sunflower to sit down. Then he patted the buffalo's head a few times and it set off back to shore, the boy still riding it and Sunflower sitting in the boat behind them.

For a while, the buffalo and the boy's legs were still under water. Sunflower looked at the boy's back— so straight, so strong—and the back of his head, so shiny, so round. The buffalo pushed through the river. The water parted at its head, rejoined over its back, parted again around the boy, then flowed together over the buffalo's rump before slapping against the boat.

The buffalo led the boat at a steady pace upriver, back toward the old elm. Sunflower's terror had dissolved. She sat in the boat, excited by the river scenery before her. The glints of sunlight on the water rippled into a golden glow that rose and fell with the river. The reeds on either side were bathed in sunlight too. When a cloud moved in front of the sun, the sky would darken, the golden glow would vanish, and the river would be an expanse of dark-blue water. But when the cloud moved on, the reeds would glow brighter and sharper, more dazzling than before. If smaller clouds drifted in front of the sun, stripes would appear across the reed lands: bright emerald in the sunlight, dark green in the shade. The reeds in the distance looked black. The clouds, the sunshine, the water, and the never-ending reeds were changing with every second. Sunflower was enchanted.

Then the buffalo huffed, reminding her where she was. A long reed with a feathery panicle came floating down the river. The boy leaned forward, grabbed it, and held it upright. It looked like a giant ink brush with its wet tip pointing to the sky. In the breeze, the wet tip loosened and began to fluff out, catching the light with a silver shimmer. The boy held it up like a flag.

As they neared the old elm, Gayu and his flock of ducks appeared. He was on a flat duck keeper's boat with a long pole and could go anywhere he wanted. At the sight of the buffalo and the little boat, he doubled over with laughter, his deep throaty laughs matching the guttural quacking of his drakes. He lay on his side in the boat, propping up his head on his hand, and watched them go by: the boat, the buffalo, the boy, the girl.

The boy did not even glance at Gayu. His only

concern was to keep steady on the buffalo, to drive it forward, and to tow the little boat to the old elm. Sunflower's father was standing under the tree, watching anxiously. Once at the shore, the boy stood on the buffalo's back and tied the boat to the tree. Then he climbed down, grabbed the side of the boat, and pulled it close to the bank.

Sunflower jumped out and clambered up the slope toward her father, who leaned forward and reached down to her. The earth was loose and Sunflower struggled to keep her footing. The boy came over and gave her a big shove from behind. Her hands met her father's, and with one pull she was on the bank.

Clutching her father's hand, she looked at the boy and at the buffalo and the boat. Tears ran down her face. Her father sank to his knees, wrapped his arms around her, and patted her reassuringly. Then he noticed the boy was looking up at them. A strange feeling took hold of him, and his hand froze on Sunflower's back.

The boy turned and began to walk back toward the buffalo.

"What's your name, child?" Sunflower's father asked.

The boy looked back at Sunflower and her father but said nothing.

"What's your name?" Sunflower's father asked again.

The boy suddenly went red, lowered his head, and walked away.

"He's called Bronze. He can't speak. He's a mute!" yelled Gayu.

The boy climbed onto the buffalo and drove it back into the water. Sunflower and her father watched him go.

On the path back to the Cadre School, Sunflower's father seemed lost in thought. They had almost arrived when suddenly he grabbed her hand and hurried back to the riverside. The boy and his buffalo were gone. Gayu and his ducks were gone too. There was just the open river flowing on.

That evening, when he was putting out the light, Sunflower's father said, "I can't believe how much he looked like your brother."

Sunflower had heard her father talk about her brother before. He had died of meningitis when he was three. She had never met him; it had been before she was born. She nestled her head against her father's arm and stared into the dark for a long time.

In the distance she could hear the faint sound of the river and the dogs barking in Damaidi.

Sunflower Fields

It had happened the year Bronze turned five. He'd been swept from his bed in the middle of the night and had felt himself jiggling up and down in his mother's arms, vaguely aware of her hurried breathing. But it was the cold, rich air of the late-autumn night that woke him. An air filled with terror.

He saw the sky as red as the morning sunrise. He heard dogs barking for miles around. There were wails and screams, and pounding footsteps. Panic and chaos shattered the peace.

"The reeds are on fire! The reeds are on fire!" people shouted until they were hoarse.

The villagers ran from their homes to the safety of the river. Parents carried their infants; older siblings took the little ones by the hand; adults helped the elderly to walk or carried them on their backs.

As they fled the village, Bronze saw the crimson beasts hissing and screaming, lashing out at Damaidi, and buried his head in his mother's chest.

"Don't be frightened," she said. She could feel him shaking and patted him gently as she ran. He could hear children crying.

There hadn't been time to untie the buffaloes from their posts. As the fire glowed in the night sky, the animals struggled for their lives. Some uprooted the tethering posts, others managed to escape the rope through their noses. Those that broke free charged off into the wild.

Chickens and ducks flapped about in the sky. Pigs squealed and ran amok. Goats and sheep rushed with the crowd to the river or ran wildly around the fields. One child saw two goats heading for the fire and, thinking they belonged to his family, raced to save them. He was hauled back. "Do you want to die with them?" shouted an adult. The helpless child watched in tears as the animals ran into the flames.

Bronze's father took the water buffalo and nothing else. It was a strong, obedient creature that had come to them as a calf, covered in sores. They'd treated it well, given it the sweetest grass, washed it every day in fresh water from the river, picked medicinal herbs and pounded them to a liquid to smear on its sores. The sores had healed quickly, and since then its coat had been sleek and glossy. It didn't charge off like the other buffaloes, but followed calmly behind its master. They were a family, and in times of crisis, a family sticks together. Bronze's grandmother Nainai walked slowly, and every so often the buffalo stopped to wait for her. The five of them—Bronze in his mother's arms, his father, Nainai and the buffalo—walked together, and if other people wanted to go faster, they and their livestock had to pass around them.

Now and again Bronze would peer out. He saw the fire reaching the edge of the village, the first buildings turning gold in the light of the flames. The dry reeds burned furiously, spitting and popping like firecrackers. Some chickens flew too close, flashed gold for a moment, then fell into the ashes. A rabbit darted in front of the fire. As it dodged the flickering tongues, its shadow loomed as large as a leaping horse. Then it vanished; the fire had swallowed it up. Soon those buildings had caught alight. A flock of ducks rose into the air: some were caught in the flames; others flew off into the dark.

The villagers ran to the river. Boats went back and forth, taking people to the other side, where the fire could not reach them. In the scramble to get on board, some people fell in the water. Shouts and cries filled the air. Those who could manage it stripped off their clothes, held them above their heads, and swam across. One man put his four-year-old son on his shoulders and waded into the river. When the boy saw the water flowing around him, he wrapped his arms around his father's head and howled. The man continued to swim. When they reached the other side, he lifted the boy down; he was now as quiet as a mouse, frozen with terror.

The fire rolled in waves down the streets and alleys until the village became a sea of flame.

Having managed to get Nainai onto a boat, Bronze's father led the buffalo to the water's edge. It knew exactly what to do and, without needing to be told, headed straight into the water. Bronze's father helped his wife climb onto the buffalo, then held the rope as they swam across the river. Bronze was cold and scared. He trembled in his mother's arms.

A child fell into the river. Screams of shock and cries for help rang out in the dark. But how could they find him? Even if he surfaced, no one would see him. The fire raged closer. A few people waded into the water to look for the boy, but most stayed on the shore, waiting for a boat. Those already on a boat were desperate to get to the other side. The boy's mother's screams tore through the sky.

Just before dawn, the fire began to subside. The villagers looked back across the river at Damaidi. The remains of their village lay wretched and black.

Bronze had been so cold, but now that the fire was out, he began to burn with heat. His temperature raged for five days. When it returned to normal, he was so thin that his big eyes bulged from his face, but in every other way he seemed well. Then his family discovered that their child, who had always talked so easily, was now mute.

After that, Bronze's world changed. He didn't start school with other children his age. It wasn't that he didn't want to; the school wouldn't take him. When he saw all the other children skipping off to school with their bags on their backs, he could only watch from a distance, while a hand—Nainai's hand—stroked his head. She didn't say anything; she knew what her grandson was thinking. She just stroked his head over and over again with her wrinkled hands that were now a little stiff. He'd offer her his hand and she'd take it, and they'd turn around and walk home or to the fields. They would go to look at the frogs in the ditches, at the "weaver girls"—the grasshoppers in the reeds by the river—at the long-legged wading birds, at the sailing boats, at the windmills. Wherever Nainai went, she took Bronze with her, determined to give him some company. Sometimes, when she saw how lonely her grandson was, she'd turn away to hide her tears. But to him, she always looked happy.

Bronze's parents were out all day working on the land, with no time to watch him. After Nainai, Bronze's closest companion was the buffalo. When his father came home from the fields, Bronze would take the rope from him and lead the buffalo to the sweetest fresh grass. The villagers grew as used to seeing Bronze leading the buffalo to graze as they were to seeing him out and about with his grandmother. They would stop and watch, always with a twinge of sadness.

Bronze looked at the buffalo as it grazed, its long and supple tongue rolling the grass into its mouth, its tail swinging rhythmically. At first, he let the buffalo eat the grass on the ground, but as the animal grew bigger he began to feed it grass he had cut, always the freshest, and the buffalo became the strongest and most handsome in Damaidi.

The villagers said it was because "the mute" fed it so well. They didn't call him mute to his face, and when they said his name, Bronze smiled at them, a pure and simple smile that brought tears to their eyes and a lump to their throats.

Sometimes when Bronze was out grazing the buffalo, he could hear the children reading aloud in class. He would hold his breath and listen as the rise and fall of their voices drifted over the fields. To him it was the most beautiful sound in the world, and he'd stand there gazing rapturously toward the school. At times like these, the buffalo would stop grazing and gently lick the boy's hand with its soft tongue. In answer, Bronze would throw his arms around the buffalo's head and dry his eyes on its mane.

Best of all, the buffalo loved to lower its head and invite Bronze to grab its horns and climb up onto its back. It wanted Bronze to ride through the fields of Damaidi like a king, with all the other children watching. And Bronze was happy to oblige.

As he rode on the buffalo, high above the world, all he could see was the sky, the reeds swaying like waves, and the windmills towering in the distance. Then, when no one was looking, he would wriggle down and lie on the buffalo's back and let it carry him wherever it liked. But Bronze was lonely. As lonely as the only bird in the sky, the only fish in the river, the only horse on the steppes.

Until the little girl appeared, and he realized he was not the loneliest child in the world.

After that, Bronze would take his buffalo to graze by the river. And Sunflower's father would tell her to go and play by the tree, so they both had a friend on the other side of the water.

Sunflower would sit beneath the old elm, resting her chin on her knees, and gaze quietly across at the opposite bank. Bronze would do as he always did when grazing the buffalo: he'd cut some grass and guide the buffalo to the best patch. Every now and then he'd glance over at her.

The days passed, and Bronze wanted to do something for the little girl across the water. He would have liked to sing her one of the songs that the village children sang, if only he could sing. He would have liked to ask her to come hunting for duck eggs in the reeds, if only he could express himself. In the end, he turned his riverbank into a stage and performed for her. He had an audience of one. And his audience always sat in the same way, with her chin resting on her knees.

Bronze would ride on the buffalo, then pull the rope tight and squeeze his heels against its belly. The buffalo would speed off, its hooves clattering along the riverbank, kicking up mud.

Sunflower barely moved, her head turning just enough to follow him with her eyes.

The buffalo charged into the reeds, causing them to rustle and sway. When it seemed they had disappeared, Bronze pulled on the rope, turned the buffalo around, and returned, galumphing along the riverbank. It was all for show, and he was the showman. Sometimes the buffalo roared to the sky, sending tremors across the water. They would run back and forth like this a few times, then Bronze would flip himself off the buffalo, toss the rope to one side, and lie down in the grass. The buffalo would pant and flap its ears, then lower its head and begin to graze leisurely.

It was during one of these quiet restful times that Sunflower heard a sound she had never heard before. It was Bronze whistling through a reed leaf, and it seemed to go on forever. She looked up at the sky and saw a flock of ducks flying off to the west.

Bronze climbed onto the buffalo and stood on its

back, whistling with the reed leaf. She worried that he might fall if it started to move, but the boy was remarkably steady. Then he threw aside his whistle and did a handstand on the buffalo's head, opening and closing his legs. Sunflower was enchanted. But when Bronze slipped off the buffalo's head, she sprang to her feet in shock.

After what felt like an age, he reappeared, covered head to foot in mud, two bright eyes peeking out through the grime. Sunflower burst out laughing.

When the sun slipped deeper over the farthest part of the river, the two children headed for home. Sunflower sang as she skipped along. Bronze sang too—in his heart.

On summer evenings, when there was a southerly breeze, Sunflower's father caught the scent of sunflowers wafting over the river from Damaidi. They were his favorite plants, and he loved their fragrance as they grew in the fields. They smelled so different from the ones that grew in pots. It was the scent of the sun's breath, and it made him feel warm and alive. He had a special bond with sunflowers; they'd played such a big part in his life, such a big part in his work.

Before he had come to the Cadre School, he had been a sculptor, and his most successful works had been sunflowers cast in bronze. It was the best material for making sunflowers, he felt. Its cold gleam had an ancient air about it that touched something primitive inside him. The coolness of the bronze and the warmth of the sunflowers came together to create a new life. He loved the vibrancy and serenity of these flowers. He would become so absorbed in them that he would lose all track of time.

His bronze sunflowers were famous. They stood in the center of the square and had become the symbol of the city. Gradually, they started to decorate and define it. They appeared on the gates of hotels, on the walls of buildings, on the columns of colonnades, on the railings in the park. The tallest sunflower reached almost ten feet, the smallest less than half an inch. Some pieces had a single stalk, some two; some were groups of four or five, or more—all leaning at different angles, each one slightly different. Then sunflowers were produced as handicrafts and laid out on shop counters for tourists to buy. They were made in workshops large and small, as many different sunflowers as you could imagine, but always in bronze. Sunflower's father thought it was too much, but there wasn't a lot he could do about it.

It was this passion for sunflowers that inspired him to give his daughter a country girl's name. To him, it was beautiful, evoking the thought of sunshine lighting up the world. And his daughter seemed to love the name too. When he called her, she would shout back, "I'm here — Sunflower's here!"

Sunflowers were in his heart. They were in his soul. And here, in this remote part of the world, he caught their beautiful scent. As evening fell and dew damp filled the air, the plants and flowers of Damaidi released their perfume. And her father could discern among all these different fragrances the particular scent of sunflowers.

"Not just one or two," he told his daughter, "but hundreds and thousands."

Sunflower sniffed the air, but no matter how hard she tried, she could not pick up the scent. Her father smiled, then took her hand. "Let's go to the river," he said.

The river was calm that night. The moon hung low in the sky, sprinkling silver across the water. Fishing lamps flickered by the overnight moorings. If you stared at the lamps long enough, they went still, and it seemed instead as if the sky and the earth, the reeds and the river were moving, as though that summer night in Damaidi were a dream, an illusion. Her father drew the air into his nose. The scent of sunflowers from across the river was even stronger. Sunflower thought she could smell it too.

They sat by the river for a long time, until the moon began to move to the west. As they walked back, the air was thick and damp and filled with night scent. They felt heady — perhaps tired or intoxicated by the perfume — as though the world were drifting and floating around them.

When Sunflower woke the next morning, her father had already left the house. He'd crept out of bed while it was still dark, picked up his easel, brushes, and paints, and followed the scent of the sunflowers through the night, across the river, to Damaidi. As he left the Cadre School, he asked his good friend Uncle Ding, the gatekeeper, to keep an eye on Sunflower.

He walked through Damaidi village and on through another stretch of reeds until he came to the sunflower fields. They were enormous, beyond his wildest dreams. He had seen sunflower fields before, but never as big as this. He climbed to a high place to look out over them. They went on and on forever. It took his breath away.

He chose the perfect place to set up his easel and unfolded his seat. A red semicircle was emerging on the horizon, like a mushroom pushing through the earth.

Sunflowers were such wonderful plants, he mused — those long, rough pencil-straight stalks holding up large round flower heads that tilted up and down like smiling faces. When night fell, the sunflowers stood solemn and still in the moonlight mist, like people, like an army.

These sunflower fields had been created from reed marshes. The soil was rich, and the sunflowers grew vigorously. Sunflower's father had never seen them so tall, with such thick stalks or such large, strong flower heads, as big as enamel washbasins.

In the early morning, before the sun's rays crept over the land, this forest of sunflowers was drenched in dew. Droplets of water hung like jewels from the heart-shaped leaves and the drooping flower heads.

The sun rose higher in the sky. On the ground, the sunflowers seemed like giants, with feeling and sensitivity, with lives and minds of their own. Their faces were turned to their god. They were the sun's children. All day long they followed it, moving imperceptibly, full of quiet love and devotion.

Sunflower's father watched as the sun rose and the flower heads woke and gradually straightened. When the sun floated high in the sky, it charged through their soft, crumpled petals, filling them with energy. They opened, bigger and brighter than ever.

A circle of gold spread its light over the sunflower fields. Petals of gold fluttered and dazzled. As the huge sun shone silently down and the little suns looked silently up, Sunflower's father was overwhelmed with emotion. These flowers, so childlike and innocent, were at the same time so resilient and strong. He loved them with all his heart.

He thought about the city, and his sunflowers cast in bronze. He felt as if he were the only person on this earth who truly understood these flowers. What he saw that day was impossible to describe in words. He must think about them, understand them, and one day, when he returned to the city, he would make bronze sunflowers that would be even more striking, even more graceful than before.

As the heat of the sun increased, the heat in the fields rose too. The sun burned, and the petals danced like flames. He daubed paint onto the canvas, stopping now and then as the magical scene before him absorbed all his attention.

At midday the sun's rays were at their strongest and the sunflowers were at their most magnificent. The flower heads competed for the sun's attention and seemed to grow ever taller. They were like balls of fire burning beneath the blue sky. Against the white feathery reeds in the background, these golden balls of fire seemed even more vivid and alive. A pale-lilac haze shimmered above the sunflower fields. Birds flying through the haze shimmered too, their shapes shifting as though in a dream.

Sunflower's father painted constantly, splashing paint onto one sheet after another. He didn't want to paint with precision; he wanted to paint with his heart, to open his heart and let everything out.

He forgot about his daughter, forgot about lunchtime, forgot about everything. The only thing in his heart and mind was the vast expanse of sunflowers in front of him.

Eventually, he grew tired. His eyes, scanning the field, came to rest upon a single sunflower. He looked at it carefully: the beautiful flower head was bursting with seeds at the front, and the back seemed green until he looked more closely and saw the soft white center. Behind the petals were the light triangular sepals, shorter than the petals, overlapping to make a green zigzag trim. The flower head itself was concave, the seeds growing darker toward the middle, which was little more than brown fluff. In this one flower alone, there was almost too much for him to take in. He had to make one!

He felt fortunate that his life was linked to these plants. He felt lucky and rich. He thought of his city and the pleasures of life reflected in his bronze sunflowers.

He was preparing to head back when he had an idea. He put down his easel, leaped into the sunflowers, and started walking. The plants were taller than he was, and the flower heads towered above him. He walked and walked and was soon submerged in the sea of gold. When he finally reappeared, he was covered from head to toe in golden pollen. Even his eyebrows were golden. Bees buzzed around his head and made him feel dizzy.

Sunflower's father walked back through Damaidi. His footsteps were slower than before. It was afternoon, and people were out working on the land. There was almost no one in the village, just a few lazy dogs stretched out in the sun.

He felt strange, as though his feet were sticking to the streets, as though a mysterious force were urging him to stop and explore.

Damaidi was a large village. There were a few brick houses with tiled roofs, but most were thatched. The newer buildings were thatched with wheat straw, which glistened like gold thread and dazzled the eye. In the summer sunlight, a blue haze hovered over the rooftops. The streets were narrow and paved with dark bricks, many of them old, uneven, and worn smooth.

It was a plain, ordinary village. To Sunflower's father it seemed strange and familiar at the same time. It was as though he had something to tell this village—something important that he had to pass on. But everything was a blur. A dog raised its head and watched as he walked past. It had a kind look in its eyes, which was unusual for dogs around there. He nodded at it, and the dog seemed to nod back. He smiled to himself. A flock of pigeons flew over the village, casting a dark shadow over the houses. They circled above him a few times before landing on one of the roofs.

By the time he left the village, he had been walking for a while. He glanced back, still with the vague feeling there was something he should leave with the village, though he couldn't say what it was. Only when he'd walked back through the reeds did this peculiar feeling begin to subside.

As he reached the river, he looked for his daughter under the old elm on the opposite bank. But there was no sign of her. Maybe Bronze had come over and they'd gone off to play. He needed to see her. He felt guilty: he hardly had any time in the day to spend with her, and when he did, he had spent it thinking about sunflowers. He had let her down. But at the same time he felt a warmth gurgling inside him like springwater. As he sat on the bank, waiting for a boat that could take him across the river, his mind filled with memories of his daughter. After her mother died, he'd brought her up by himself. There were only two things in his life now: sunflowers and his daughter. She was such a clever, beautiful, adorable little girl! When he thought of her, his heart melted.

One memory after another floated before his eyes, adding layer upon layer to this summer scene.

He remembered the time he'd been working late one evening on his bronze sunflowers, and his daughter was tired. He'd carried her to bed, tucked her in, patted her shoulder, and whispered softly, "Good little Sunflower, go to sleep. Sleep, little Sunflower. Go to sleep."

She'd opened her eyes wide and looked at him. But he couldn't stay; he was worrying about the sunflower that he still had to finish. When he couldn't get her to sleep, he had to leave her on her own.

"Baba's got to work. Try and go to sleep," he had said before going back to his workshop. She didn't cry or make a fuss. After a while he went to check on her. He tiptoed to the door and heard her little voice saying, "Good little Sunflower, go to sleep. Baba's got to work. Try and go to sleep." And when he peered around the doorway, he saw her gently patting her shoulder as he had done. Eventually, her little hand stopped on her chest, like a tired bird resting in a tree. She had put herself to sleep. He'd gone back to his workshop, but when he thought of his daughter asleep in her bed, he couldn't help smiling.

Sometimes his daughter would fall asleep while she was playing. He would carry her in his arms, her arms and legs flopping, and when he laid her on the bed, a smile would creep from the corner of her mouth and ripple across her face. To him, her face was like a flower, a peaceful flower.

When thunder crashed outside, she'd burrow her head in his chest and curl up tight. He'd press his cheek to her head and pat her trembling back with his large, firm hand. "Don't be afraid," he'd say. "The thunder's telling us that spring is on its way. When spring comes, the grass will be green and the flowers will open, and the butterflies and bees will arrive." Gradually, he would calm her. But when she peered out and saw a streak of blue lightning split the heavens and the trees bending in the wind, she would hide her face in his chest again. He would comfort her until the thunder and lightning no longer frightened her and she could look out the window and watch the storm in the sky.

Day by day, his daughter grew. He knew her better than he knew himself. He knew her face, her arms and legs, her temperament. Recently he'd been working so hard that he mostly saw her when she was asleep, when he tucked her arms under the cover. Her skin was soft as warm silk. As he lay in bed thinking of bronze sunflowers, he would suddenly be overcome with love. He would wrap his arms around her and hold her tight, taking in her smell as he nuzzled her porcelain-smooth cheeks.

In daylight, when he saw her skin as flawless as the purest white jade, the thought of even a scratch on it tormented him. He insisted she take care as she played. But she did not always do as she was told, and sometimes she scraped her arm, nicked her finger, or grazed her knee. Once, when she was not looking where she was going, she'd tripped and cut her face on a brick. It bled, bright red. He had been angry and terrified. He couldn't bear to think of a scar on her beautiful face. For days, he nursed her wound, full of worry, until the skin healed and her face was like porcelain again, and he could relax.

Now he was desperate to see her. The feeling was intense, as though he might never see her again. As though he had something urgent to tell her.

She did not come. She must be with Bronze. He liked Bronze, and hoped the pair would play together often. He felt she was safe with him. But at that very moment his need to see her was overwhelming.

He saw a little boat by the shore, one he'd seen earlier that day. It was too small for him, so he decided to wait for a bigger one. Time passed, but no boats came. As the sun moved to the west, he decided to cross the river in the little boat after all.

The little boat carried him, and his easel and his materials, steadily across the water. It was the first time he'd steered a boat, and he enjoyed it. He punted with the bamboo pole, and the boat glided easily across the water.

As the high riverbank came into view, a clamor of crows rose up. Their raucous caws took him by surprise, and as he looked up, down it fell—a glob of white sticky liquid—and landed on his face. He put down the pole and managed to keep his balance as he crouched in the boat, scooped up some water, and washed his face. He was just about to dry his face on his sleeve when he saw it—a tornado spinning toward him from the far end of the river.

Judging by all the dry leaves and sand that were whirling inside, the tornado must have come from over the fields, sucking up everything in its wake, including a large bird, which was thrashing about madly. The monster descended and hit the river like a drill, shooting a vortex of water nine feet into the air, sending spray in every direction and driving a channel through the water as it spun toward him. Sunflower's father shook in terror. The tornado was heading straight for the little boat.

It didn't slice the boat in half as he feared. Instead, waves hit the prow and whipped his folder of paintings up into the air, where a blast of wind caught it and wrenched it open. The cardboard folder flapped like the wings of a giant bird and released his paintings to the sky. The painted sunflowers fluttered briefly, then floated down, one by one, onto the water. One yellow flower after another, they landed face upward, drifting on a river of jade. As the golden sun filled the sky, casting its brightness far and wide, he felt intoxicated, invigorated, liberated.

Forgetting that he was in the little boat on the river, he bent down and reached out as far as he could to grab the nearest sunflower. The boat rolled over. As he struggled in the water, his eyes were fixed on the riverbank. He wanted so badly to see his daughter. But there was only the old elm tree.

The sunflowers drifted in the sunlight. A man traveling in another boat had been watching from a distance. He pulled on the mainsail and steered his boat toward the scene. He found the upturned boat half under water and the folder, paintings, and materials floating on the surface. Everything was still. The river flowed on and a few waterbirds circled above. The boatman searched the water, then yelled as loudly as he could, "Man overboard! Man overboard!"

On both sides of the river people heard his shouts. The news spread, from one man to ten, from ten to a hundred. They came running to see what had happened, and soon both banks were lined with people, shouting and jostling for space.

"Who is it? Who is it?"

No one knew who had fallen in, until the people from the Cadre School saw the easel and the paintings.

Sunflower had been at the Cadre School fishpond, watching Bronze catch river crabs. When they saw the adults running to the river, they ran after them and found the shore crowded with people. Some men had jumped in and were searching frantically underwater. The moment she saw the sunflowers floating on the water, Sunflower knew.

"Baba!" she screamed, running through the crowd. She scanned the faces for news. "Baba!"

Someone caught her and held her tight. She fought to break free, waving her arms furiously in the air.

"Baba! Baba . . . !"

There was no answer.

Some women hurried her away from the river and back to the Cadre School. They didn't want her to see any more. They tried to comfort her, but she was too upset. She cried and howled, and tears poured down her face.

Bronze watched from a distance.

Eventually, Sunflower's throat was dry with exhaustion. Icy teardrops ran down her nose, past the corners of her mouth, and down her neck. She stretched her hands out to the river, convulsed with sobs.

Bronze stood by the wall of the Cadre School and did not move.

There were a dozen or more boats out on the river, and too many people to count. They searched and searched, but by nightfall, Sunflower's father had not been found.

The search continued all week, but still they couldn't find him. They found no body either. It was a mystery.

While the hunt continued, the women in the Cadre School, Sunflower's "aunties," took turns looking after her. She had stopped crying, but her face was pale and the life was gone from her eyes. When she cried out for her father in her sleep, the women had to wipe away their own tears.

A week after her father fell into the river, Sunflower disappeared. The Cadre School people searched every corner. They widened the search to two miles beyond the Cadre School, but still there was no sign of her. Perhaps she'd gone to Damaidi? Someone crossed the river to ask, and when the villagers heard that the little girl was missing, they sprang into action and joined the search. They scoured the entire village, inside and out, but they couldn't find her either.

They were about to give up hope when Bronze had a flash of inspiration and leaped to his feet. He threw himself onto the buffalo and charged through the crowds, then raced off down the road out of the village and on past the reed marsh. There they were — field upon field of sunflowers, basking in the midday sun, a forest of gold, bees, and butterflies hovering overhead.

Bronze jumped down from the buffalo, threw the rope to the ground, and ran into the sunflowers. The stalks grew so close together, he could barely see where he was going. But on he ran, panting loudly, sweat dripping from his brow.

He spotted her deep in the sunflowers, lying on her side in a little hollow in the ground. She seemed to be asleep. He ran to the nearest hill and waved his arms until people in the village saw him and, hoping for good news, hurried over to the sunflower fields. Bronze led them to Sunflower.

They watched her quietly for a while, not wanting to disturb her. No one knew how she had crossed the river or how she had gotten to the sunflower fields. When one of the men lifted her from the ground, she opened her eyes slightly and mumbled, "I saw him. He's here in the sunflower fields."

Her cheeks were bright red. The man put his hand on her forehead. "It's burning!"

They took her straight to the hospital. As they pounded along the dust road, their footfalls sent shudders across the land.

That afternoon, a dark cloud moved in front of the sun. A fierce wind picked up and a heavy rainstorm set in. In the evening, when the sky calmed, the fields of golden sunflowers were gone. Flower heads hung from their stalks, staring at the petals on the ground. Their dazzling beauty was no more.

The Old Tree

The people in the Cadre School had traveled hundreds of miles to come to these reed marshes. They had come to work, to do hard physical labor. The people of Damaidi, who had been working hard—and dreaming of not working hard—for generation after generation, couldn't understand this. Why didn't these city people stay where it was nice and comfortable instead of moving to this bleak wilderness where life was hard? What was the attraction of physical labor? The villagers had no choice; their lives were bound to this land. Surely these city people, who enjoyed good lives, had other options. How strange it was. So often the villagers packed up their tools at the end of the day and saw the Cadre School people still hard at work. So often they were woken by the Cadre School people singing and shouting as they labored long into the night. "They're mad!" muttered the villagers, rolling back to their dreams.

The stronger the wind and the rain, the harder these crazy people worked. And they didn't seem to be able to keep themselves clean like the villagers. There was always mud on their clothes.

Little did they know that the Cadre School people had no choice.

And working as hard as they did, what were they going to do with the little girl who kept running off to the sunflower fields? They couldn't spare anyone to look after her. Her parents had been only children, and there were no relatives who could take her in. The situation couldn't continue for long. The Cadre School managed for two or three weeks, then they contacted the village to see if a family in Damaidi might be willing to take her in. They had a good relationship with the village: among other things, they'd let the villagers use their tractor and had helped build a new bridge. The villagers would probably be willing to help.

The Cadre School people knew it was a big responsibility for the villagers, and some suggested that they should send her back to the city to live with a family there. But her father's friends disagreed.

"Better for her to grow up with a family in Damaidi. It's only across the river, and if anything happens, we can be here for her."

The night before they took Sunflower across the river, the head of the village made an announcement over the loudspeaker. He repeated the information three times. Representatives from the Cadre School would bring the little girl to the big tree at the end of the village at half past eight in the morning. He sincerely hoped that all the villagers would come.

Bronze was inside eating his supper when the loud-speaker broadcast the solemn message. He might have been mute, but there was nothing wrong with

Bronze's ears. He heard every word. He put down his bowl, leaving the rest of his supper untouched, went outside, took the buffalo, and headed off into the night.

"Where are you going?" his father asked, but Bronze didn't look back.

All the villagers knew that Bronze was intelligent but that he could behave very strangely. He felt the four emotions like all the other children—happiness, anger, grief, and joy—but he expressed them in his own way. A few years ago, if something upset him, he'd take himself deep into the reeds and wouldn't come out, no matter how much they called him. Once, he was there for three days, and was as thin as a monkey when he reappeared. Nainai had cried so much she almost ran out of tears. When he was happy, he'd climb to the top of the windmill, look up at the sky, and laugh, all by himself. And up until he was ten, when he was really excited he'd take off his clothes and leap around naked.

The villagers remembered one winter's day when nine-year-old Bronze had gotten very excited about something (although they rarely knew what excited him), stripped down to his underpants, and run outside. The snow was deep on the ground, and it was snowing heavily. Everyone rushed out to see what was happening. Bronze was thrilled to see all these people looking at him, and ran about even more wildly. His parents and Nainai chased after him, telling him to stop. But he wouldn't. He ran around and around, then took off his underpants, threw them aside, and pranced off like a young colt through the falling snow. Some young men chased after him and eventually managed to catch him. Then his mother had to force his arms and legs back into his clothes.

The villagers had no idea what had set him off that time. They struggled to guess what could capture his imagination like that. Mostly, it was little things that excited him. Once when he was grazing the buffalo, he found a nest full of shiny green eggs in a mulberry tree. For days afterward he hid behind the reeds and watched two birds with gorgeous plumage take turns sitting on the eggs. Then, one day, the birds weren't there. Bronze became worried. When he went to check the nest, he found that the eggs had turned into skinny little chicks and he was beside himself with joy. Another time, he was cutting grass by the river, close to a willow tree that had been dead for years. When he looked up and saw two tiny green leaves growing on one of the branches, quivering timidly in the cold wind, he was overcome with emotion.

Bronze did his own thing, lived in his own little world. He was very different from the other children in the village. He could spend hours by the river, gazing through the clear water, watching a crab creep imperceptibly along the bottom. He would fold reed leaves into boats, ten or more at a time, and watch them race down the river, feeling sad for the ones that the wind or the waves pushed over. There was something about him, something quite mysterious.

The villagers saw him catch fish—big ones—in ponds where they thought there were none. He would go to the reed marsh, stand by the water, and clap his hands until a dozen or so birds flapped out of the reeds, circled above him, then flew down to land on the water. The villagers had never seen such beautiful birds before.

It seemed that Bronze didn't much like playing with

the village children and wasn't particularly concerned whether they wanted to play with him or not. He had the river, the reeds, the buffalo, and more plants, flowers, birds, and insects than he could count, or name. One child said he'd seen Bronze walking through a patch of grass that was wilting, and when he passed by, holding out his hands with the palms facing down, the grass straightened up again. No one believed him.

"But it's true," he said. "I swear it's the truth."

The villagers still didn't believe him. But when they saw Bronze in the fields, walking along holding a willow branch strung with fish, they had to admit there was something extraordinary about him.

That evening Bronze appeared on the long main street, riding on the buffalo.

"What's he doing now?" the villagers wondered.

No one knew where Bronze and the buffalo were going. Bronze didn't know either. He let the buffalo lead the way. He'd go wherever it wanted. He just needed to be outside, to have time to think.

Bronze looked lost in his thoughts. If he was aware

he was riding on the buffalo, he was surely unaware of the curious faces peering out the doorways at him. The buffalo waddled along, rocking Bronze from side to side like a boat on the waves. He was looking not at the village but at the sky, the late-summer, early-autumn sky, dark blue and twinkling with the thousands and thousands of stars of the Milky Way. The buffalo's hooves clattered on the bricks of the empty street.

The buffalo walked through the village and on through the fields. Bronze saw the river. It seemed bigger at night, so much longer and wider. He saw the Cadre School on the other side and the lamps flickering in the reeds. In the morning, the little girl from the Cadre School would cross the river and arrive at the old tree at the end of the village.

Moonlight spilled over the river and the land. Cicadas screeched in the grass. Startled birds rose from the reeds, cried out, and flew away. There was a chill in the air. Bronze jumped down from the buffalo and stood barefoot in the grass. It was wet with dew. The buffalo looked up at the moon, its eyes shiny as jet. Bronze looked at the moon too. Its light was soft that night.

When the buffalo lowered its head to graze, Bronze knelt in the grass and spoke to it with his hands. He was always talking to the buffalo with his eyes and his hands, and he believed that the buffalo understood him.

"Do you like Sunflower?" he asked the buffalo.

It chomped away at the grass, but Bronze heard its answer.

"Shall we bring her home, then?"

The buffalo looked up. Again, Bronze heard its answer.

He patted it on the head and wanted to throw his arms around its neck and hug it. He didn't think of it as a buffalo. In fact, they all treated it like a member of the family. Bronze's parents and Nainai talked to it too. Sometimes they told it off, just as they would a child, and the buffalo would look at them with its kind, gentle eyes.

"Then we'll say yes." Bronze patted it on the head again and climbed onto its back.

The buffalo took him back to the village and stopped by the stone slab under the old tree. In the morning, Sunflower would sit there and wait for one of the families to take her in. Bronze pictured her, a cloth-wrapped bundle by her side, her head down, staring at the ground.

The moon moved above the old tree and threw shadows everywhere.

At half past eight exactly, the representatives from the Cadre School brought Sunflower to the old tree.

The aunties had gone to a lot of trouble to make her look nice. They had brushed her hair, braided it, and tied it with a red ribbon. Not a hair was out of place. She was a clean, tidy, and presentable little girl.

She sat perfectly still on the stone slab, her cloth bundle by her side. Her big black eyes and her thin little face gave her a timid look.

For days, the aunties and uncles at the Cadre School had been preparing her for this. They had explained what would happen.

Sunflower didn't cry. She told herself not to.

Some of the aunties stayed with her. They brushed away the specks of dust or dirt that landed on her clothes, and stroked her head. One of them noticed a tearstain by her ear and went to the river, dabbed a handkerchief in the fresh water, and carefully wiped it away.

They looked at the villagers. "She's such a good little girl!" was the message in their eyes.

A crowd was gathering, and more people were on their way. "Where is she? Where is she?" they muttered as they drew closer, but as soon as they reached the old tree and saw little Sunflower, they went quiet.

People kept on coming—men and women, young and old. They filled the clearing as though arriving at market. But the hubbub of a market was missing; there was just a low murmur from the crowd.

Sunflower raised her head bashfully, but when she saw all those people looking at her with kindly faces, she forgot for a moment about her situation. For a while, it was Sunflower who was looking at them. Then, remembering why she was there, sitting on the stone slab, she looked down at her feet again—in the new shoes and socks that the aunties had bought for her.

The autumn wind blew and yellow leaves fluttered down from the old tree. A few landed in Sunflower's hair. She didn't know they were there, and when the aunties leaned in to blow them away, she flinched at the touch of their breath. The crowd saw this tiny movement, and it touched their hearts.

The sun rose higher and the autumn sky grew bigger and brighter.

But still no one said a word. Not a single family had stepped forward and expressed an interest in taking Sunflower in. Most of the villagers already had children. The women were healthy and strong—they had fresh air and sunshine, fresh fish from the river and fresh rice from the paddy fields—and had no trouble getting pregnant.

"Zhuguo has been married for years and still doesn't have any children. He should take her."

"Says who? His wife's pregnant right now. You should see the size of her belly!"

"Are there any families with only boys and no girls?"

And so they continued, considering every family,

one by one. Gayu's family had only one child—Gayu—and from the looks of things, his mother wouldn't be having more. They were also the wealthiest family in the village, having raised ducks for generations. But Gayu's family wasn't there.

The crowd considered Bronze's family too. They had only one son, and he was mute. But no one expected them to take Sunflower; they were too poor.

Bronze's family had come to see the little girl as well. But with the jostling of the crowd, Nainai had trouble keeping her footing. Once she found a good place, she stopped, leaned on her stick, and stayed there. Bronze and his parents went to find somewhere else to stand.

Nainai loved Sunflower from the moment she set eyes on her. Sunflower had never seen Nainai before, but she seemed familiar. They looked at each other. She loved Nainai's silvery hair, which quivered in the breeze and glistened in the sunlight. She had never seen hair quite so beautiful. And as Nainai looked back at her, the little girl felt the soft caress of her eyes upon her cheeks and seemed to hear her trembling voice telling her not to be afraid. Nainai's eyes were quietly drawing her closer. Then Nainai turned and

73

walked away. She needed to find her son, daughter-in-law, and grandson. She had something to say to them.

By midday no one had come forward. The head of the village was getting worried. He walked through the crowd. "Such a good little girl!" he said to the onlookers.

But his words had the opposite effect of the one he intended. For everyone had fallen in love with this little girl! They were so charmed by her that they didn't dare to take her in, afraid that they'd never be able to bring her up as well as they should. Some families who would have been happy to take in a little girl took one look at Sunflower and withdrew to the back of the crowd.

"She's too good for us," they sighed. Damaidi was a poor place, and the villagers had little to spare.

The aunties who had brought Sunflower to Damaidi were desperate for someone to step forward. By the time the sun was directly above their heads, as high as it could go, some of them turned away to hide their tears.

"Let's go," they said. "We can take turns looking after her. We won't leave her here if she's not wanted."

Sunflower's head hung even lower.

The head of the village looked at Bronze's family. He walked over to them and said, "You're good people, and it would be ideal if you could take this child, but . . ."

He didn't finish his sentence, didn't say "you're too poor," just shook his head and walked away. As he passed Bronze, he reached out and, with sadness, stroked the boy's head with his large hand.

Bronze's father, who had been squatting on the ground all this time, stood up and said, "Let's go home."

The rest of the family said nothing. Nainai, remembering what the head of the village had said, did not glance back at Sunflower. They wanted to leave as quickly as possible. All except Bronze, who didn't move. His father had to drag him away.

The buffalo, which had been grazing nearby, let out a long cry.

Everyone stopped and turned to see where the noise was coming from. The sight of Bronze's family leaving was one that the villagers would never forget. There, under the midday sun, was Nainai, tottering at the front, followed by Bronze's mother, then Bronze's father pulling Bronze, who clearly didn't want to go, and the buffalo, who didn't want to go either and kept digging its heels into the ground and pulling back.

As Sunflower watched Bronze's family head off into the distance, a tear ran down the side of her nose.

Then, as the crowd started to disperse, Gayu's family turned up.

Gayu and his father had been out all morning with the ducks. They came and stood close to the stone slab. Every so often Gayu glanced at his parents. He could see in their eyes and from their faces that they liked Sunflower, that they might consider taking her. He grinned at her.

Gayu's father looked up at the sun and said a few words in his son's ear. Gayu ran off, and soon came back with a hard-boiled duck egg in each hand.

His mother motioned to him to place them in Sunflower's hands, but Gayu felt too awkward. He put them in his mother's hands instead.

His mother went up to Sunflower, leaned forward,

and said, "Little girl, it's the middle of the day. You must be hungry. Have these two duck eggs."

Sunflower refused. She put her hands behind her back and shook her head.

Gayu's mother tucked the eggs inside the pockets of Sunflower's jacket.

After that, Gayu's family stood by the old tree. Occasionally a few people wandered past, and Gayu's parents would mumble a few words. They continued to watch Sunflower and slowly, imperceptibly, they moved closer and closer to her.

The aunties who had been standing next to Sunflower eventually sat down on the stone slab. They could wait a bit longer.

When Bronze's family arrived home, no one said a word. His mother brought the food to the table, but no one came to eat. She sighed and walked away.

In the meantime Bronze had vanished.

His mother went out to look for him. "Have you seen Bronze?" she asked a child on the road.

The child pointed to the river, east of their home. "That's him, over there."

She turned to look and saw Bronze sitting on a cement column in the middle of the river.

A few years ago there had been plans to build a bridge here. The cement column had been made, but the funds had run dry and the plans had been scrapped. The cement column remained in the river, all on its own. Weary waterbirds sought refuge on it, which explained why it was covered in white bird droppings.

Bronze had taken a little boat to the cement column, then climbed up. He deliberately didn't tether the boat, and by the time he had reached the top of the column, it had drifted off. He sat on the top like a big bird, looking over the water.

When his mother saw him, she went to fetch his father. He took the little boat, which had floated back to the bank, and punted it over to the cement column.

He looked up at Bronze. "Get down!" he shouted.

Bronze didn't even glance at his father. He sat completely still, perched precariously on top of the cement column, his expression frozen, staring out over the river. Although Bronze didn't move, his shadow rippled on the water, stretching and shrinking like an illusion.

A crowd soon gathered. It was lunchtime and many had brought their bowls of rice with them. They were used to Bronze creating scenes, but this was completely out of the ordinary, even for him.

His father was furious. He threatened his son with the bamboo pole. "If you don't come down right now, I'll thrash you."

Bronze ignored him.

"Bronze, come down!" his mother shouted.

When Bronze's father realized that shouting wasn't going to work, he lost patience. He thrust the pole toward his son's bottom and tried to knock him into the water. But Bronze was ready. He wrapped his arms and legs around the cement column and clung on so tightly he could have been growing on it.

"It'll take more than that to knock him off," someone shouted from the bank.

"Then you can stay up there!"

There was nothing his father could do, so, in a rage, he punted back to the bank, climbed ashore, and led the buffalo off to plow the fields.

The crowd had seen enough and began to drift away.

His mother had had enough too. "If you've got any sense, you'll stay up there and never come down!" she declared. And she went home.

Bronze felt everything go calm. He sat with his legs dangling, his chin cradled in his hand, and the river breeze ruffling his hair and his clothes.

Back home, his mother was tidying the house and worrying about her son. She tidied here and tidied there and then stopped, suddenly conscious that she was behaving a little strangely. Why was she making up a small bed? Why had she taken the mosquito net down from Bronze's bed and put it to soak in a washbasin? Why was she taking clean bedding out of the cupboard? Why was she plumping up a pillow? She sat on the edge of the little bed that she had just made up.

Out on the road, Bronze's father was getting annoyed with the buffalo. It was usually very compliant, but today it was being awkward. It kept stopping to relieve itself. It dragged its feet. When finally it did move, it kept stopping to eat other people's crops.

Eventually they arrived at the field, but when Bronze's father put the yoke over its neck, it jerked its head and threw it to the ground. When he raised the whip in the air, the buffalo raised its head, looked him in the eye, roared, and then snorted. And when he managed to fasten the yoke, the buffalo charged ahead before he could grab the plow. When he finally caught it, Bronze's father was livid and thrashed the whip on the buffalo's head. It didn't recoil, didn't make a sound, just lowered its head. Bronze's father almost never used the whip. He saw the buffalo's eyes moisten with tears and immediately regretted what he had done.

"You can't blame me," he said to the buffalo. "You wouldn't do as you were told."

He didn't ask any more of the buffalo, but removed the yoke and wrapped its rope around its horns, as if to say, "You can lead the way."

But the buffalo just stood there.

Bronze's father sat down on the ridge between the fields and anxiously smoked a cigarette.

Nainai was standing by the wicker fence in front of the house, leaning on her stick, looking toward the old tree.

Bronze's mother went back to the riverbank.

Nainai went too. She looked at her grandson without saying a word. She understood him better than anyone else. She looked after him while his parents were out in the fields. He'd slept in her bed until he was five. On wintry nights they had kept each other warm. She took him everywhere she went. The villagers would see them chattering away endlessly. Bronze talked with his eyes and with his hands, and she understood everything, no matter how complicated or subtle. Nainai was the only person who could fully enter his special world, and she loved being with him.

Nainai looked up at Bronze. "What's the point of sitting up there? If you've something to say, go and say it to your father—he's the head of the family. If you don't, someone else will take her in. I can see your father likes her," Nainai continued, "but he thinks we can't afford it. Now, if you were to stop playing around and start earning a bit of money, then you could change that. Come on, get down." Nainai shuffled to the water's edge, picked up the bamboo pole, and gently pushed the boat toward the cement column. Bronze slid down to the boat.

Bronze's father came home early.

"Back so soon?" said Bronze's mother.

He didn't respond.

Bronze went up to his father and, using his eyes and hands in a way that only his family could understand, talked excitedly.

"She's a good little girl, such a wonderful little girl. I want her to come and live with us. . . . From now on, I'll work hard, really hard. . . . I don't need new clothes for New Year's. . . . And I promise to stop complaining that there's not enough meat. . . . I really want her to be my sister. . . ."

Tears were welling up in his eyes. And in his mother's eyes. And in Nainai's eyes too.

His father crouched on the ground, his head in his arms.

"We might be poor," said Nainai, "but we're not so poor that we can't feed that little girl. If we all ate a little less, we could manage it. I've always wanted a granddaughter!"

Bronze took Nainai's hand and they headed off to the old tree.

His father took a deep breath.

Bronze's mother went after them, and his father soon joined them.

Up at the front, leading the way, was the buffalo.

When the villagers asked where they were going, they didn't answer, just headed straight for the old tree.

The sun was moving toward the west. Most of the crowd was gone, but the aunties from the Cadre School were still sitting with Sunflower on the stone slab under the old tree.

Gayu's family had moved closer. His mother was now sitting on the stone slab with her hand on Sunflower's shoulder, facing her as though she were talking to her. It seemed as though it would all be settled soon. The head of the village looked both pleased and anxious.

Gayu's father was crouching down, drawing something with a stick in the earth. He was trying to figure out how many more eggs the ducks would have to lay in a year if they were to take in the girl. He'd been at it for ages and still hadn't come up with an answer.

Gayu and his mother were getting impatient. So were the head of the village and the remaining villagers. Every now and then Gayu's father would stop and look up at Sunflower. Then he'd smile and return to his calculation.

Then Bronze's family arrived.

"You're back!" the head of the village said, surprised.

"Has the little girl been taken?" Bronze's father asked.

"We're still waiting for the final decision," said the head of the village. The aunties sitting beside Sunflower nodded in agreement.

"Good!" said Bronze's father with a sigh of relief.

When Gayu's father heard this, he didn't even look up. He couldn't believe that Bronze's family was thinking of taking Sunflower in. How on earth would they manage?

But Gayu glanced at Bronze and could feel some kind of shift taking place. He nudged his father with his foot.

Gayu's mother could feel the tension rising. "Hurry up and make a decision," she snapped at her husband.

"We'd like to take this little girl!" announced Bronze's father.

At last, Gayu's father looked up. "You want to take her in?"

"Yes, we do," said Bronze's father.

"Yes, we do," said Bronze's mother.

"Yes, we do," said Nainai, banging her stick on the ground.

The buffalo threw back its head and roared so loudly that it echoed in their bellies and shook leaves from the trees.

Gayu's father stood up. "You want to take her in?" He snorted with disdain. "Well, you're too late. We're taking her."

"The head of the village said he was waiting for a final decision. We're not too late. We said we wanted her before you did."

"She's not going anywhere," said Gayu's father. "You can't afford to take her in!"

When Nainai heard this, she stepped forward. "You're right; we're poor. But we'd sell everything we owned in order to raise this child."

Everyone in the village respected Nainai. The head

of the village could see that she was agitated and quickly slipped his arm through hers. "It's not good to get worked up at your age. Come on, let's discuss this." He pointed his finger at Gayu's father. "Haven't you finished your sums yet?"

But Gayu's father had made up his mind. The two families started arguing and shouting. People heard the noise and came to see what was happening.

The head of the village didn't know what to do.

"Why not let the child decide for herself?" someone suggested.

The crowd thought this was an excellent idea.

"Would you be willing to let Sunflower decide?" the head of the village asked Gayu's father.

"Yes!" Gayu's father felt it would give him an advantage. He pointed to the only tiled brick house in the western part of the village. "That's our house, over there," he told her.

"Would you be willing to let Sunflower decide?" the head of the village asked Bronze's family.

"We won't let this child down," said Nainai.

"Good," said the head of the village. Then he went over to Sunflower.

"Little girl, the people of Damaidi are very fond of you. They want you to have a good life, but they are concerned about doing what's right for you. They don't want to let you down. Everyone here is a good person, and both of these families would be kind to you. We'd like you to choose."

Bronze stood, clutching the buffalo's rope, staring at Sunflower. Sunflower looked at Bronze and stood up. There was silence. All eyes were on Sunflower, waiting to see which way she would turn: east to Bronze's family, or west to Gayu's. She picked up her bundle. The aunties began to sob.

Sunflower looked at Bronze, then began to walk to the west. The crowd watched her. Bronze hung his head. Gayu grinned from ear to ear. Sunflower walked over to Gayu's mother. She looked at her gratefully, put her hands in her pockets, took out the two duck eggs, and placed them in the woman's pockets. Then she took a few steps back, still looking at Gayu's family, before turning around and walking away.

Everyone watched intently. Everyone except Bronze. Nainai touched her stick against his head. Bronze looked up and saw Sunflower slowly heading toward them. Nainai flung open her arms to welcome the little girl as her granddaughter, her own flesh and blood.

Soon afterward, the villagers watched quietly as the little group made its way through the village, Bronze at the front, leading the buffalo with Sunflower on its back, followed by Nainai holding Sunflower's bundle, then his mother, and finally his father. The buffalo's hooves clattered on the gray bricks, crisply tapping out the good news.

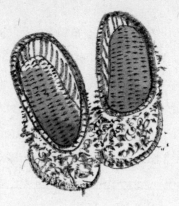

Woven-Reed Shoes

To the villagers' surprise, the little girl blended effort-lessly into her new family. The moment Sunflower stepped over the threshold, she became Nainai's grand-daughter, Baba and Mama's daughter, Bronze's little sister.

She would follow Bronze wherever he went, just as Bronze had once followed Nainai. In no time at all, she could talk to him about anything, whatever was on her mind. They began to share things as easily as water flows.

The villagers often saw them together in the bright sunshine out on the ridges between the fields, looking for wild plants, mostly walking but sometimes sitting for a while or lying back in the grass. Bronze would come home with a big string bag full of plants on his back, Sunflower with a basket on her arm, also brimming with plants.

When it had rained in the night and there was water everywhere, they would set off, Bronze in a woven-bark rain cape holding a fishing net, Sunflower in a round bamboo rain hat with a fishing creel on her back. There would be just the two of them in the wide-open fields, silvery screens of rain still falling, everywhere drenched in silence. They would walk and stop, and stop and walk. Then the boy would disappear from view. He'd be down in a water channel with the fishing net, and she'd be crouching at the edge, her arms around the creel. When he popped up again, dragging the net behind him, they'd lean together and pick out the fish. Then they'd run around in the rain, wild with excitement at their catch. Until Bronze would slip—on purpose. And Sunflower would slip too—on purpose.

They'd come home with a creel full of wriggling fish.

They would go to the sunflower fields too. Without

the bright leaves and petals, the fields seemed bare and bleak. The sunflower heads were packed tightly with seeds. They hung heavily on the stalks, no longer rising in the sunshine, no longer turning to follow the sun. It was Sunflower who wanted to go there, and Bronze was happy to take her. They would sit for a long time on the high ground, looking out over the fields, searching. Then she'd stand. She'd see her father, over there by that sunflower. Bronze would stand too, but when he looked in the same place, all he could see was row upon row of sunflower stalks. But he would believe her, believe that she'd seen him. Some of the villagers said they'd also seen him there, in the moonlight. Bronze believed them too. Whenever he saw in her eyes that she wanted to go to the sunflower fields, he dropped everything and took her there.

The pair were always together: in the daytime, at night, in the sun, in the rain. When he was covered in mud, so was she. And when the villagers saw them out in the fields, walking and having fun, something stirred inside them. They felt a warmth course through their bodies, a pure and gentle warmth that melted and softened their hearts.

Having spent all summer out in the fields, the village children suddenly realized that school would be starting soon. They wanted to play as long as they could under the crisp, bright autumn sky.

The adults had already started calculating all the things they would need to pay for when school started. It wasn't a large amount of money, but for most of the villagers the expense was significant. Some families sent their children to school as soon as they were old enough. Others couldn't afford it. One year lost wouldn't matter, they thought. It would only be reading and writing, and as long as their children could write their names, that was enough. So instead the children would feed the pigs, herd the sheep, and drive the ducks. But for some children many years would go by without them ever going to school. Finally, when they reached their tenth or eleventh birthday, their parents would grit their teeth and send them. For this reason, a single class would be made up of children of very different ages. To look at them standing in a line, you would see a jumble of different heights.

There were also families who never sent their children to school. And some children who'd missed so much school that they refused to go even when their parents wanted them to. They felt too big, and too embarrassed, to be in the first year with the little ones.

"Don't blame us when you're an adult and can't read," their families would say when their children decided to take their futures into their own hands.

For those who did attend school, things didn't always go smoothly either. The school was strict about fees, and if money was owed, action was taken. If the fees were not paid, the teacher would tell the child to pick up his stool and go home. And the child would pick up his stool, in front of the whole class, and cry all the way home. If the fees were then paid, he might go back . . . or he might not.

For the last few days, Baba and Mama had not slept well. Their minds were heavy with worry. They had put aside a sum of money to send Bronze to the school for deaf and mute children in town. He was eleven now, and he couldn't keep on like this, not going to school. They had a distant relative in town who had agreed that he could sleep and eat there. But Sunflower was seven, which was the age to start school. Some families in Damaidi sent their children to school as young as five. Whatever else the family did or did not do, they had to send Sunflower to school.

The adults took out the wooden box where they kept their money. They had earned every cent, from each hen's egg, each fish, each basket of vegetables they had sold, and each mouthful of food they had saved for the next meal. They tipped out the money, counted it, then counted it again. They did their calculations over and over, but no matter how hard they tried, there was not enough to send two children to school. They looked at the pile of money, with its stench of sweat, and wondered what on earth they should do.

"We could sell some chickens," said Mama.

"We don't have much choice," said Baba.

"The chickens lay eggs," said Nainai. "If we sell the chickens, we still won't have enough. But as long as the chickens are laying, we can sell the eggs."

"We could borrow some money," said Mama.

"Who's rich around here?" said Baba. "And it's an expensive time of year."

"Starting tomorrow, the children can have rice every tenth day," said Nainai. "We can sell the rest and raise some money that way."

They did all of these things, but they still couldn't find enough money to send both children to school. They discussed it again and again, and came to the same conclusion: this year they could only send one child to school. But which? Bronze? Or Sunflower? It was a terrible decision to have to make.

In the end they decided they would send Sunflower to school. They reasoned that Bronze was mute, and it didn't matter so much if he went to school or not. He'd already missed so much; he could miss another year or two. They could wait until things were a bit better, then he could go too. As long as he could write a few characters, that would do.

The children had seen it coming.

Bronze had wanted to go to school for years. He'd been so lonely walking through the village and out in the fields, all alone in his private world. He used to graze the buffalo near the school and listen to the children reading out loud. He was captivated by it. He knew he'd never be able to read aloud like the other children, but he could sit with them and listen. He wanted to learn to read. He looked at those characters with wonder, drawn to them as if to lights glowing in the wilderness at night. For a while he collected scraps of paper with writing on them, then hid himself away and pretended he could read them. When he saw boys scribbling characters in chalk on someone's wall, he felt envious and ashamed—so ashamed that he had to keep his distance.

Bronze had once tried to sneak into school to learn a few characters, but before the teacher even had time to chase him out, he was laughed at by the other children.

"Mute!" shouted one of them, and all heads turned to look. Then they crowded around him, shouting, "Mute! Mute!" He felt awkward and embarrassed. He tried to break through the wall of children, raising squeals of laughter when he finally burst through, rolled across the floor, scrambled to his feet, and fled.

Bronze dreamed of being able to go to school for

real. But the facts could not have been clearer: only one of them, he or Sunflower, could go. He lay in bed at night, his eyes wide open, unable to sleep. But in the morning, as he wandered around the fields with Sunflower, he behaved as though nothing were bothering him.

Sunflower seemed carefree too, always by his side. They watched the swallows flying south. They punted one of the little boats through the reeds and picked up gorgeous feathers dropped by wild geese, wild chickens, and mandarin ducks. They went hunting for insects in the dry grass, following their lyrical songs.

Then, one evening, the adults called them over to tell them their plans.

"Let Bronze go to school!" cried Sunflower once they had spoken. "I can go next year. I'm little. I can stay home with Nainai."

Nainai pulled the girl to her chest and wrapped her arms around her. There was a lump in her throat.

Bronze seemed to have prepared what he wanted to say. He expressed himself with his hands and his face, and there could be no mistaking his meaning.

"Let Sunflower go to school. I don't need to go; there's no use to it. I have to graze the buffalo. I'm the only one who can do it. Sunflower can't—she's too young."

As the two children continued to argue, the adults grew more and more upset. Mama hid her face and burst into tears.

Sunflower buried her face in Nainai's chest and started to cry too. "I'm not going to school. I'm not going to school!"

"We'll see" was all Baba could say.

The next day, when they were still unable to resolve the situation, Bronze left the room and returned holding an earthenware jar. He put it on the table and took two ginkgo nuts out of his pocket: one dyed red, the other green. The village children dyed them pretty colors and played games with them—if you lost, you handed over a ginkgo nut. Most children always had a few in their pockets.

Bronze explained, "I'll put one red and one green in the jar, and whoever picks out the red one will go to school."

The three adults looked at him doubtfully.

"Don't worry," he gestured.

Bronze's family knew he was clever, but they couldn't decide if he was up to something.

"Nothing will go wrong," he gestured again.

The adults looked at one another and then agreed.

"Do you understand what this means?" Bronze gestured to Sunflower.

She nodded.

"And you agree?"

She looked at Baba, Mama, and, finally, at Nainai.

"I think it's a good idea," said Nainai.

Sunflower looked at Bronze and nodded.

"And what's decided is final?"

"Yes!" she said.

"No tricks, please, you two. We're watching," said Mama.

Bronze wanted to be completely sure that everyone agreed. He put out his hand and curled his little finger around Sunflower's little finger.

"Cross my heart," said Nainai.

Sunflower turned and smiled at Nainai. "Cross my heart."

"Cross my heart," said Baba and Mama.

Bronze held the jar upside down and shook it to show there was nothing inside.

Then, one by one, he showed them what was in the palm of his hand: a red ginkgo nut and a green ginkgo nut.

Everyone nodded. One red. One green.

Bronze closed his hand into a fist and pushed it inside the jar. A few moments later, he pulled his hand out, placed it over the top of the jar, held the jar up to his ear, and gave it a good shake. They could hear the two ginkgo nuts bouncing about inside.

When he stopped shaking the jar, he put it down on the table and asked Sunflower to take one.

Should she go first? she wondered. She glanced at Nainai.

"*On the ridge, picking grass: young grass first, old grass last.* Sunflower's younger, so it's right that she should go first," said Nainai.

Sunflower went up to the jar and pushed her little hand inside. The two ginkgo nuts were lying there in the dark. Which one should she choose? She hesitated, then made her choice.

"There's no going back!" Bronze declared in gestures.

"No going back," said Nainai.

"No going back," said Baba and Mama.

"No going back," said Sunflower quietly, her voice trembling. Slowly, she pulled her hand out of the jar, like a bird afraid to leave the nest. Her hand was clenched tight, and she didn't dare open it.

"Open up!" said Nainai.

"Open up!" said Baba.

"Open up!" said Mama.

Sunflower closed her eyes and slowly opened her hand.

"We can see it!" said the adults.

Sunflower opened her eyes. There in the palm of her clammy hand was the red ginkgo nut.

Bronze reached inside the jar, felt around, pulled out his hand and opened it. In his palm was the green ginkgo nut. He smiled, but he was holding back his tears. He would never be able to tell them his secret.

Sunflower was a timid little girl, and she was scared of going to and from school on her own. They lived a long way from the village school, and she had to cross a stretch of wasteland to get there. Some other children went the same way, but she didn't know them well yet. They still felt that she was an outsider and different from them, so they tended to keep their distance.

The adults were also anxious, but Bronze already had the answer: he would take her and bring her back himself.

It was probably the first time in the entire history of Damaidi that a little girl had gone to school by buffalo, escorted by her brother. They left the house promptly in the morning, and at the end of the school day, Bronze and the buffalo would be waiting at the school gate. In the mornings, Sunflower would sit on the buffalo, reading the lesson out loud, and by the time they reached school, she knew it by heart. On the way home, she would do some math in her head so that once she got home, it didn't take long to finish her homework.

Every time Bronze dropped her off in the morning, she'd run into school, then run straight out again and check that he would be there to pick her up later. She was worried that he'd forget. On the one occasion that he was a little bit late getting the buffalo from his father, he arrived to find her in tears by the school gate.

On rainy days, the earth road became a slippery, slimy mud bath. The children who walked to school arrived with their shoes covered in mud and, if they'd slipped on the way, with splashes of mud on their clothes. But Sunflower would arrive pristine. The other girls were envious, and almost resentful.

There was another reason Bronze was eager to take Sunflower to and from school, and that was to prevent Gayu from bullying her.

Gayu was the same age as Bronze, and he did not go to school either—not because his family couldn't afford it, but because he wouldn't buckle down and take it seriously. He'd repeated the first year three times and had still been at the bottom of the class. When his father saw that he wasn't going to learn more than a handful of characters, he'd tied him to a tree and beaten him.

"Three years in school, and what do you have to show for it?"

"Nothing. I gave it all back to the teacher," Gayu answered.

He didn't care about learning but enjoyed being a troublemaker at school. Every day there was something, whether it was fighting with one child or arguing with another, breaking a classroom window or snapping the trunk of a newly planted tree. Eventually the school paid his father a visit.

"About your Gayu, would you like to take him out of school . . . before we expel him?"

His father thought about it. "He won't be going to school anymore," he said. And after that, Gayu was free to hang around the village all year long.

Gayu made a point of driving his ducks at exactly the same time that Sunflower was on her way to and from school, often blocking the road with his flock. There were so many of them and they waddled along so slowly. Every now and then Gayu would glance back at Bronze and Sunflower with a nasty look on his face. It seemed as though he was waiting for an opportunity, when Bronze wasn't there. But Bronze was determined not to give him one.

It seemed that Gayu was a bit scared of Bronze. When Bronze was there, he looked uneasy and inhibited, and he took it out on his ducks. He drove them all over the place, and when he hurled mud at a duck, it would start quacking and flapping its wings, causing others to do the same.

Bronze and Sunflower would pay no attention to him and would continue on their way.

Bronze's family was like an old cart that has rolled for years along bumpy roads and through wind and rain. The axles need grease, the wheels need fixing, the parts seem a bit loose, and the cart creaks forward as though everything is a big effort. But it still works, and it still gets to where it needs to go on time.

With Sunflower now on board, the cart seemed even heavier. And she knew she added to the family's load.

One day, toward the end of the semester, the teacher made an announcement. "Tomorrow afternoon Limping Liu from the studio in Youmadi is coming to our school. He'll be taking photos of the teachers. It's a wonderful opportunity to have your photo taken too. But you'll need to pay for it in advance."

The news was announced in all the classes, and soon the school was bubbling with excitement, like rice porridge bubbling in the pot.

For the village children, it was a luxury to have their photograph taken, something they only dreamed of. Those who knew they could ask for money at home leaped about, whooping and laughing. Those who thought they might be able to ask for money, but who knew how hard that money was to come by, were excited but apprehensive. Then there were some who knew very clearly that they could not ask for money—not because the adults wouldn't give it if they could, but because there simply wasn't a spare cent at home. These children kept quiet and stood to one side, sad and dejected. A few of them wanted a photo so badly that they secretly borrowed from the children who had money, promising to do things in return: to carry their stools for them, to do their homework, to steal one of the family pigeons for them. Those who had managed to borrow some money were happy. And those who hadn't were annoyed with the people who refused to lend. Cries of "I'm not your friend anymore!" could often be heard over the bubbling excitement.

It was the girls who were most excited about having their photos taken. They huddled together in small groups, chattering away about the shoot the next day, choosing a nice landscape as a backdrop and deciding what to wear. Those who didn't have nice clothes tried to borrow from those who did and were delighted when they got a yes.

Both inside and outside the classroom, the photos were the topic of every conversation.

Sunflower stayed at her desk, all alone. The excitement in the schoolyard was beginning to affect her. Of course she would have liked to have her photo taken. She hadn't had a photograph taken since she'd arrived at the Cadre School with her father. She knew she was pretty, and everyone had always admired her photos. She liked to look at them too, and was always a bit surprised: she never quite believed the girl in the photos was her.

Sunflower sat at her desk reading. At least she was trying to read, but nothing would go in. Every now and then, the other children would glance over at her. She could feel their stares and buried her face in her book.

When Bronze came to get her, he could see that all the children were more excited than usual, like at New Year's — all, that was, except Sunflower.

On the way home, Sunflower sat on the buffalo and watched the sun setting over the river. It was as big and round as a winnowing basket, an intense red disk burning silently in the sky. It stained the fluffy white panicles of the reeds, which stood in rows like torches.

Sunflower stared at the scene with an expressionless face. Bronze wondered what was wrong. He glanced up at her, and she noticed and smiled at him and pointed to the sky in the west. "Did you see that wild duck coming down to the river?"

It was almost dark when they reached home. Baba and Mama had just returned from working in the fields. Sunflower saw how tired they looked and went to fetch a scoop of water from the water barrel. Mama took a few sips, then handed it to Baba. She really is a thoughtful girl, thought Mama as she lifted the corner of her jacket and wiped the gleam of sweat from Sunflower's face.

The family drank their rice soup, as they did every evening. There was no lamplight, just the clear, crisp sounds of them eating their supper in the gloom. As she drank, Sunflower told them about interesting things that had happened at school that day, and everyone laughed.

But Bronze took his bowl and went to sit on the wooden threshold. The pale moon shimmered on the surface of his thin rice soup.

The following afternoon, Limping Liu of the Youmadi Photographic Studio appeared at the gates of the school, rocking from side to side as he walked, his bag of photographic equipment slung across his shoulders.

"Limping Liu's here!" shouted the sharp-eyed child who spotted him first.

"Limping Liu's here!" everyone shouted, whether they'd seen him or not.

No one could think about schoolwork now. The classroom doors opened like the gates of a sheep pen, the sheep streaming out, desperate for fresh grass, pushing and shoving. The desks were swept to the side. Some boys couldn't wait for the jam to clear; they pushed open a window and jumped out.

"Limping Liu's here!"

The photographer didn't mind that the children called him Limping Liu. After all, he did walk with a limp.

Youmadi was the only town for miles around that had a photographic studio. As well as taking his customers' photos in the studio, once a year Limping Liu would spend two weeks visiting the villages around Youmadi, alone and on foot, his arrival causing as much commotion as a traveling theater or a circus. Wherever Limping Liu went, he seemed to take a festival with him.

In the villages, most of his business was in the schools. Sometimes the older village girls would hear he was there and rush to the school, and between taking photos of the teachers and children, he'd squeeze them in somehow. He charged less in the villages than he did in the studio.

As always, he photographed the teachers first, then the children. He photographed them class by class, and everyone had to line up. Any bad behavior and Limping Liu would let his black cloth drop over the lens and refuse to continue, at which point a teacher would come and put the children back into line.

As soon as everything was in order and Limping Liu was happy, he would concentrate on taking the photographs. Once his heavy old camera was set up on his heavy old tripod, he would busy himself, adjusting the camera, then shouting, "That girl first! Next! Next! Head this way a bit! Chin up! Relax! Did you wake up with a stiff neck?" And when a person couldn't do what he asked, he'd limp over, pull their shoulders back, and move their head until he had what he wanted.

Most of the children had paid to have one photo taken, and a few had paid for two or even three. Limping Liu was very pleased. He talked louder than ever and said amusing things that made everyone howl with laughter. It was always fun when Limping Liu was in school.

Sunflower stayed in the classroom. The noise from outside reached her in waves.

"Why aren't you having your photo taken?" asked a girl who'd run inside to fetch something. Sunflower didn't know what to say, but fortunately the girl was busy looking for whatever it was and ran out as soon as she'd found it.

Sunflower was afraid someone else might see her, so she slipped out the door into the school yard. There were people everywhere, but no one noticed her. Keeping low, she sneaked past the classrooms and vanished like a wisp of smoke into the lush forest of bamboo behind the office. The laughter seemed far away now.

She waited, hidden in the bamboo, until the school had gone completely quiet. When she crept back to the school gate, she found Bronze waiting for her, sweating with worry. As soon as she saw him, she started to sing one of the songs Nainai had taught her:

> *"Little Sister Meimei, we combed your hair*
> *And now you look like a lady!*
> *Big Sister Jiejie, we combed your hair*
> *And now you look like a baby!"*

She laughed at the words as she sang them.

"What's funny?" he asked.

Sunflower didn't reply, just laughed until the laughter turned to tears.

A week later, when Bronze came to pick up Sunflower, he saw the other children walking along with photos in their hands. Whether they were stealing glances at them on their own or showing them to friends, they were clearly all delighted with them. Sunflower was the last to appear.

"What about your photo?" he asked.

She shook her head.

Neither of them spoke on the way home. As soon as they arrived at the house, Bronze told the adults about it.

"Why didn't you say something?" Mama asked Sunflower.

"I don't like having my photo taken," said Sunflower.

Mama put her hand to her daughter's face and took a deep breath. Then she pulled her into a hug and combed her fingers through her wind-tangled hair.

That night, Sunflower was the only one who slept well. The others tossed and turned. They had promised to do their best for her, and they felt they had broken their promise.

"Surely we must have a little bit of money?" Mama asked Baba.

"Nobody said there wasn't any."

After that, Bronze's family worked even harder. Although she was getting older, Nainai tended the vegetable garden and gathered firewood. Often she wasn't back until after dark. When Bronze and Sunflower went to look for her, they would find her stooped over in the half-light, struggling home with a mound of firewood on her back. With patience and determination, the family saved every cent they could.

In the wintertime, the villagers could seldom afford to buy cotton-padded shoes, so they wore shoes made of reeds. First, you had to pick the finest reed panicles, then twist them as evenly as you could into a grass rope, which you then used to make the shoes. They were known locally as "fluffy birds' nests" because they were thick and sturdy like a bird's nest, and the fluffy panicles kept your feet warm, even in the snow.

When the autumn harvest was in, the family decided that in the winter months, when they weren't busy in the fields, they would work together to make a hundred pairs of reed shoes that Bronze could take to sell in Youmadi. By the New Year they would have made a good amount of money! They were excited just thinking about it. Their future felt bright.

Bronze started to gather reed panicles as he grazed the buffalo. He took a large cloth sack and wove his way into the deepest part of the marsh. He found the thickest, fluffiest, shiniest reed panicles and stripped them from the stalks. He worked only on this year's panicles, not last year's. The reed fluff was like duck's down, and he felt warm just looking at it. There were reed marshes as far as the eye could see, but Bronze was very particular. Whatever he picked had to be the best, and it took him a long time to fill the sack.

On Sundays, Sunflower would go with him. She would look up at the tall reeds, searching and searching, and when she found a particularly pretty one, she would call Bronze to take a look.

"There's one here!" she'd say, and he'd rush over, smiling in delight when he saw how good it was.

When they had enough reed panicles, the whole family set to work making the shoes. Bronze started by beating the fresh golden reeds with a wooden mallet. They had to be beaten again and again, to turn the raw grass into what was called worked grass. Worked grass was soft and strong, and because it didn't break or split, it was easy to twist into rope, which could be braided. Bronze held the mallet in one hand and turned the grass over with the other. The mallet thudded down, and the ground shuddered like a drum.

Nainai twisted the grass into rope. Her rope was well known in Damaidi: it was neat, strong, and beautifully shiny. But this rope was different from usual because she had to tuck the fluffy heads into it as she went. Nainai's hands worked their magic, and the fluffy rope flowed through her hands like water, like a living creature.

Sunflower would take a little stool and sit beside Nainai. Her job was to wind Nainai's rope into a ball. It felt lovely and soft as it passed through her hands. When the rope was long enough, Baba and Mama began to make the shoes. Baba made shoes for men and Mama made shoes for women. Their work was good too. Baba's shoes looked stockier; Mama's shoes looked prettier. But the technique was the same for both: the rope had to be woven tightly enough to keep the rain out. The soles had to be particularly sturdy or they wouldn't last long.

When the first two pairs of shoes were finished — one men's pair, one women's pair — the family was wild with joy. They passed them around and around, unable to take their eyes off them. They were covered in a soft fluff that seemed to grow all over them. When the wind blew, it ruffled the fluffy hairs, revealing the golden straw beneath, just as the wind ruffles the downy feathers of a bird. The two pairs of shoes looked like four birds' nests and, at the same time, like two handsome pairs of birds.

The family kept on beating grass, twisting, winding, and braiding rope. The work was hard, but no one made a face or complained. They talked and laughed. They worried about today but looked forward to the future. This horse cart might be creaking, but it was still going strong. It might be slow, but they could clearly see the road ahead and the scenery around them. They couldn't abandon it. So, if they hit a storm, a muddy patch, a bumpy road, or a steep hill, they would get out, lean in with all their strength, and push as hard as they could.

Nainai would sing as she sat twisting rope in the moonlight. She could sing forever. The family loved to hear her. It made them feel alive and full of energy. When she sang, they worked better. Nainai would stroke her granddaughter's head, smile, and say, "This is for our Sunflower:

"*When roses bloom in the spring*
And the silkworm season begins,
The women go out to pick mulberry leaves
In pairs, in pairs.
Their baskets hang from the mulberry trees
And they strip the branches bare
In tears, in tears."

Eventually the family finished making their hundred pairs of shoes. Then they made another pair for Bronze. It was only right that he should have new shoes.

Sunflower wanted some too, but Mama said she would make her some padded cotton shoes instead. "They're so much nicer," she said.

Every day, Bronze would take a dozen or more pairs to sell in Youmadi. It was a big town, with a pier for the steamboat, shops, a food-distribution center, a grain-processing plant, a hospital, and all kinds of different stalls. People came and went all day long. It was a busy place.

The shoes were tied together in pairs by means of a thin hemp string. Bronze hung them over his shoulder, with one shoe from each pair hanging down his chest and the other down his back. They swung as he walked.

The people of Youmadi and the various traders who came to sell their goods would see Bronze approaching from the bridge in the east. "The mute's here again, with his shoes," they'd say.

Sometimes he'd hear them, but he didn't care; after all, he *was* mute. He just wanted to sell the shoes and go home. All day long he made hand gestures, beckoning them to come and see the beautiful reed shoes for themselves.

And many people did go and look, and perhaps because they liked the quality of the workmanship, or his sincerity, they bought the shoes, one pair after another.

At home, the little wooden box was filling up. Every so often the family would crowd around and look at the heap of creased bills. When they'd seen enough, Baba would lift up one of the boards of the bed and hide the box inside. They'd agreed that when all the shoes were sold, they'd go to the Youmadi Photographic Studio and ask Limping Liu to take a photograph of the whole family, and then one of Sunflower, and that they'd have them specially tinted too.

With the hopes and dreams of his family never far from his mind, Bronze would get up very early so that he could go and stand in the best spot in Youmadi — by the river. He'd tie a rope between two trees and hang the shoes over it. They would sway in the breeze and glisten in the sunlight, and were so appealing that even people who'd never normally wear reed shoes couldn't help admiring them.

When winter set in, it turned very cold. It was particularly chilly by the bridge. The north wind blew across the water and slashed Bronze's skin like a knife. He would jump up and down to stop his feet from going numb, and when he jumped he spotted things that he couldn't see from the ground. He could see beyond the first row of roof ridges to the one behind, where a flock of pigeons had landed. Their soft feathers seemed to dance in the breeze. It amused him to compare the pigeons with his shoes, however crazy an idea it was. When he stopped jumping up and down, he still thought the shoes looked like pigeons, and it crossed his mind that they might be getting cold too.

At midday, he pulled a cold, hard flatbread from his inside pocket and chewed on it. The family had begun by telling him to buy some *baozi*—steamed buns with a hot savory filling—for his lunch, but, wanting to save the money, he had ignored them and stood there all day with an empty stomach. So the family had started making him a packed lunch to take with him.

Bronze was a straightforward salesman. He had a price, and if people tried to haggle, they'd soon find that he wouldn't budge by even a cent. There'd be no haggling over such beautiful shoes! Every time he sold a pair, he felt sad to see them heading off into the distance, as though someone were walking off with his pet dog or cat.

At the same time, he hoped the shoes would sell quickly. If someone was on the verge of buying a pair, then hesitated and walked off, Bronze would take down the pair they were looking at and hurry after them. When they sensed they were being followed and saw who it was, sometimes they'd buy the shoes on the spot, and sometimes they'd say they weren't buying and keep walking. Bronze would continue to follow them. The person would feel uncomfortable and would stop again. This time, they'd see him holding up the shoes and feel his big black eyes urging them to buy. They'd scratch their heads, then buy the shoes, saying, "These are very well made. . . ."

As the New Year approached, Bronze had sold most of the shoes.

One night it snowed very heavily. Snow was still falling in the morning, and there were drifts two feet high. The family had difficulty pushing the door open.

"Don't go to town today," said Nainai.

"There are eleven pairs left," said Baba and Mama.

"One pair's for you, so that leaves ten. If we can't sell them, we'll keep them and wear them ourselves."

Bronze took Sunflower to school.

"Don't go to town today," said Sunflower before she ran into school. Then she came straight out again. "Don't go!" she shouted to him in the distance.

But Bronze was determined. Back at home, he gathered his things together. It was cold, he said, and people would come to buy shoes. Baba, Mama, and Nainai knew that once Bronze had decided to do something, it was very difficult to get him to change his mind.

"In that case, you'd better choose a pair for yourself."

Bronze agreed and found a pair that fit. Then he picked up the other ten and waved as he headed out into the blustery snow.

The streets of the town were almost deserted. There was only the snow falling constantly, quietly. He stood where he always stood, by the bridge. Now and again someone would walk by and say, "Go home. You won't have any business today."

Bronze ignored them.

The ten pairs of shoes hanging from the rope were soon covered in snow.

A man walked over. "How much a pound?" he asked.

Bronze had no idea what he was talking about and looked around. The man pointed to the shoes. "These ducks of yours, how much a pound?"

This time Bronze understood. He lifted a pair of shoes from the rope, brushed off the snow, and held them out in front of him. The man burst out laughing. From a distance, they'd looked like white ducks hanging there! Bronze laughed too. People walking past laughed as well. But as they hurried through the snow, they thought of the pitiful sight of Bronze standing in the cold and sighed.

Meanwhile, Bronze couldn't stop laughing. He only had to look at the ten pairs of shoes hanging on the rope and he began again. Once he started, it was hard to stop. Doubled up with laughter, he crouched on the ground, his body shaking so much that the snow slipped off his hair and slid inside his collar.

Some people were watching him from across the road. They were inside, keeping warm by a roaring fire.

"The boy's gone crazy!" they muttered.

Eventually Bronze stopped laughing. But instead of getting up, he stayed in the same crouching position. He was completely still. The snow was beginning to settle on him. The people across the road were worried.

"Mute!" they called out, quietly. When there was no response, they raised their voices. "MUTE!" they shouted.

Bronze must have fallen asleep, and their shouting startled him. As he looked up, a mountain of snow slid down his back. The people across the road waved in a friendly way. "Come inside and keep warm! You can keep an eye on your shoes from here."

Bronze waved back, but he preferred to stay outside with his shoes.

The snow was falling heavily, and by midday the small flakes had become big white clumps. The people across the road shouted, "Go home, mute!"

Bronze huddled deeper inside his clothes and stood there, expressionless.

Then two people ran across the road, grabbed him by the arms, and dragged him inside. They didn't give him a chance to object. While he was warming up by the fire, he saw someone stop and look at his shoes. He ran out to seize his chance.

The person looked for a while, then started walking away.

"Perhaps he thought they were ducks!" said one of the people inside, and everyone started laughing.

This time Bronze didn't laugh. He desperately wanted to sell the last ten pairs of shoes, but the morning was gone and he hadn't sold a single pair. He gazed up at the sky full of snow. "Come on! Come and buy my shoes! Come on! Come and buy my shoes!" he repeated over and over in his head.

Eventually, it stopped snowing. Bronze took the shoes off the line one pair at a time, brushed the snow off them, and hung them up again.

A group of people appeared on the road. They didn't look local; they were from one of the Cadre Schools and were taking the steamboat back to the city for New Year's. Some had big backpacks, and others were carrying bags, probably full of local produce. They were chatting and laughing as their feet crunched through the snow.

Bronze didn't think these city people would be

interested in buying reed shoes. After all, city people had cotton-padded shoes or leather shoes. So he didn't beckon them over.

He was right. These city people didn't wear reed shoes, but when they came past him, some of them stopped. The others wondered why and stopped too. One or two of them must have been artists. They were enchanted by the ten pairs of fluffy reed shoes in the white light of the snow. The artists saw beauty—an extraordinary beauty—in these shoes. It was difficult to explain. One by one they stepped closer and touched the shoes—and when they touched them, they liked them even more. Some of them held a pair up to their nose and sniffed, a whiff of straw, which was especially strong in the cold air around them.

"They'd look so good on the wall at home," one of them said.

The others nodded and reached to grab a pair, afraid of missing out. There were nine in the group. They each took a pair, and one person took two. All ten were in their hands. Until they asked the price, Bronze wasn't at all sure that they were really going to buy them. He told them his price — the price that never changed. So cheap! thought the city people, and they handed over their money. They were delighted with their purchases, which they would bring back to the city, and took great pleasure in examining them as they walked on.

Bronze stood there in the snow with a handful of cash. He'd done it! Then someone yelled from across the road, "Hey, mute, best get home now that your shoes are sold! You'll freeze to death out here!"

Bronze stuffed the cash into his inside pocket, untied the rope from the trees, and fastened it around his waist. He looked across the road. There was a crowd of people watching him. He waved to them and started running through the snow like a madman.

The sky was clear and everything was bright. Bronze took the usual road home. He wanted to sing, to sing the song that Nainai sang when she was twisting rope. He couldn't sing out loud, so he sang in his head:

Fishing for prawns in trees? Oh, put away your net!
Looking for gold in mud? There's only sand as yet!

Oranges grow on the black locust tree.
Oh, when will we see the pe-o-ny?

Someone was following him.

"Hey, shoe boy, stop!"

Bronze stopped and glanced around warily. He didn't recognize the man and was suspicious. When the man caught up with Bronze, he said, "I saw them buying your shoes. Have you got any more? I'd like some too."

Bronze shook his head and felt a bit sorry for him. The man wrung his hands and sighed in disappointment. Bronze looked at him and wished he could do something. The man turned and headed toward the pier, and Bronze turned and headed for home.

After a while Bronze slowed down. He saw the reed shoes on his feet. He heard the snow crunch beneath them. He stopped walking, looked up at the sky, then down at the snow, and, finally, at the reed shoes, which felt warm and snug on his feet. Nainai's song warbled through his mind. After a moment or two, he pulled his right foot out of his shoe and put it down on the snow. The cold jabbed like a needle.

He did the same with his left. Immediately, the cold shot through his bones. He bent forward, picked up the shoes, and held them up to inspect them. They'd only been worn once in the snow, and there were no dirty marks on them. They looked like new.

Bronze smiled, then turned and ran after the man. His bare feet sent snow spraying as they hit the ground.

The man was stepping down to the pier to catch the steamboat when Bronze appeared in front of him, holding up the pair of reed shoes. The man couldn't believe his luck and reached out to take them. He wanted to pay Bronze extra, but Bronze would only take his usual price.

Bronze waved at his last customer, then headed for home. He ran all the way, without once looking back. His feet were washed clean by the snow but were frozen red. Bright, bright red.

Golden Thatch

Bronze liked to sit beside Sunflower when she was doing her homework. As she concentrated on writing her characters and doing her math, his eyes were full of envy and hope. When Sunflower discovered this, she had an idea: she would teach him to read. It came to her like a flash of lightning and took her completely by surprise. She was so excited and wished she'd thought of it earlier.

She used the money Mama had given her for buying ribbon to buy a pencil for Bronze.

"Starting today, I'm going to teach you how to read."

Bronze looked at her as though he hadn't heard right. But Nainai, Baba, and Mama had, and stopped what they were doing. Sunflower put the sharpened pencil and a little notebook in front of him and repeated, "Starting today, I'm going to teach you how to read."

Bronze was stunned. He was excited but also a little embarrassed and unsure. He looked at Sunflower, then at the adults, and finally back at Sunflower. It was a bolt out of the blue, and for a while no one said a word.

Sunflower picked up the pencil and notebook. Bronze shot out the door. Sunflower ran after him. "Bronze . . . !" she shouted. But he ran and ran. "Bronze!" she cried, chasing him.

This time he looked back, but his hands and eyes said, "No! No! I can't! I won't be able to."

"But you will! You will!"

He kept running, and Sunflower chased after him. But her foot caught on a tree root sticking out of the mud, and she tumbled onto the riverbank and went rolling down. Noticing that he could no longer hear Sunflower's footsteps, Bronze looked around and saw her on the shore. He raced over, leaped down, and helped her to her feet. She was covered in mud and bits of grass, but she had held on tight to the pencil and notebook as she rolled, and the notebook still looked new. As Bronze brushed the mud and grass off her, she repeated, "Starting today, I'm going to teach you how to read."

Bronze felt his eyes well up with tears, which rolled down his nose. He bent his knees so she could climb onto his back, then slowly carried her up the bank. They sat together under a big tree, the setting sun staining the river a bright orange. Sunflower pointed to the glowing ball in the sky, then found a stick and wrote two characters in the earth:

太阳

She read them out loud: "*Tai yang* . . . the sun." She retraced the strokes of the characters over and over again, naming each of the brushstrokes as she wrote. "*Heng* (a horizontal line), *pie* (descending to the left), *na* (descending to the right), and finally *dian* (a dot). That's *tai*. . . ."

She found a stick for Bronze and made him copy what she had written. Bronze concentrated. He was used to being the older one, and it felt strange being taught by Sunflower.

Slowly, the sun was setting. Slowly, a leaf fell from the tree. Sunflower pointed to the fluttering leaf, and as she watched it, she said, "*Luo* . . . falling, *luo xia qu* . . . falling down." It settled on the grass like a butterfly. Sunflower wrote three more characters after the first two:

太阳落下去

She read them out loud: "*Tai yang luo xia qu* . . . the sun is setting."

Bronze had a good memory, and once he had grasped the names of the strokes, and knew that they had to be written in a particular order, it was astonishing how quickly he learned.

By now the sun had sunk low, and it was getting more and more difficult to see the characters in the earth.

"It's time to go home," said Sunflower.

But Bronze shook his head and kept writing with the stick. As the moon rose, it shone a different kind of light — a pure, soft light — over the ground.

Bronze pointed to the moon.

"We've finished for today," said Sunflower.

Bronze kept pointing at the moon until she taught him how to write *yue liang* . . . the moon; *yue liang sheng shang lai* . . . the moon is rising.

月亮升上来

It was getting late, and Mama was calling them.

All the way home, Bronze was remembering and writing in his mind, *tai yang luo xia qu* . . . *yue liang sheng shang lai*.

太阳落下去
月亮升上来

Bronze was hungry to learn and gobbled up every character Sunflower knew, writing them out on the ground and in his notebook. The two of them never stopped. Wherever they went, whatever they saw, Bronze wanted to know what the characters were. He learned how to write the characters for buffalo and sheep. He also learned how to put characters together to build sentences.

牛	niu	buffalo
牛吃草	niu chi cao	the buffalo is eating grass
羊	yang	sheep
羊打架	yang da jia	the rams are fighting

And so it went on:

天	tian	sky
地	di	earth
风	feng	wind
雨	yu	rain
鸭子	yazi	duck
鸽子	gezi	pigeon
大鸭子	da yazi	big duck
小鸭子	xiao yazi	little duck
白鸽子	bai gezi	white pigeon
黑鸽子	hei gezi	black pigeon

Bronze saw the beautiful world around him transform into the magical world of characters. The sun became more gorgeous, more vivid, more enticing than ever. Likewise, the moon, the sky, the earth, the wind, the rain . . . everything took on a new life. And Bronze, who was used to careering around the fields whatever the weather, was changing too. He was calmer than he used to be.

Sunflower devised her own special ways of teaching Bronze. These clever little tricks engraved the characters so deeply into his memory that he would never forget them. His characters were a bit wonky and rough compared with Sunflower's nice neat ones, but they had a flavor all their own.

No one in Damaidi knew anything about it.

One quiet afternoon, when Bronze was taking the buffalo to graze, he passed one of the teachers writing a slogan on someone's wall in whitewash. He tethered the buffalo to a tree and went to watch.

"Come here," said the teacher, holding the dripping brush in his hand. "I'll teach you a character."

Bronze shook his head.

"You'll have to learn a few characters one day, you know."

A small crowd gathered and began to comment.

"That mute, he stands there watching as though he can write too."

"Hey, mute, come and show us what you can write."

Bronze waved his hand at them and backed away.

"Then what are you watching for? Go and graze your buffalo, you stupid mute."

Bronze turned around and walked toward the buffalo. As he was untying the rope, he heard raucous laughter break out behind him. He leaned close to the buffalo, taking his time, then stood and walked back over to them. The teacher was busy writing and didn't notice him approaching—until Bronze snatched the brush from his hand. Everyone went quiet. Bronze grabbed the bucket of whitewash with his other hand and wrote on the wall in huge characters:

我是大麦地的青铜

Wo shi Damaidi de Qingtong

I am Bronze from Damaidi

The silence was deafening. Bronze looked at them, put down the bucket, threw the brush to one side, and walked off. He didn't look back.

The characters were a bit higgledy-piggledy, but every single one of them was written correctly. The crowd could barely believe their eyes. The news spread throughout Damaidi, and by the end of the day all the villagers knew that something strange was going on. They remembered all kinds of mysterious stories about Bronze and came to the conclusion, as they had in the past, that there was something extraordinary about this mute boy.

Sunflower was happy with her new family. She had been pale when she arrived, but the fresh air and fresh food had given her a healthy glow. With her cotton shoes, her hair in braids, her trousers worn short, and her jacket fastened tightly around her waist, she could have been a local. The villagers soon forgot how she had arrived in Damaidi. The family talked about "our Sunflower" as though she had always been one of them.

And the family had such fun! At night, after the lights were turned out, they talked and talked, and the sound of laughter flew out the window of their little thatched house and into the night. Anyone passing by would wonder what on earth could be so funny.

Working and playing together like this, time passed quickly. There was no place better than Damaidi in the springtime. Dazzling spring flowers appeared at the edges of the fields, by the ponds, and along the riverside, their colors brightening the landscape. Everywhere was green, a rich lush hue. Big blue magpies and their smaller azure-winged relatives and all kinds of other birds with different names and some with no names flew about the fields and villages, crying out. The river had been quiet during the winter, and now boats with white and brown sails were beginning to pass by again. March was a busy month, full of activity, and the sounds of people singing while they worked, of dogs barking, and of girls cheerfully collecting mulberries infused the land with new life.

But the buffalo was restless. It had been restless for a few days. There was fresh grass everywhere, but it didn't seem to be interested. It would take a couple of mouthfuls, then look up at the sky—in the daytime at the sun, at night the moon. Every now and then it would give a deep bellow that rumbled so much it rustled the leaves on the trees.

Then, one evening, it refused to go into its pen. It pulled the rope from Bronze's hand but didn't go far, just circled around and around the house. Eventually Bronze and Baba managed to get it into the pen. There was a light breeze that evening, and the moonlight was as soft as water—it was a quiet and peaceful spring evening. But deep in the night, when the villagers were fast asleep, the weather changed, and in no time at all, a wild wind hurtled in from the horizon, swirling and thrashing like an army of screaming black demons, their mouths gaping, their tongues flicking. It crashed over the land, stripping branches and leaves from the trees. It swept along the ground, whipping sand and dust into the air. It ripped planks from the wooden bridge and hurled them into the river, crashed little boats into the bank, snapped reed stalks, knocked over crops, tore down electricity cables, blew birds' nests out of trees and birds to the ground . . . and changed the world almost beyond recognition.

Sunflower woke with a start. When she opened her eyes, she wasn't sure where she was. She looked up to see the black sky of night and the stars shining brightly, yet there were four walls around her.

Mama came rushing over. "Sunflower, Sunflower! Get up! Quick!" she said, pulling her out of bed and hurriedly pushing her arms and legs into some clothes. In the darkness they heard Baba shout, "Bronze, help Nainai out of the house. Quick!"

Then Nainai's trembling voice. "Where's Sunflower? Where is she?"

"She's here with me!" shouted Mama.

Sunflower didn't know what was happening. As Mama dressed her, she looked up at the sky: all those branches and leaves flying around.

"The wind's blown the roof off," said Mama.

Was that even possible? Sunflower wondered. Then, when she realized that what Mama was saying was true, she burst into tears.

"Don't be afraid, don't be afraid," said Mama, hugging her tight.

The gale stormed across the sky, spreading debris and dust in its wake. The buffalo had long since crashed its way out of the pen and was quietly waiting for them by the door. The five of them helped one another out of the house, struggling against the raging wind.

Once outside, they could hear faint sounds over the howling wind: the shouts and cries of the villagers of Damaidi.

The wind was growing stronger and stronger, and it had started to rain.

"Head for the school!" yelled Baba. The school was a brick building with a tiled roof, the strongest building in Damaidi. Lightning cracked through the sky, and when the family looked back, they saw that the four walls of their house had collapsed. They hurried to the school. Other people were gathering there too. The wind gradually began to subside, but the rain fell harder and harder. At one point it seemed that the sky was a river, and it was leaking. The villagers crowded into the classrooms and, helpless and heavyhearted, watched as rain ruled the sky. No one said a word.

At dawn it was still raining, but not so heavily. The fields and the crops were flooded, and although the village was still recognizable as Damaidi, a lot of houses had fallen down. The first people to venture into the fields were Gayu and his parents, looking for their ducks. They walked along, calling and searching. The wind had carried off the fencing of the duck pen, and the ducks had gotten out. The people who had sought shelter at the school heard Gayu's parents' shouts and thought about their own chickens, ducks, pigs, and sheep, and their belongings at home. They headed out in the rain, many to homes that were in ruins.

"I left my schoolbag at home," said Sunflower.

"It won't be any use now," said Nainai. "The books will all be soaked."

"I have to go and find it," said Sunflower.

Baba and Mama were also worried about the things they had left at home. They urged Nainai to stay at the school with the items they'd brought with them, and headed home with the children. The road was deep in water. Bronze helped Sunflower onto the buffalo and off they went.

The water stretched before their eyes like a lake. The tips of broken reeds peeked out and swayed like countless tails sticking up in the air. The tall trees were half underwater and looked short and dumpy.

If you were on a boat, you could reach out and touch the birds' nests that had withstood the wind. Floating about on the water were pan lids, shoes, chamber pots, mats, buckets, ducks without a home to go to—all sorts of everyday things.

The family went home. But it was no longer a house, just some broken-down walls. Bronze went in first, determined to find Sunflower's schoolbag. He poked about with his foot underwater, and every time he felt something, he'd hook it up with his toes: a bowl, a wok, an iron shovel. Sunflower watched him pull out one thing after another, wondering what he'd find next. She asked Baba to help her down from the buffalo and stood trembling in the water. The next time Bronze fished something out, she cried out in delight.

"Bronze! Give it to me!"

Baba and Mama were standing in the water too, watching dejectedly, barely moving. Then all of a sudden something flew out of nowhere and hit Sunflower. It almost knocked her over. She gave a startled cry, then saw something swimming away fast underwater, stirring up waves. A fish! An enormous carp! Bronze hurled himself forward and hurried to close what was left of the door, to trap the fish inside the house. The whole family watched as the fish swam around and around. Every so often it would crash into the remains of one of the walls, or into Bronze's or Sunflower's legs, and whenever it hit something, it would leap out of the water.

Bronze ran around trying to catch it. Sunflower squealed.

The fish leaped out of the water again, splashing Sunflower's face. She put her hands up to keep the water off, and when she looked up again, everyone was laughing. Bronze was grinning and leaning back, laughing, not paying attention, when the fish thrashed against his leg and knocked him off balance. He staggered backward and tumbled into the water.

"Bronze!" shouted Sunflower.

He clambered to his feet, dripping with water. He looked so funny that Sunflower started to giggle and giggle and giggle, unable to stop. As he was already wet, Bronze simply plunged back into the water and began to feel around with his hands. Sunflower had dodged out of the way and was standing on the corner of a broken wall, watching him anxiously, expectantly.

He almost caught the fish several times, and it annoyed him when it got away. He knew he could catch it. He huffed and puffed as he felt around for it. Then the enormous carp swam straight into his arms. All he had to do was hold on tight. The fish struggled for its life, its tail splashing water all over Bronze's face. Sunflower was so excited.

"Bronze! Bronze!" she cried.

Eventually the fish had no strength left, but Bronze didn't dare loosen his grip. He held on tight and stood up. The fish had red whiskers, and they quivered as it opened and closed its mouth. Bronze beckoned Sunflower to come and touch it. She walked through the water, reached out her hand, and lightly ran her finger over its cold, slippery body.

The next moment they were jumping for joy at their catch, leaping and splashing about in the water. Mama looked at the two children, who hadn't a care in the world, and at the house that barely had walls. She turned away and wept. Baba's hard, rough hands rubbed his hard, rough face over and over.

When the flood receded, the family put up a shelter on the foundations of their old house. From now on, they would have to live even more frugally. They would need to build a new house, and with two children to look after, there was no time to lose. Besides, people would look down on them if they lived in a shelter.

But building a house would be expensive, and they barely had any money. Within days, Baba's hair turned gray and Mama's face became more wrinkled. Nainai grew even thinner than before, so thin that Bronze and Sunflower were afraid the wind might blow her over.

"I'm not going to school anymore," said Sunflower.

"Oh, yes, you are," said Mama.

Nainai pulled Sunflower close. She didn't say anything, just stroked her hair over and over. But Sunflower could hear the voice deep in Nainai's heart: "Don't say such ridiculous things."

Sunflower never mentioned it again. Instead she worked harder than ever and became the top student in her class in everything. "If only all the children in Damaidi were like Sunflower!" sighed the teachers.

In the evenings Sunflower would do her homework,

but she was worried about burning up too much paraffin in the lamp, so she would say she was going to play at Cuihuan's or Qiuni's house. In fact, she was going there to do her homework, sharing their lamplight—although she was careful to let the others have the light and she didn't chatter or distract them. Cuihuan liked people to do things for her. She was always asking Sunflower to pass her the eraser or draw lines in her exercise book, and Sunflower did what she asked. With Qiuni she'd try not to appear too smart. It annoyed Qiuni that Sunflower did her homework faster and better than she did, so Sunflower kept quiet. She didn't say, "All done!" when she'd finished or "I know!" when Qiuni couldn't answer the questions. If Qiuni asked for help, she would talk the question over with her tentatively, as though they were figuring it out together. This way, Qiuni could appear to answer it before her, and when Qiuni said smugly, "Maybe you're not so clever after all!" Sunflower would stay silent.

One day, the teacher was particularly critical of Cuihuan's and Qiuni's work, and tore up their homework books in front of the class. Then she opened up Sunflower's pristine homework book, stepped down from the teacher's platform, and passed it around. "This is Sunflower's. This is what I call homework!" Sunflower kept her head down.

That evening, after the family had eaten, Sunflower wondered if she could still go to Cuihuan's or Qiuni's to do her homework. It was dark outside and there was no light in the shelter. They'd barely lit the lamp since the house fell down. They ate in the dark and went to bed in the dark. But she still had a lot of homework to do. She thought it over and told her family she was going to play at Cuihuan's.

It was unusual to find Cuihuan's door closed. Sunflower knocked.

"I'm already in bed," called Cuihuan.

But Sunflower could see through the crack in the door that Cuihuan was sitting doing her homework by the lamp. She walked around the village, her head hanging. She didn't want to go and knock on Qiuni's door, so she decided to head home. After a while, however, the thought of the homework she still had to do made her turn back in the direction of Qiuni's house. The door was open, but she stood in the doorway for a few minutes before going inside.

"Hi, Qiuni," she said.

Qiuni kept doing her homework as though she hadn't heard. Sunflower saw a stool on the other side of the table and went to sit down.

"My mother will be here soon, and she'll need to sit there while she stitches soles for the cotton shoes she's making."

Sunflower froze.

"Don't you have a light at your house?" asked Qiuni without looking up.

Sunflower didn't reply.

"Do you ever light the lamp at your house?" Qiuni still didn't look up.

Sunflower picked up her homework book and hurried out of Qiuni's house as fast as she could. She ran down the street that stretched the entire length of the village, eager to get home as soon as she could, tears streaming down her face all the way.

But she didn't go straight home. Instead, she went and sat on the stone slab under the old tree at the end of the village, the same stone slab she had sat on a few years earlier, before riding to Bronze's house on the back of the buffalo. She looked up at the old tree and saw its branches heavy with early summer leaves. She longed to throw her arms around the tree and weep. Instead, she gazed through teary eyes at the dark sky and the moon above.

Meanwhile, Bronze went looking for her. He stopped at Cuihuan's house first. From the street, he could hear her mother telling her off. "Why didn't you open the door and let her in?"

"I don't want her using our light."

Then Cuihuan started crying. Perhaps her mother had slapped her.

"I just don't want her using our light!"

"You know, Sunflower is one in a million. You and the other girls don't even begin to compare!"

Bronze decided that Sunflower must have gone to Qiuni's. But as he approached her house, he heard her crying too. She seemed to be talking to herself. "If you can't afford school, then don't go. How dare you come to our house and use our light?"

Qiuni had probably been slapped this evening too. Bronze started to run through the village. He raced down one street, then another, and eventually found Sunflower beneath the old tree. She was lying on her front on the stone slab, struggling to do her homework in the moonlight. Bronze stood very quietly behind her. When she realized he was there, she grabbed her homework book in one hand and placed the other hand in Bronze's.

Neither of them said a word as they walked hand in hand by the river and then headed back to the shelter in the pale milky light of the moon.

The following evening Bronze went to the vegetable garden and picked ten or more stems of pumpkin flowers that were just about to open. When Nainai asked what he was doing, he just smiled. Then he took a boat to the reed pond. As he steered through the dense patch of reeds to the pool of water, there they were: hundreds and hundreds of fireflies dancing about in the grass. They cast their glow on the water and lit up the sky. It took his breath away and reminded him of the time his father had taken him into the city. In the evening they'd climbed up a tower and seen all those thousands of lights shining below them. He stood for a while and drank it all in.

The fireflies seemed to dance aimlessly, free to go wherever they liked, their magical trails crisscrossing the sky. There were so many of them, he couldn't help wondering what drew them to this pool of water. Their light was so bright that he could spot a dragonfly on the tip of a blade of grass: its eyes, its feet, and the pattern on its wings.

Bronze stood in the shallow water beside the grass and began to catch fireflies. He went after the biggest, brightest, and most beautiful. When he caught one he put it inside one of the tight pumpkin flowers. It lit up like a lantern. He put a dozen or so fireflies in each flower lantern; the more fireflies he put in, the brighter it glowed. As soon as he completed a lantern, he placed it in the boat and started on the next. He wanted to make ten lanterns. He wanted to fill their temporary shelter with light and illuminate every single character in Sunflower's homework book.

He had identified the biggest and brightest firefly, but it kept flying over the middle of the pool and didn't look as though it had any intention of landing on the grass. Bronze wanted this one most of all. He started clapping his hands. All the village children knew that fireflies like the sound of clapping. Sure enough, the fireflies started dancing around him. As long as he kept clapping, they kept coming, and soon he was surrounded by rings of light, as though caught in the middle of a glowing whirlwind. He chose the biggest and brightest ones, between ten and twenty per lantern, but he was really after the magnificent one that kept flying over the middle of the pool. No matter how much he clapped, it would not come. Bronze was annoyed.

By now he had ten lamps. They were all lying on the boat, at different angles to one another, and looked like a massive lamp in the shape of a branch. Bronze got back into his boat and prepared to go home, but he couldn't get that firefly out of his head. He plunged the bamboo pole into the water at the stern of the boat and headed for the middle of the pool instead. He was determined to catch that firefly.

As the boat approached, the firefly flew off. Bronze chased after it, but the firefly only flew higher. Bronze's chin rose as he watched it flying higher and higher. There was nothing he could do. Then, after a while, it started to hover and circle downward again. Bronze kept as still as a wooden post and waited patiently. The firefly was attracted by the lanterns and darted close to investigate, then just as quickly darted away again. It did this a few times, growing in confidence each time, until it was flying right in front of Bronze. He could see its wings, shiny and brown, but he couldn't reach it. If he could just hold out, he thought, this little creature would come close enough. . . .

Eventually, the firefly began to fly above his head, as though it had mistaken Bronze's hair for a patch of rough grass. The firefly flew around him, lighting up his face whenever it passed in front of him.

Bronze waited for the right moment. The firefly was just above him to the side. He figured he should be able to jump up and catch it unawares. He held his breath, waited until it came closer again, then leaped up, clapped his hands together in the air, and . . . Got it!

But as he'd pressed his feet into the boat, it had slid across the pool. He landed in the water and swallowed a couple of mouthfuls, but still he managed to keep his hands together tightly. He scrambled out of the water, the firefly safely inside his hands, which were glowing from the light within. He climbed back onto the boat and slipped the firefly inside one of the pumpkin lanterns.

Bronze headed home. When he got back, he hung the lanterns from a string and, holding one end of the string in each hand, arms outstretched, he went inside.

The dark shelter filled with light. Everyone's faces lit up, and for a moment they stood staring—Nainai, Baba, Mama, and Sunflower. They were at a loss for words.

Bronze tied the ends of the string to a couple of the shelter posts and grinned as if to say, "Look! We've got light!"

It was the brightest, most beautiful light in Damaidi, perfect for doing homework.

The family could not spend the winter in the temporary shelter. They had to build a house before the cold weather arrived. The adults had decided that they should build a good house and build it well.

They spent the summer making plans. They would

sell whatever they could. They cut down some of the large trees at the front of the house and sold them. They sold a fat pig. They also had a pond full of lotus root, a plot of arrowhead, and a smaller plot of white radish, which they would harvest and sell. But when they added it all up, it was still a long way from what they needed.

They put pride to one side and borrowed from relatives and neighbors, promising to repay it all with interest. They didn't care if people looked down on them; all they wanted was to be able to move the children into the new house before winter came. Nainai wanted to contribute, but Baba and Mama wouldn't hear of it: she was getting old and deserved respect, not the scorn of the neighbors. But watching the two children playing outside made her even more determined. She glanced at Mama and Baba, took up her stick, and went out to ask for loans. Most people were alarmed, and embarrassed, to see such an elderly lady asking for money. "Of course," they said. "When do you need it?"

Nainai had a nephew. She thought she might be able to borrow a little from him, so she went to ask him. He refused, snapping at her that he didn't have any money. She had never expected he would be so nasty, so heartless. As a senior member of the family, she was entitled to get angry at his disrespect, but she bit her tongue and hobbled away with her stick.

Although some of the newer buildings in Damaidi had tiled roofs, everyone knew that the best roofs were those made from cogon grass. Cogon grass grew by the sea, over sixty miles away, and the family had planned to go and rent a plot of ripe cogon grass and harvest it themselves. But first they needed to find the money.

"We could use straw instead," said Baba and Mama.

"No," said Nainai. "We agreed that we would have the best: a cogon-grass roof."

"It doesn't matter," said Mama.

"We are having a cogon-grass roof!" insisted Nainai, shaking her head.

Nainai left the house early the next morning. No one knew where she had gone. She didn't come home at lunchtime. It was evening before she appeared, staggering along the main road by the village.

"Nainai, where have you been!" shouted Sunflower as she ran to meet her.

Her grandmother looked exhausted, but there was joy in her eyes.

Nainai had always been the smartest old person in Damaidi. She was tall, with silver hair, and she kept herself immaculate, washing in cold water throughout the four seasons. She folded her clothes carefully at night, so they always looked neat and had crisp lines in the morning, never a crumple. Although there were patches on almost all of her clothes, they were sewn with such fine stitching and such a closely matching color of thread that it seemed they were part of the garment, that it would look strange without them.

To the villagers, Nainai was a kindly, elegant old lady. She was also very strong willed. She'd told Sunflower that she'd been born into a rich family and had enjoyed a good childhood. Pale jade earrings dangled from her ears; she wore a gold ring on her finger and a jade bangle on her wrist. She'd wanted to sell them, or at least some of them, but Baba and Mama wouldn't let her. One day, she'd pawned the earrings, but as soon as they heard about it, Baba and Mama sold some of their grain and went into town to buy them back.

Today, as Sunflower walked home with Nainai, her grandmother looked different. Sunflower wasn't sure why. She kept wondering what it could be.

"What are you looking at?" Nainai smiled.

Eventually Sunflower realized that Nainai wasn't wearing her earrings. Her hand hovered in the air as she pointed to one ear and then the other. Nainai said nothing, just smiled.

Suddenly Sunflower ran on ahead. "Nainai's earrings are gone!" she cried as soon as she saw Baba and Mama.

So that was where Nainai had been all day! They pressed her to tell them which pawnshop she'd taken them to, but she wouldn't. She had only one thing to say: "We have a home to build!"

Mama looked at the money on the table and burst into tears. "You've worn those earrings all your life. You can't sell them."

"We have a home to build."

Mama wiped away her tears. "You're too good to us. How can we ever repay you?"

"Don't talk nonsense!" said Nainai impatiently. Then she wrapped her arms around her grandchildren and smiled up at the moon in the sky. "Let's build a big house for Bronze and Sunflower!"

Baba borrowed a large boat, and early one morning he and Bronze set out from Damaidi. Nainai, Mama, and Sunflower went to the river to see them off.

Sunflower waved at them until the last bit of the boat disappeared around the bend of the river, then she walked home with Nainai and Mama, looking back after each step. And they began to wait.

All day and all night, Baba and Bronze steered the boat down the river to the sea, adjusting the sail to take the wind. Two days later, early in the morning, they reached the sea. It didn't take long to rent a decent plot, and everything seemed to be going well.

By now it was autumn and, as they had hoped, the frost had turned the cogon grass a beautiful golden red. The straight stems looked like copper wire. When the wind blew, they moved against one another, producing a metallic sound. Waves crashed on either side of Baba and Bronze — white waves on one side, copper waves on the other.

Bronze spotted a wild animal he had never seen before. Baba said it was a river deer. It looked straight at Bronze and his father, then dipped low into the grass and disappeared.

They started to build a shelter, and by the time they had finished, there was a bright moon in the sky. They sat in the entrance to the shelter, eating the dry food they had brought with them from home. There was a light breeze. It was quieter at night: the sea was calmer, and the cogon grass rustled gently.

There seemed to be a lamp shining far in the distance.

"Can you see?" said Baba. "Over there. Perhaps they've come to cut grass too."

The coast was so vast that the tiny light flickering in the distance was a source of comfort to them; they were glad to know they were not completely alone. It had been a long and tiring journey. With the waves lapping against the shore, and Damaidi in their thoughts, they soon fell fast asleep.

The next morning, they were up before sunrise, all set to cut grass. Baba had a big scythe with a long curved blade and an even longer handle. He kept the end of the handle at his waist, holding it tight with both hands, then moved his body with a steady rhythm. The blade sliced through the air and into the grass.

Bronze's job was to gather up the cut grass, tie it into bundles, and stack them up.

The scythe danced ceaselessly in Baba's hands. Soon his clothes were drenched, and beads of sweat dripped from his forehead onto the grass.

Bronze was soaked too.

They urged each other to rest, but neither would stop. As they looked out over the vast grassland around them, they thought of the house they were going to build: a big, tall house, with a golden-red roof. And as they worked, they pictured it towering before them in the sky.

Their life by the sea was simple: they ate, they cut grass, they slept. Every so often, they would put down their tools and bathe in the water, which was still warm from the summer. It was so different from swimming in the river. Here they felt light; they floated. Just the two of them, father and son, in the huge sea.

When Baba saw Bronze having such fun, it brought a lump to his throat. He felt he'd never done enough for his son, especially after Bronze lost his speech. But life was hard, and they were always so busy that they seldom had any time to spend with him. What else could they have done? Time had passed and he'd grown up. Bronze didn't have what other children had, but he had never complained about anything—in fact he always tried to find ways to help the family.

"That child suffers!" Nainai had told Baba and Mama, again and again. Now Baba had taken his son away from home to this lonely wilderness. It pained his heart. He drew Bronze near and briskly began to brush the dust and dirt off him. The boy was so thin, it brought tears to his eyes.

"We'll spend just a few more days here, then we'll have enough grass to build the house, a really big house, with a room for you and a room for Sunflower." The words seemed to catch in his throat.

"And one for Nainai," Bronze said with his hands.

"Of course." Baba washed the dirt off his son with clean water.

The sun shone warmly over the sea, and a few gulls circled gracefully above the surface of the water. The days passed, and Bronze began to miss Mama, Nainai, and Damaidi, but most of all he missed Sunflower. He was beginning to feel overwhelmed by the vastness of the sea and the enormity of the grassland. Sometimes he would stand with a bundle of grass in his arms, wishing he were a bird and dreaming that he could fly back to Damaidi. The grass would rustle as it slipped to the ground, and Baba would say, "Come on, we're almost there."

Behind them stretched the bare ground they had already stripped. And by the sea towered two gold mountains of grass they had already cut.

Bronze had another job to do every day. He had to take an iron bucket across the high sea dike and fetch a pail of fresh water. It felt such a long way, and when Baba disappeared from view, he felt all alone—as though the sea would swallow him up.

But one day something wonderful happened. As he

was walking along, he saw a boy about the same age, also climbing up the dike with an iron bucket.

The boy was delighted and surprised to see Bronze. Bronze put down his bucket and waited. The boy stopped for a moment, then ran up to the top of the dike. They stood there, facing each other, like two wild animals sizing each other up.

"Where are you from?" the boy asked first.

Bronze blushed and used his hands to show that he couldn't speak.

The boy pointed to his mouth. "You're mute?"

Bronze nodded with embarrassment.

Then they sat on top of the enormous dike and began to talk. It wasn't easy.

Bronze used a stick to write the two characters of his name on the ground:

青铜

Qingtong

Then he patted himself on the chest and pointed to the boy's chest.

"You're asking my name?"

Bronze nodded. The boy took the stick from Bronze's hand and wrote the two characters of his name on the ground:

青狗

Qinggou

With his finger, Bronze drew a line under the first character of his name and the first character of the boy's name and laughed. Qinggou laughed too.

He told Bronze that he'd also come here with his father, to cut grass to take home and build a house. "Those are ours," he said, pointing to two haystacks in the distance. They were about the same size as the ones Bronze and Baba had made.

When the boy stood up to go, Bronze gestured to him to stay a while longer.

"I can't," said Qinggou. "I've got to get back with the water. If I take too long, my father'll lose his temper."

Bronze was taken aback. It had never occurred to him that a boy could be scared of his own father.

"See you here tomorrow, same place, same time?" said Qinggou.

Bronze nodded, and reluctantly they went their separate ways.

Bronze walked back to the shelter with a spring in his step. He couldn't wait to tell Baba that he'd met a boy on the dike.

Baba was delighted. "Really? That's wonderful!" He'd never expected his son might meet another child here.

From then on, the two boys met on the dike every day. Bronze learned that Qinggou had no mother, only a father, who had a foul temper. He wanted to tell Qinggou how kind his father was, but he didn't. In any case, it would have been very hard to explain. At one of their last meetings, he was shocked to learn that Qinggou's mother had abandoned him before his first birthday, eleven years previously, and gone off with an opera singer. Apparently, when she'd married Qinggou's father he'd promised to build her a three-roomed house with a thatched roof, but he'd never been able to do it. His father had told him that she was very beautiful, and that when she was leaving, he'd been on his knees with Qinggou in his arms, begging her to stay, promising that the house would be built within three years. She'd just laughed at him, and off she'd gone. But Qinggou didn't hate her for it.

Bronze realized how lucky he was to have such a warm and loving family. As he was picking up the grass and tying it in bundles, he couldn't help glancing at Baba. He was a generous, kind man, and just thinking about this made Bronze work even harder.

Eventually, they had made a third haystack. That evening, as the sun set over the sea and the glow from the water filled the air, Baba rolled the long handle of the scythe in his hands and wiped the sweat from his brow. He looked up at the sky, let out a long sigh, and looked at Bronze. "Son, we've got enough."

Bronze stared at the three haystacks bathed in the evening sun. He felt like dropping to his knees and touching his head to the ground to worship them!

"Tomorrow, go and say good-bye to the boy and then we'll go home."

On their last night by the sea, the sky was clear, the moon was bright, the breeze was light, and the sea was calm. It felt more autumnal than when they had arrived, and the sound of insects all around seemed plaintive, as though they were singing their last song. Bronze and Baba were exhausted and soon fell asleep.

In the early hours, Baba stepped out of the shelter to relieve himself and caught sight of something in the distance: three large fires were burning away, as high as the sky. The color drained from his cheeks. He wondered if he was dreaming, but when he took a second look, the fires were still there. He rushed into the shelter and woke Bronze. "Get up! Get up! There's a fire!"

Baba dragged Bronze outside. The three mountains of fire were raging in the sky—they were Qinggou's haystacks. Bronze thought he could hear his friend shouting for help.

The fire had started in the shelter while Qinggou and his father were sleeping. His father had been drinking that evening and had fallen asleep smoking. The cigarette had slipped from his fingers and landed in the grass. Luckily, the fire had woken Qinggou, and he'd quickly woken his father. They had gotten out in time, but the shelter had gone up in smoke. The fire had hissed and wriggled like snakes heading for the haystacks.

By the time Bronze and Baba arrived, the mountains

of fire had more or less died down, and in the dark light they saw Qinggou and his father walking toward the sea.

That evening, as Bronze and Baba set sail for home in their boat piled high with cogon grass, Bronze stood at the front looking toward the shore. He spotted Qinggou at the water's edge in the chill sea breeze, and at that moment felt he was the luckiest child in the world. He waved to his friend but could barely see him through the tears in his eyes. He wished him and his father good luck, over and over again. He wanted to tell him that everything would be all right.

Since Bronze and Baba had set out on the boat, Sunflower had been counting the days till their return. Every morning when she got up, the first thing she did was chalk another line on her counting post. Baba had said they'd be away for a month.

After school, instead of going straight home, she would go and stand on the bridge and look down the river that led to the sea. How she longed to see

Bronze and Baba and their boat full of grass appear in the late-afternoon light. She would stay there such a long time that Nainai had to come and get her.

"Let's go home," she'd say. "They won't be here yet."

The last few nights, Sunflower had been calling out Bronze's name in her sleep, which had woken Nainai and Mama. Nainai made a game of talking to her while she slept.

"Where's Bronze?" she'd ask.

And Sunflower would answer in her sleep, "He's on the boat."

"And where's the boat?" Nainai would ask.

"It's on the river."

As Nainai continued asking questions, Sunflower's answers would become more and more vague and indistinct, until there was only the sound of her little mouth opening and closing, and then no sound at all.

"Look at her, answering questions in her sleep!" Mama would say.

One day, Sunflower was sitting on the bridge as usual, looking into the distance where the river bent to the west. The sun was inching its way down into the river, and the western sky was a rosy pink. Birds circled in the evening light, their shadows making beautiful silhouettes in the sunlight as they searched for food.

All of a sudden a mountain of grass appeared at the bend in the river. At first Sunflower was not sure what it was, but when she saw the sail, she knew. Baba and Bronze were back! She leaped to her feet, her heart pounding with excitement. As the boat sailed up the river, the mountain of grass grew higher and higher, the sun disappearing from view.

Sunflower ran home, shouting at the top of her voice, "They're sailing up the river! Baba and Bronze are here!"

Mama slipped her arm through Nainai's and walked with her to the river. The boat drew closer and closer. Bronze was sitting on the top of the enormous mountain of grass, as high as the buildings on either side of the river. As the evening sun fell on the cogon grass, it dazzled like a boat filled with gold, lighting up the faces of the people watching from the bank.

Bronze took off his jacket and waved it around in the air—at Damaidi and at Nainai, Mama, and Sunflower.

The Ice Necklace

The new house was finished just as the swallows were leaving. It was a large house, quite magnificent to behold both at close quarters and from a distance, and the villagers kept coming to take a look. There were few houses to compare with it, and it made the villagers feel that the poorest family in Damaidi was on its way to prosperity.

Then Baba did something that almost scared the life out of Bronze and Sunflower. He climbed onto the roof, struck a match, held it up for everyone below to see, then tossed it onto the cogon-grass thatching. A thin line of fire broke out and immediately tore from one side of the roof to the other, burning everything in its way.

Bronze leaped about in panic on the ground.

"Baba! Baba!" shouted Sunflower.

Bronze was beating his fist into his chest, and Sunflower bit into her hand so hard that she left a line of teeth marks. But Baba stood on the roof laughing at them, as though it were the most normal thing in the world. Then, one after another, the people on the ground started to laugh too. Bronze and Sunflower were confused. Had the adults gone mad?

Nainai explained, "There's enough cogon grass on that roof to cover two houses. The stalks are pressed together so tightly that there's not a hair's breadth between them. Just now when the fire tore across the roof, it wasn't burning the cogon grass, it was burning off the crumbs. Tightly packed cogon grass doesn't catch fire in the same way as wheat straw. And it looks so much better when it's been burned."

Sunflower looked up at the roof. Baba was holding a broom and sweeping away the ash. And, just as

Nainai had said, the roof looked better after the fire. It shone and glistened in the sun.

Baba sat down on the roof. Bronze looked up at him, a little enviously. When Baba beckoned to him to join him, Bronze ran up the ladder and pulled himself onto the shiny cogon grass.

Sunflower waved from the ground. "I want to come up too!"

"Can she?" asked Bronze, looking at Baba.

Baba nodded.

The adults helped Sunflower up the ladder, and Baba put out his big hand and pulled her onto the roof. She was scared at first, but Baba put his arm around her, and soon she wasn't afraid anymore.

More people gathered around and stood gaping up at them.

"My goodness, look at them all!" said Mama.

Bronze and Sunflower had a fabulous view from the roof. Even sitting down, they could see the whole of Damaidi: the windmill on the other side of the village, the Cadre School across the river, and the reeds that went on forever and ever.

"Nainai, come up here!" Sunflower called down.

"Don't be silly!" said Mama.

No matter how many times Nainai and Mama told them to come down, the three on the roof stayed exactly where they were, side by side, quietly looking at the village and the countryside all around.

They had done it—they had built the house before winter arrived.

That night, the family was so tired they could barely move. When it started to rain, they came inside, locked the door, and went to bed without bothering to eat. They slept right through to the following evening.

Nainai woke first. She made some food, then woke the others. Bronze and Sunflower were so sleepy they could barely sit up straight, and kept yawning as they ate.

Baba turned to Mama and said, "The children have been working so hard lately. They're so thin too. They should rest, and then we should let them play and have some fun."

Bronze and Sunflower did indeed need to rest. It

was several days before they had enough energy to do anything.

Then, not long after, someone passing through Damaidi brought news that the traveling circus was in Daoxiangdu, and there would be a show that night. When Sunflower heard this, she ran all the way home and told Bronze.

Bronze suggested that he could take Sunflower.

"Good idea!" said the adults.

Nainai toasted some sunflower seeds and stuffed them into their pockets, to eat while they were watching the show.

"You must look after Sunflower," said Nainai.

Bronze nodded.

That evening the family ate much earlier than usual, then Bronze and Sunflower joined a crowd of other children from the village and walked the three miles to Daoxiangdu.

"We're off to see the circus! We're off to see the circus!"

The children chattered and laughed all the way, and every so often the villagers could hear their voices in the distance.

It was dark by the time they reached Daoxiangdu, and a crowd was already gathering on the threshing ground where the show would take place. Bronze and Sunflower were a long way from the stage. The four paraffin lamps hanging from the beam above the stage were so bright they hurt their eyes. They walked around the threshing ground, but all they could see were people shuffling from one leg to the other. Bronze held Sunflower's hand tightly. He was hoping to squeeze through the crowd and get closer to the stage, but there were no gaps—it was like trying to break through a wall of steel. There were so many people that the air was stifling. Bronze and Sunflower began to sweat and had to back away from the crowd to get some air.

More and more people were arriving. People were getting separated in the crowd. Brothers and sisters were calling out to each other, and they could hear one little girl left behind in the fields, sobbing and screaming for her brother.

Sunflower gripped Bronze's hand tighter than ever. He wiped the sweat from her forehead with his sleeve.

There was no room in the trees around the

threshing ground. They were already filled with children, perching on the branches like enormous birds. Bronze and Sunflower kept walking.

Then a branch snapped, and two children crashed to the ground. There were cries and wails. People in the crowd turned to look, but no one rushed to help. They didn't want to lose their places.

Bronze and Sunflower walked around another couple of times. They still couldn't find a good place. So they went a little bit farther out and looked for something they could stand on to get a better view. In the dark, they found a stone roller lying in a grassy patch not too far from the threshing ground. It was the kind that a buffalo would pull over the threshing ground to remove the husks from the wheat and rice. Bronze was excited, and surprised that no one else had seen it. He pulled Sunflower with him, and they perched their bottoms on it to claim it. They sat there for a while, looking left and right, until they were sure no one would snatch it from them. Then they began to push the stone roller toward the threshing ground. They had to use all their strength just to get it to move. They leaned their bodies into it, shifting it forward inch by inch. It was slow, but it worked.

The other children looked at them enviously. Bronze and Sunflower glanced around anxiously, worried that someone might try to take their prize from them. As soon as they had pushed the stone roller onto the threshing ground, they sat down on it. Sweat dripped from their foreheads and stung their eyes. For a while, they struggled to see.

Suddenly, there was movement on the stage, and it looked as though the show was about to start. Bronze stood up and pulled Sunflower up too. Standing on top of the roller, they had a clear view of the stage. Sunflower looked around and saw children still wandering about, trying to break through the crowd. She couldn't help feeling sorry for them. Bronze nudged her, directing her gaze toward the stage. There was a performer preparing to come on. Sunflower stood as close as she could to Bronze and opened her eyes wide.

There was a beating of drums and a clashing of gongs. The crowd cheered, then settled down. The performer waved to the audience as he walked onto the stage with a monkey. The monkey looked wary at first, but it had done this performance many times before and immediately started its tricks. It leaped about, full of life, jumping onto its master's shoulders, then down to the ground. It blinked constantly, drawing attention to its big, round, shiny eyes.

Then, following its master's instructions, this wiry, agile monkey began a hilarious routine that had the audience laughing out loud.

Another child fell out of a tree — he'd laughed so much, he'd forgotten where he was. The children still perched in the branches roared with laughter. It was hard to tell if they were laughing at the monkey or at the child on the ground, who was clenching his teeth and rubbing his buttocks.

Suddenly, something whacked across Bronze's legs. He turned and saw a boy who was a full head taller than him, and stockier. He was holding a stick and glaring. Behind him were more boys, looking equally menacing.

Sunflower was scared. She grabbed Bronze's hand.

"Whose roller is this?"

Bronze shook his head.

"So you don't know whose it is, but you're standing on it anyway?"

Bronze tried to explain with his hands. "My sister and I . . . we found it in the grass and pushed it over here. It was hard work."

The boys didn't understand. Then their leader's lip curled in contempt. "Hey, he's a mute!" He banged his stick against Bronze's leg again. "Come on! Get down!"

"But we pushed it all the way here!" protested Sunflower.

He looked her up and down, then from side to side. "That's not good enough."

Then a boy at the back asked, "Where are you from?"

"Damaidi," said Sunflower.

"Well, this is Daoxiangdu and this is our roller. Why don't you go back to Damaidi and get one of your own!"

Bronze edged himself between Sunflower and the boys. He wouldn't let them spoil their evening. They had a good view of the stage. They could see the monkey performing. With a little straw hat on its head and a little hammer in its hands, it looked like an old man heading off to work in the fields. The audience howled with laughter.

Bronze and Sunflower burst out laughing. Then Bronze felt the full force of the stick across his ankle. Pain seared through his body. He looked around at the leader.

The boy stared back at him. "What? Want to fight?"

All Bronze wanted to do was stay on the roller so that Sunflower could enjoy the circus. The pain made him break out in a sweat, but he gritted his teeth. He wasn't going to get off the roller and fight.

"Are you OK?" asked Sunflower.

Bronze nodded and told her to watch the show.

But the boys weren't going to go away. Bronze could see it in their faces.

He scanned the crowd, looking for other children from Damaidi who might come over and help him. But he couldn't see any except for Gayu, and he didn't want to ask him. He wasn't sure if Gayu would help them anyway. Bronze was going to have to deal with the boys alone.

The gang was dying to see what was happening

on the stage. The audience seemed to be having such fun! When the crowd burst out laughing again, they couldn't wait any longer.

"Are you going to get off or not?" yelled the boy, brandishing the stick.

Bronze glared at him. He was not going to give in.

The boy pointed at Bronze with the stick. "Pull them off!" he told the boy behind him.

The gang swarmed around. Sunflower was stunned to find herself watching the stage one minute and on the ground the next. It took her a moment to realize what had happened. Bronze clapped the dust off his hands, helped Sunflower to her feet, led her to a safe place, and told her to stay there. Then he turned and made his way back to the gang.

"Bronze!" cried Sunflower.

But Bronze didn't look back. He found the boys crammed together on top of the roller, thoroughly enjoying the show. Bronze stood with his legs apart, tucked his chin into his chest, spread his arms, and charged, just as his buffalo would do. The boys were sent flying.

Bronze climbed back onto the roller and stood

there, ready to fight for his life. The boys stared blankly at their leader. He was on the ground, waiting for them to help him up. Eventually a few of the boys realized what he wanted and went over, but he was so annoyed now that as soon as he was on his feet, he swept them aside with his arm. They looked ashamed.

The boy started slapping the stick against the palm of his hand. He walked around the roller and all of a sudden raised the stick and brought it crashing down toward Bronze. Bronze managed to dodge it— instinctively he turned to one side and put his arms up to protect himself. The next time the stick came slashing through the air, he leaped up and wrestled the boy to the ground. The two of them rolled over and over, like the roller that everyone seemed to have forgotten about.

But Bronze was no match for this boy, who was on top of him now, pressing him to the ground. Panting, the boy motioned for the others to pass him the stick that had fallen from his hand. He tapped it very lightly on Bronze's forehead. "You need to show me some respect, mute! Otherwise, I'm gonna throw you and that girl into the river."

Bronze struggled, but he couldn't break free.

Meanwhile, Sunflower, who had stayed where he left her, was in tears, worrying that something terrible might have happened to him.

"I want to go home," she sobbed. "I want to go home." She waited a little longer for Bronze to return, then ran back toward the roller. When she saw the gang dragging Bronze by his arms from the threshing ground, she charged forward, screaming his name and punching at the boys. They didn't fight back—they didn't fight girls. They kept dragging Bronze and dodging Sunflower's little fists.

The gang dumped Bronze in a grassy area beside the threshing ground, then ran back to the roller. Sunflower crouched beside her brother and helped him to sit up. Bronze wiped the blood from his nose and staggered to his feet.

"Let's go home, Bronze. We've seen enough of the circus," she said, helping him to move away from the crowd. Bronze would have fought for the roller, but

Sunflower's safety came first. He swallowed his pride and walked toward the road.

Another peal of laughter rang through the crowd. Sunflower couldn't help taking a look.

The villages in this area were so remote and so poor that life was usually very quiet. The villagers often had to travel up to six miles or so just to see a film or a show. So whenever there was an event, the children were so excited. When they'd heard that the traveling circus was in Daoxiangdu, they could think of nothing else.

Bronze took a few steps, then stopped, grasped Sunflower's hand, and headed back to the threshing ground.

"Let's go home, Bronze; we've seen enough," said Sunflower, afraid that he might try and snatch the roller back from the gang.

In the light of the moon, Bronze gestured with his hands, "I'm not going to fight them. Honestly, I'm not going to fight them." He set off again, pulling her with him. They found a place that was not too crowded. Bronze bent his knees and crouched. He patted his shoulders, telling her to climb up.

Sunflower didn't move. "Let's go home," she said again.

But Bronze was insistent. He would only get up if she did as he asked. He kept patting his shoulders, until she finally put her hands in his and slid her legs over his shoulders.

As Bronze stood up, he placed his hand on the back of the man in front for support. The man turned around but didn't mind at all. Bronze could see it in his eyes. He even leaned forward to offer more support. As Bronze pulled himself up to full height, Sunflower rose higher and higher. She saw the upper back of the kind man in front, then the back of his head, and finally the bright lights of the stage. What's more, there was a nice fresh breeze blowing over the heads of all these people.

A black bear was performing now. Sunflower had never seen one before and couldn't help feeling a little scared. She gripped Bronze's hand tighter. The bear was a greedy so-and-so and would only perform when it was given food. Otherwise, it would just lie on the ground and sulk, which had the children in stitches.

For a while, Sunflower was captivated by the performance. All her attention was on the stage. She felt comfortable and secure on Bronze's shoulders and kept steady by holding on to his ears. She watched the bear, then a little dog, then a big dog, then a little cat, then a big cat. She watched the big cat and dog playing together, then a girl on horseback came riding in. One act followed another, delighting the audience. A dog jumping through a ring of fire, a cat riding on a dog's back, a man on horseback balancing a stack of plates on his head . . . In moments of excitement, Sunflower clapped her hands against Bronze's head, completely forgetting that she was on his shoulders.

Bronze held on to Sunflower's legs. At first he stood very still, but as he grew tired, he began to sway. He gritted his teeth. There were people packed in close in front of him and more behind, so there was little fresh air circulating. He felt stifled. He wanted to take Sunflower away, but he couldn't find a route through the crowd. Sweat was dripping off him.

And then everything went black.

The threshing ground, Sunflower, the circus . . . it all slipped from his mind. He was on a little boat at dawn. In the misty light of the early morning, a breeze was blowing over the river, rippling the water. The waves rocked the boat, and as the boat rocked, the riverbanks started to sway, and then the villages and trees along the river began to sway too. A little bird appeared, a black bird that he'd met when grazing the buffalo in a remote stretch of reeds. He looked at the bird, and the bird looked at him. It was like a dark spirit, here one minute and gone the next. He saw a spider, spinning its big web between the mulberry and the melia trees at the back of the house. A beautiful spider, a rich deep red. When it rested on its web, it was like a little safflower. Tiny dewdrops hung from the gossamer threads, and as the sun rose the web glistened and sparkled. . . .

As Bronze drifted in the dark, his thoughts floating, his body weightless, he somehow managed to stay on his feet.

Meanwhile, Sunflower hugged Bronze's head with the same contentment she felt when hugging the big tree by the river as she watched the waterbirds in spring. The circus had been magical. It was one of the happiest evenings of her life.

Bronze felt a cool wind on his forehead. He was still light-headed. Although things were blurry, he could see that the crowd was beginning to disperse. He could hear voices shouting. They roared in his ears like waves on the sea. Some people walked in front of him: the Damaidi children and Gayu. Still dazed, Bronze started to follow them.

As they left, Sunflower's thoughts were still on the circus. It had given her such pleasure. She rested her chin on Bronze's head. "What did you like best?" she asked him. "The black bear? One of the dogs? Maybe the black dog?"

Silence.

"I liked the black dog; it was so smart, it could read! Did you see the dog leaping through the ring of fire? Were you scared? I was scared it wouldn't make it and its fur would catch fire."

Bronze rocked from side to side as he walked. In the fields, in the dark of night, there were paraffin lamps and torchlights everywhere. It was like being in a dream.

"What did you like best, Bronze?"

Then the questions stopped and Sunflower went

quiet. She remembered that she'd been sitting on his shoulders. Standing on the threshing ground, he hadn't seen a thing. And she hadn't given him a thought.

And it wasn't just this evening. He'd been carrying her on his shoulders for years now.

She looked at the dark fields ahead of them and wrapped her arms tightly around his neck.

"That's the last time we go to see the circus," she said, as one tear after another landed in his sweat-soaked hair.

The family had borrowed money to build the house, and they had to pay it back by the date that had been agreed. Bronze's father was a man of his word. Fortunately, they'd gotten a good price for the lotus root they'd cut in the pond. They'd gotten more or less what they expected from the white radishes. And they still had the arrowhead corms to collect from their paddy field.

Baba had been spending a lot of time in the paddy field recently. Arrowhead was one of the things people of that region ate at the New Year, along with sweet potato and water celery. Arrowhead leaves are shaped like arrowheads, but it is really the corms that are special. They are tubers that grow in mud but, when washed, they look as round and white and smooth as mushrooms. If Baba waited until just before the New Year and took the "lucky mushrooms" to Youmadi, he was bound to get a good price for them. He would put some of the money toward the debt, but the adults also wanted to buy material to make new clothes for Bronze and Sunflower for the New Year. They had spent days and nights figuring out how they might afford it.

Baba pushed his hands into the slimy mud and felt the corms. They were round and smooth, and getting bigger by the day. He couldn't bear to pull up a single one, not just yet. He wanted to keep them all in the ground for a bit longer. When the time was right, he'd drain the land, pick them out of the mud, lay them out on a bamboo tray, and rinse off the dirt. He pictured himself walking across the fields, the yoke over his shoulders, taking his top-quality arrowhead corms to Youmadi. He could imagine people saying,

"There's money in those baskets!" and "Now, that's what we call lucky mushrooms!" But it wasn't just Baba—the whole family was depending on that field of arrowheads.

One day, on his way home from inspecting the arrowhead field, Baba noticed a flock of ducks on the river. Why had it never occurred to him that the ducks might go into the arrowhead field? Ducks love arrowhead corms and gobble them up whenever they can. Their tails go up in the air as their beaks plunge deep in the mud. With their long flat beaks, a flock of ducks could clear this field in no time! The thought of it brought him out in a cold sweat. Thank goodness it hadn't happened already.

When he got home, he made scarecrows to stick in the field. He took some rope and marked out the boundary, winding it around one tree and then the next. Then he hung bundles of grass from the rope, and watched them sway back and forth in the wind. But Baba was not convinced this was enough. From now on the family would take turns watching the arrowhead field, until the very last corm had been harvested.

One Sunday afternoon, it was Sunflower's turn to keep watch. Baba and Mama had gone with some other villagers to dig a water channel miles away from Damaidi. Nainai was at home, preparing food and looking after the pig and the goats, and Bronze had taken the buffalo to graze near the reeds and to pick fluffy reed panicles. They were going to make another hundred pairs of shoes this year, and they were already counting on this income as they planned their accounts.

Sunflower took her homework with her to the arrowhead field. She had a long bamboo pole beside her, which Bronze had made to chase away the ducks. The pole had a piece of string tied to one end and a bundle of grass hanging free from the string.

Although it was winter, it was a warm, sunny afternoon. The arrowhead field was filled with water, as were the fields around it, and the sunlight bounced off the surface, dazzling Sunflower's eyes. A few wading birds were searching in the water for food. They looked so elegant. As soon as a bird caught one of the little fish that were in the water, it would hold it tightly in its beak, thrash it from side to side, crane its neck up to the sky, and slowly gulp it down.

From time to time, the wind picked up, sending ripples running across the water. The algae on the surface was a brilliant green, like emerald silk, despite the water being bitterly cold. On the ridges between the fields, there were dark-skinned beets growing half in and half out of the mud. It was tempting to go and pull one up, rinse it in the water, and take a bite. Sunflower felt very content, watching the field full of water in the bright sunshine.

Sunflower thought she could hear ducks. She looked around and saw a flock heading toward her on the little river that ran alongside the field. Behind them was a little duck boat, and steering it was none other than Gayu.

The moment she saw him, Sunflower began to panic.

Gayu knew she was there. He turned his back to her and peed in the river, delighting in the contrasting colors as it spattered in the water. He remained there for ages, lost in thought. Then he had an idea.

Gayu turned, glanced at Sunflower sitting on the ridge of the field, and shouted to his ducks to stop. While he had been messing about, they had swum on ahead. The ducks knew his voice and his commands. They stopped where they were or swam off toward the reeds at the side of the water.

Gayu steered the boat to the side of the river, tied it to a tree, climbed onto the bank, and, clutching the long-handled shovel he used to drive the ducks, sat down at the edge of the field.

He was wearing a loose black padded jacket and equally loose black padded trousers. Sunflower kept an eye on him as he sat there. An image of the black bear at the circus came to mind. She wanted to laugh, but didn't dare. She was always wary of Gayu. She continued to sit by the side of the field, reading her book, but she couldn't concentrate. She wished Bronze would appear.

When Gayu saw that Sunflower was ignoring him, he stood up, sank his shovel into the ground, dug out a piece of mud, and hurled it through the air. It landed in the calm water with a great big splash. The wading birds were startled and flew into the air.

They circled overhead a few times, and when they saw that Gayu wasn't moving on, they flew off to another paddy field.

Now there were just the two of them, Gayu and Sunflower, sitting by the paddy field. The edges of the fields were covered in loose, dry winter grass. Gayu decided to rest for a while and stretched out on the ground. The grass felt good, like a soft mattress. The sun was in his eyes, so he closed them.

When the ducks on the river lost sight of their master, they started quacking. Gayu ignored them. But they were anxious, quacking and flapping their wings. They tried to climb up the bank, but it was steep and they kept slipping back into the river. They shook the water off their feathers, flapped their wings, and started climbing again. Fearless, one by one the whole flock climbed up onto the bank. As soon as they saw Gayu, they relaxed and began to look around in the grass for food.

The moment Sunflower saw the ducks on the bank, she put down her book, grabbed the long pole, and leaped to her feet.

The ducks seemed to have heard her. They stopped

searching for food and huddled together at the side of the paddy field. They were quiet; they seemed to be looking at something. A speckled drake lowered its head and, as it did so, saw its reflection in the water.

Sunflower clutched the bamboo pole. She didn't dare take her eyes off the ducks.

The speckled drake was the first to jump into the paddy field, and after that, the other ducks started jumping in too.

"SHOO! SHOO!" shouted Sunflower.

There were still a lot of ducks on the bank, hesitating before they jumped. But they soon made up their minds when Sunflower ran over waving the pole at them. They flapped their wings and flew into the paddy field. Before long it was completely covered with ducks.

Sunflower tried to shoo them away, but the ducks didn't care. The smarter ones started pulling fresh white corms out of the mud, stretching their necks and gobbling them down. The others quickly followed. They dodged Sunflower's pole, dragging their long flat beaks through the mud. Now that they had tasted the corms, they weren't going to leave that easily! And why should they? Their master was lying at the side of the field, showing no concern about their activity. He was giving them permission to help themselves.

In the winter sunlight, while the rest of the world was at peace, Gayu's ducks were making the most appalling racket as they raided the family's arrowhead field.

Gayu didn't lift a finger. He lay stretched out on the grass, soaking up the warm sunshine, keeping one eye on Sunflower as she ran up and down in a panic. It was exactly what he'd been hoping for: panic and fear. He remembered the day she had sat under the old tree and gone home with Bronze's family—it was in the afternoon and in the sunshine, just like today. He heard Sunflower's shoo-shooing and happily closed his eyes. The sunlight filtered through his eyelids, and the sky seemed red.

As soon as Sunflower had chased away one group of ducks, another group poked their beaks into the mud somewhere else. The paddy field was full of the sight of stubby ducks' tails pointing to the sky, and long ducks' necks gulping down corms. The water that had been calm and clear was now a muddy pool.

The ducks had stirred it up so much that there were little fish gasping for breath on the field ridge.

Sunflower was in tears. She was getting tired.

"How could you?" she screamed at the ducks.

But the ducks were shameless. They plunged their beaks — so many beaks — into the mud, plowing it up, turning out the corms, their faces covered in slime, beady black eyes peering out. Why would they stop now?

Sunflower watched helplessly as the ducks feasted on the family's crop. Each corm — each lucky mushroom — was as precious as gold. She wanted to run home and get someone, but the paddy field was a long way from home, and by the time she got there, the ducks would have finished everything. She looked around her, but apart from a few birds flying overhead, there was no sign of life.

"Your ducks are eating our arrowhead corms!" she yelled at Gayu.

But Gayu lay there, as still as a dead dog.

Sunflower took off her shoes and socks, rolled up her trouser legs, and, ignoring the iciness of the water, waded in. This time the ducks really did get a fright.

They flapped their wings, quacked loudly, and fled into the next field. But this one was just a paddy field, and once the ducks had searched about in the mud and discovered there was nothing to be eaten, they came back to the surface, where they sat motionless, watching Sunflower. When the wind blew, they were blown off to one side.

Sunflower stood in the arrowhead field, holding the bamboo pole. She had pins and needles in her legs and feet. The water was cold enough for a thin layer of ice to freeze over the surface at night. Soon she was shivering all over and her teeth were chattering. But she would not give up. She would stay there until Bronze came.

In the next field, the wind had blown the ducks into the distance. They looked contented — with their bellies full, they were probably sleepy — and many had tucked their heads under their wings to rest. It didn't look as though they would come and invade the arrowhead field again, so Sunflower scrambled up the bank. As she washed the slime from her legs and feet, she saw how red they had turned. She rubbed them, then jumped up and down in the sunshine to get warm, all the while looking in the direction in which Bronze had gone to collect reed panicles.

But the ducks came floating back, against the wind. They flooded back into the arrowhead field.

Again Sunflower went down into the water, but this time they weren't scared of her at all. When she slashed the bamboo pole through the air, they just jumped out of the way. They soon realized that she couldn't lift her feet out of the mud easily, so there was no need to hurry away. They simply dodged the pole, then floated back again.

Sunflower stood in the mud and felt helpless. All around her the ducks were noisily gobbling down the arrowhead corms. She climbed onto the bank and again screamed at Gayu, "Your ducks are eating our arrowhead corms!"

Everything around her was moving: the water, the grass, the leaves on the trees. Everything but Gayu. She poked him with the bamboo pole.

"Did you hear me?"

There was no response. She moved closer and gave him a hard push.

"Your ducks are eating our arrowhead corms!"

Gayu still didn't move.

She grabbed his arm to pull him up. But he was sleeping like a pig. When she let go of his arm, it flopped to the ground as though it didn't belong to him. Sunflower flinched and stepped back.

Gayu lay there, completely still, his eyes closed and his hair blowing in the wind like the grass. Sunflower crouched on her haunches, reached forward, and pushed his head. It rolled to one side and then stopped, just like a watermelon.

"Gayu," she said quietly.

"GAYU!" she shouted. Then she leaped to her feet and ran back to the village, screaming, "Gayu's dead! Gayu's dead!"

She had almost reached the village when Bronze appeared. In fits and starts she told him everything. Bronze was suspicious and ran back with her to the paddy field. Just before they got there, they heard Gayu's peculiar way of singing. They followed the sound and saw him steering his little boat and driving his ducks toward the big river. The sun was in the west, and the ducks were calm, as though they hadn't a thought in their heads. The evening breeze blew ripples across the water, which flowed onto their bodies and ran down their tails back into the river.

Bronze devised a story and made Sunflower agree to it. They told the family that he'd taken over from Sunflower that afternoon so that she could go and do her schoolwork. He was watching the arrowhead field but went chasing after a wild rabbit, and that was when Gayu's ducks had gotten in.

Baba crouched by the side of the devastated arrowhead field. He held his head in his hands and for a long time was completely silent. Then he went down into the field and fished around in the mud with his foot. Before, he would have immediately felt several corms, but now there wasn't a single one. He grabbed a handful of mud and hurled it into the distance. Bronze and Sunflower hung their heads and stood very still at the edge of the field.

Baba grabbed another handful of mud, turned around, and looked at Bronze. Then he hurled it. Bronze didn't try to dodge, and the mud splattered on his chest. Sunflower looked anxiously at Baba. He grabbed another handful of mud and hurled it at Bronze. He hurled a string of foul language at Bronze too. He couldn't control himself. He pelted his son with mud, not caring where it hit him. Bronze made no attempt to wipe the mud away, even when it splattered on his face. He didn't even raise his hands. He took everything that was thrown at him.

"BABA! BABA!" Sunflower was in tears.

Nainai was walking nearby. When she heard Sunflower crying, she hurried over, hobbling with her stick. She saw Bronze covered head to toe in mud, threw down her stick, and went to stand in front of him.

"Hurl the mud at me!" she called out to Baba. "Come on! What's the matter with you?"

Baba's head dropped to his chest, his hands went limp, and the mud dropped into the water with a dull splash.

Nainai slipped one hand into Bronze's and the other into Sunflower's.

"Let's go home," she said.

That evening, Bronze wasn't allowed any supper.

He wasn't allowed inside at all. Baba made him stand outside in the bitterly cold wind.

Sunflower didn't eat either. She stood up to go and join Bronze.

"Sit down and eat!" Baba roared at her.

But she was determined to stand outside with Bronze. Baba was beside himself with rage. He stormed outside, grabbed her arm with his big strong hand, and dragged her back inside. Sunflower struggled against him and somehow managed to break free. When Baba reached out to grab her, she looked at him and then fell to her knees.

"Baba! Baba! I was the one watching the arrowhead field. It was my turn. Bronze was picking reed panicles all afternoon." Tears were streaming down her face.

Mama ran outside and tried to pull her to her feet, but she wouldn't get up. She was determined to stay on her knees. It was the respectful thing to do. She pointed to the haystack in front of her. "Bronze gathered a whole sack full of reed panicles. It's behind the haystack."

Mama went to look. She returned with the sack

in her arms and placed it in front of Baba. She was crying now too.

With a lump rising in her throat, Sunflower stayed on her knees and hung her head in shame.

Baba considered going to Gayu's house to ask for compensation, but he soon abandoned the idea. Gayu's father was renowned for his love of money and for being the most unreasonable person in Damaidi. If Baba went to complain, he'd get a lot of hassle and no money. But Bronze could not forget this injustice; he would settle the score somehow. He was always looking out of the corner of his eye, watching Gayu and his ducks.

Whenever Gayu sensed he was being watched, he quickly took his ducks down to the river. He'd always been nervous around Bronze. All the children in the village were. They didn't know how the mute might react, what he might do if he was annoyed. He was a mystery to them. Ever since that gray rainy day when they'd seen him out grazing his buffalo, sitting all by himself on a mound of earth on the wasteland, they'd kept their distance or hurried away as soon as he appeared.

Bronze kept a firm eye on Gayu.

One day, Gayu took his ducks down to the river and disappeared. Bronze was hiding with his buffalo in a stretch of reeds nearby. The clever buffalo sensed that Bronze was up to something and stood without making a sound.

The moment Gayu was out of sight, Bronze leaped to his feet and jumped onto the buffalo. He slapped it on the rump, and off it ran, trampling the reeds underfoot. They charged along the river shore toward the ducks. The flock had just been fed, and the ducks were resting, half asleep. By the time they heard the thundering hooves, the buffalo was right in front of them. They shrieked in panic and fled in all directions. A few narrowly missed being trampled underfoot.

Bronze didn't hang around. He rode off into the distance, leaving the ducks in distress. They were all over the place: in the water, in the grass, quacking away on the shore.

It was nightfall before Gayu had gathered his flock again.

Early the next morning, Gayu's father set out as usual with a wicker basket to collect the eggs from the duck pen. He did this every morning, and it was his favorite time of the day. He would see the white and gray-green duck eggs on the ground and feel that life was good, very good. Carefully, he would pick them up and put them in his basket. With the New Year approaching, duck eggs were getting more and more valuable.

But that morning, something was wrong. As he walked through the duck pen, he could find only a few eggs dotted about. He collected no more than a dozen. He shook his head and wondered what was going on. It wasn't as if ducks could go on strike and refuse to lay. He looked up at the sky. There was no change there. Everything was normal. He left the duck pen with a light basket and a heavy heart.

He could never have guessed that the ducks had already laid their eggs before returning to the duck pen. They'd had such a shock the previous day that they'd laid them in the river!

Over the next few days, Bronze seized every opportunity to ride his buffalo and charge after the ducks,
disrupting their egg-laying pattern. Some of them laid
their eggs in the middle of the afternoon in the grass
by the river, and made the village children very happy
when they found them.

Then, one day, Bronze decided to stop launching
secret attacks on Gayu's ducks. He would make one
final attack in broad daylight. He wanted the whole
village to see that his family would not be cheated. He
took an old bedcover from home, which was printed
with large flowers on a red background, and tied it to
a bamboo pole. He held it up in the air and waved it
around like a flag. Then he waited for the children to
come out of school.

Gayu had taken his ducks to a paddy field that
had already been harvested, to scavenge whatever
was left. When Bronze appeared on the ridge of the
paddy field, riding tall and proud on the buffalo and
holding up his flag, Gayu had no idea what to expect.
He grabbed the iron shovel he used for driving the
ducks.

The children started to spill out of school. Many of

them were heading toward the fields. All of a sudden, on Bronze's signal, the buffalo stormed toward the ducks. The old bedcover unfurled behind Bronze like a flag and flapped noisily in the wind. The ducks couldn't have been more terrified if their nests had been on fire. They fled in all directions. Bronze and the buffalo put on a magnificent performance in the empty paddy field, racing and turning, turning and racing. The ridge by the field was crowded with excited children eagerly watching the spectacle. Gayu sat on the ground, paralyzed.

"Bronze! Bronze!" shouted Sunflower.

Bronze pulled on the rope and the buffalo turned and ran toward her. Bronze leaped down, helped her onto the buffalo, and led the way home. There was a swagger to his step. Sunflower had never felt so proud.

Gayu lay on the ground and wept.

That evening, Gayu's father tied him to the tree in front of their house and gave him a thrashing. He had planned to drag his son over to Bronze's house to sort the problem out, but they'd met someone on the way who had told him that Gayu had let the ducks eat all the corms in Bronze's family's arrowhead field. When he heard this, Gayu's father gave his son a kick in the backside, in front of everyone, then dragged him back home and tied him to the tree.

As Gayu hung from the tree, he looked at the moon in the sky and began to cry. "Go away! Get lost!" he yelled at the children who were gathering around. He kicked at them but in vain. It just made him swing even more.

There were only a few days left before the New Year. The excitement was building. The children were counting down the days, and the adults were busy preparing for the celebrations ahead. They asked the children to help.

"No going out to play today. We need you to help clean the house."

"Go to Auntie's house and see if anyone's using the millstone. We need to grind some wheat flour to make pancakes."

"Your father's going to the fishpond. Go and help him carry the creel."

The children seemed happy to do as they were told. When the first family killed their pig, its squeals were heard all over Damaidi.

Some of the village children couldn't wait any longer and crept outside with the fireworks their family had put aside for New Year's Eve and New Year's Day. They let them off: *Bang! Crack! Whoosh!*

The road running past Damaidi was busy with people on their way to and from Youmadi to get things for the celebrations. News spread rapidly through the fields.

"How much for a *jin* of fish?"

"Twice the usual price."

"So expensive!"

"But you've got to have fish at New Year's. No matter how much it costs."

"Is it busy in town?"

"It's packed. You can barely move for all the people. No idea where they're coming from."

Although they were poor, Bronze's family was still preparing for the New Year. As the house was new, they didn't need to spring-clean, but still Mama was frantically washing everything that could be washed: bedcovers, clothes, pillows, table, chairs. She spent the day traipsing between the house and the river, and the long rope in front of the house dripped constantly from the washing hung out to dry.

"Everything but the kitchen stove!" said the people who passed by.

Mama always kept everything clean. All those years ago, when Nainai had pointed her out to Baba, she'd said, "This girl's neat and tidy." And she'd been right. No matter how old or worn the family's clothes and bedding might be, they were always clean. Nobody left the house looking anything less than clean and tidy.

Nainai herself couldn't manage a day without water. She was always at the riverside, gently pushing the floating greenery to the side, then washing her hands and face in the cold water. She might be old, but she never smelled of old age.

"Clean every day of her life," said the villagers. "And she insists that the family is too."

It was traditional to have new clothes at the New

Year. Bronze's family couldn't afford new clothes this year, but they would certainly make the most of what they had. They took off the padded jackets that kept them warm through the winter — they were so worn they looked polished — and washed them, and the padded trousers too.

Bronze and Sunflower had something special to look forward to, however. The family had taken Bronze's jacket to be dyed in town, and there was going to be a flower-patterned dress for Sunflower.

The dress was adapted from one Mama had had when she was first married. She'd only worn it a few times. When she realized they wouldn't be able to afford to buy cloth to make a new dress, she'd sighed and thought suddenly of this dress at the bottom of the chest. She'd taken it out and shown it to Nainai.

"It's New Year's. I want to alter this dress for Sun-flower," she said.

"You should hold on to it and wear it yourself," said Nainai.

"Oh, it's too small for me now. And I'm too old to wear such brightly patterned clothes."

Nainai was the best seamstress in the village. She'd

been helping people cut fabric and make clothes all her life. She'd lost track of how many things she had made. She spent two days adapting Mama's old dress into a new one for Sunflower. It had a high collar and darts at the waist. Nainai added an elaborate knot fastening at the top, which none of the other villagers knew how to do.

When Sunflower put on the dress, everyone in the family told her how lovely it was. She didn't want to take it off.

"Save it for New Year's Day," Mama said.

"Can't I keep it on this morning?"

"Let her wear it this morning," said Nainai. "But you mustn't get it dirty."

Sunflower had to go to school that morning to rehearse for the New Year show. She had a crucial role in the show: she was the host as well as a performer. The teachers had been worried about her not having something new to wear and had been planning, when the time came, to ask if one of the other girls might lend her a dress. So when they saw her in this wonderful new dress, they were thrilled. The teachers and children crowded around to admire it. Sunflower began to feel uncomfortable.

"It would look perfect with a silver necklace!" said Ms. Liu, the teacher in charge of the show.

Once she'd said it, everyone pictured Sunflower in this beautiful dress, wearing a silver necklace, and in their imagination she looked more captivating than ever.

When Ms. Liu realized that her mind had drifted, she clapped her hands briskly. "OK, everybody, take your places. We need to rehearse."

After the rehearsal, Sunflower went home very happy.

"Did they like the dress?" asked Mama.

"Yes, everyone loves it!"

Sunflower was feeling pretty pleased with herself, and as they were eating lunch, she said, "Ms. Liu says I'd look even more beautiful with a silver necklace."

"You're beautiful enough already!" said Mama, tapping her on the head with her chopsticks.

Sunflower giggled.

But as they sat eating, they could all imagine how

lovely she would look wearing a silver necklace with her new dress.

As usual, the performance would take place on New Year's Day in the afternoon. Having seen out the old year, the villagers would go to the threshing ground and enjoy the New Year's entertainment.

Since the moment she'd seen Sunflower in the brightly colored dress, Ms. Liu had been wondering where she could find a silver necklace for her to wear as the host of the show. The villagers loved silver jewelry, and lots of the village girls had silver necklaces. At the morning rehearsal on New Year's Day, Ms. Liu asked Lingzi, who was also in the show, if she'd lend her silver necklace to Sunflower for the performance. She nodded, took off the necklace, and placed it in Ms. Liu's hand. Ms. Liu called Sunflower over, and fastened it around her neck. It looked even better than she had imagined. Ms. Liu took a couple of steps back to admire it and smiled. It would sparkle magnificently at the show that afternoon!

But after the rehearsal, Lingzi changed her mind. "If my mother hears about this, I'll be in such trouble.

She's told me over and over again I'm not to let anyone else wear my necklace."

Sunflower immediately took off the necklace and returned it to Lingzi. She felt her face burn with embarrassment and shame.

When she got home, she was still thinking about it.

"It's New Year's! What's the matter?" Mama asked her.

"It's nothing." Sunflower smiled.

Mama had her doubts. Soon afterward, Sunflower's friend Lanzi came to the house.

Mama said to her, "Sunflower's been very quiet since she got home from school. Do you know why?"

Lanzi told her in a whisper about the silver necklace. Mama sighed. Bronze was sitting by the door, apparently lost in thought. But he had heard every word Lanzi said, and every word had moved him. In his eyes, his sister was the most beautiful girl in Damaidi, and he wanted her to be the happiest, luckiest girl in Damaidi too. More than anything, he loved to watch Nainai and Mama helping Sunflower get ready. He loved to see Nainai comb and braid her hair, then tie ribbons around the ends. And he loved to see Mama take a freshly picked flower and tuck it into her braid. At New Year and other festivals, he'd watch Nainai dab her finger in some rouge and make a tiny red dot between Sunflower's eyebrows, and watch Mama as she painted Sunflower's nails red with a mixture of alum and balsam. And when he heard people saying how beautiful Sunflower was, he felt so proud. "The mute is such a good brother to her," said the older villagers.

Of course, there was nothing Bronze could do about Sunflower not having a silver necklace to wear. There was nothing anyone in the family could do. They simply didn't have fancy things. They had the sky and the earth, they had fresh water from the river, and they were clean from the inside out.

In the sky above, Bronze heard a dove calling. When he looked up, he couldn't see the dove, but he did notice some icicles hanging from the eaves. They were like bamboo shoots in the spring, but hanging upside down. They were all different lengths and sparkled in the light. They were enchanting. The longer he looked at them, the more excited he became, till his heart was pounding like a frog leaping about inside his chest.

He went to fetch a table, then climbed on top of it, broke off a dozen or so icicles, and put them on a large plate. Then he slid the plate under the haystack in front of the house to keep them cold and hidden from view. He went to the water's edge, cut some reed stems, then brought them back to the house and used scissors to cut them into fine reed tubes. He asked Mama for some strong red thread. Everyone in the family saw he was busy and thought he was behaving a little strangely, but they didn't ask any questions. They were used to him doing his own thing.

Bronze used a wooden stick to smash the icicles into small pieces. They sparkled like diamonds on the plate. He chose some pieces that were roughly the same size, not too big, not too small. Then he picked up a fine reed tube about two or three inches long, put one end in his mouth and the other on a piece of ice, and blew into the tube. It took a few minutes, but his soft warm breath was like a sharp drill and gradually bored a tiny hole through the middle of the ice.

He put the finished piece on another, smaller plate

and started on the next. *Clink, clink* went each piece as it landed on the plate.

Sunflower and Lanzi walked by.

"What are you doing?" asked Sunflower.

Bronze looked up and smiled mysteriously. Sunflower didn't press him, and the two girls went off to play.

Bronze sat at the bottom of the haystack, patiently working on his project. The icicles he'd chosen were all slightly different shapes and sizes, which made them glisten all the more on the plate. There was a wintry calm about them and a sense of luxury.

Bronze blew holes in one piece after another. When his cheeks went numb, he patted them to bring them back to life. As the sun moved across the sky, the intensity and color of his "diamonds" changed with the light. As the late-afternoon sun began its descent in the west, they turned a pale orange.

Before the sun went down, he picked up the red string that Mama had given him and carefully threaded it through all the icicle beads, then knotted the two ends together. He held it up with one finger.

In the last light of the day, here it was—a necklace made of ice! A long, long necklace, hanging perfectly still in the air. Even Bronze was surprised at its beauty. He held it in front of his chest, but it made him feel girlish and silly, and he laughed in embarrassment.

He didn't show it to Nainai and his parents or to Sunflower. Instead, he laid it on the plate and covered it lightly with rice straw.

That evening, after supper, almost everyone in Damaidi gathered on the threshing ground. The paraffin lamps on the stage had been lit.

Just as the performers were preparing to go out, Bronze appeared backstage. Sunflower ran over to him.

"What are you doing here?" she asked.

Bronze held out the plate with both hands. He blew away the straw and revealed the ice necklace. It twinkled in the dim glow of a backstage oil lamp. Sunflower's eyes lit up. She couldn't tell what was lying on the blue-and-white porcelain plate, but she was utterly enchanted by the way it glistened.

Bronze gestured to her to pick it up. She didn't

dare. So he held the plate in one hand and picked up the ice necklace with the other, then put the plate on the ground.

"It's a necklace . . . made of ice." He wished she would come closer so he could put it on her.

"Won't it melt?" she asked.

"It's a cold night, and we're outside. It's not going to melt."

Sunflower stepped closer and bent her head forward. Bronze placed the ice necklace around her neck. It followed the line of her high collar, then draped down her front. She ran her fingers over it and wondered what it looked like now that she was wearing it. It was ice-cold. She felt good. She looked down at it, then glanced sideways at Bronze to ask what he thought.

Bronze rubbed his hands together in delight. It was more wonderful than he had ever imagined.

Sunflower looked down again. She hardly dared believe it was real. She felt stupid and overwhelmed, and wanted to take it off. Bronze wouldn't let her.

Then Ms. Liu called her. "Sunflower, where are you? You're onstage in a moment."

Sunflower hurried over.

When Ms. Liu saw Sunflower, she was mesmerized. She couldn't take her eyes off the ice necklace.

"Oh, my goodness!" she said, lifting it gently and letting it rest in the palm of her hand. "Where did this come from? What's it made of?"

Thinking Ms. Liu was angry with her, Sunflower glanced back at Bronze and began to undo the necklace.

"Stop! Don't take it off!" said Ms. Liu, and pushed her gently onto the stage. The time had come.

In the lamplight, the ice necklace sparkled a never-ending array of colors. Nobody knew what it was made of, but the light it gave out was so beautiful, so pure, so mysterious and elegant, the audience was entranced.

For a moment, time stood still. Both onstage and offstage, everything went as quiet as the deepest forest. Sunflower wondered if the necklace had ruined the show. She stood, blinded by the light, unsure what to do.

Then someone in the audience started to clap. Immediately, others joined in, and then more, until everyone was clapping, onstage and off. On this clearest of nights, the clapping sounded like heavy rain.

Sunflower spotted Bronze — he was standing on a stool at the back. His eyes were gleaming, black and shiny.

Her eyes misted over, and for a few moments her vision was blurred.

A Plague of Locusts

When Sunflower was in the final semester of third grade, in the late spring and early summer, a plague of locusts invaded Damaidi and the whole area around.

Before the locusts came, life in Damaidi was as it had always been. The villagers' lives were busy at times and slow at others. The cows, sheep, pigs, and dogs, and the chickens, ducks, geese, and doves made their usual noises and did their usual things. Those that swim, swam. Those that fly, flew. The blue sky above Damaidi looked fresh from morning to night, and every day it was as if it were bluer than usual. White cottony clouds floated along above the fields.

This year's crops promised to be better than ever. Rapeseed fields bordered fields of wheat, patterning the land in yellow and green. The rapeseed flowers blossomed, one cluster after another, and there were bees and butterflies everywhere. The wheat grew thick and green, with its bushy squirrel-tail ears. The farmers of Damaidi were expecting a truly golden harvest. They wandered lazily through the village alleys and along the ridges between the fields as though they were half asleep or half drunk.

But forty miles away, swarms of locusts were filling the sky and covering the earth, gobbling up everything in sight. By the time they finished and moved on, the sky and earth were bare.

The reed lands, which could turn suddenly humid or dry, were a perfect breeding ground for locusts. The historical records told of numerous locust plagues there. The older people in the village could tell stories so horrific they would make your hair stand on end.

"The locusts passed over like a barber's knife, razing everything to the ground. They didn't leave a single blade of grass."

"When the locusts flew in, they cleaned out the house, including our clothes and our books. If they'd had teeth they'd have eaten us too!"

There were numerous instances of plagues of locusts in the county records:

SONG DYNASTY, third year of the Chunxi reign (1176): a plague of locusts

YUAN DYNASTY, nineteenth year of the Zhiyuan reign (1282): a swarm of locusts blocked out the sun and stripped the crops as they passed through

YUAN DYNASTY, sixth year of the Dade reign (1302): locusts covered the land and ate all the grain

MING DYNASTY, fifteenth year of the Chenghua reign (1479): drought, locusts ate all the grain, many people fled

MING DYNASTY, sixteenth year of the Chenghua reign (1480): drought for the second year in a row, emergency, no crops or grain were harvested, food rationed to one cup of millet per person

And so the list went on.

It had been such a long time since the last plague that people thought they were over for good. The children had seen locusts, but when Nainai told them about vast swarms, they didn't believe her and came out with silly things like "Hens and ducks quack and cluck; they'll eat the locusts, then lay eggs." Or, "No problem! I'll swat them like flies! *Splat! Splat! Splat!* Or light a fire and burn them to death."

Nainai would sigh and shake her head. These children would never understand.

The villagers were growing more and more anxious about the current reports. The loudspeakers in the village and across the river at the Cadre School were constantly broadcasting news about the swarm: how big it was, how far it had gone, how close it was to Damaidi. It was like listening to battle reports in wartime. But, besides worrying, there was nothing they could do. The crops were green and growing; they wouldn't be ripe enough to harvest before the locusts came. The villagers looked out over the fields, praying and praying that the locusts would fly in a different direction and leave them alone.

The village children were excited.

When Bronze was riding on his buffalo, he'd look up at the sky, wondering when the locusts were going to come. He thought the adults were ridiculous. How could these fully grown people be so scared of tiny insects? How many locusts had he killed in the grass and reeds and fed to the chickens and ducks at home? Then one day he saw a black cloud approaching in the western sky. It looked ominous, but it turned out to be a flock of sparrows.

When Sunflower and her friends came out of school, they talked about nothing else. They seemed scared, but at the same time were enjoying the drama. Every now and then one of them would suddenly shout, "The locusts are coming!" and they'd jump and look up at the sky. And the joker would rock back and forth with laughter. Despite the adults' warnings, the children couldn't wait.

Sunflower kept bothering Nainai. "When are the locusts coming?"

And Nainai would say, "Do you want them to come and gobble you up?"

"But locusts don't eat people!"

"They eat the crops, though. And if there are no crops left, *then* what will you eat?"

That was when Sunflower realized how serious it was. She couldn't stop thinking about the locusts.

When they heard that the locusts were twenty miles from Damaidi, everyone grew tense. At the Cadre School and in the village, pesticide sprayers stood lined up, ready for battle. Then it was announced that the authorities might send planes to spray pesticide from the air. The adults were excited to hear this. None of them had ever seen airborne chemical warfare against a plague of locusts!

The children ran around like crazy, spreading the news.

"Calm down," said some of the older people. "The locusts are twenty miles away. If they fly fast, they might be here in a day and a night. But they might not come to Damaidi at all. It depends which way the wind is blowing. Locusts like to fly against the wind," they explained. "The stronger, the better."

The children ran to the river and under trees to check which way the wind was blowing. They were disappointed to find it was blowing toward Damaidi, which meant the locusts might not come. They kept checking throughout the day.

But during the night, the wind suddenly changed direction and began to pick up strength. In the early hours of the morning, there were shrieks of panic in the village. "The locusts are coming! The locusts are coming!"

Soon the shouts and screams woke the whole village. People leaped out of bed, ran outside, and looked up at the sky. But there was no sky, just a seething mass of screeching locusts blocking out the early-morning light. The rising sun was like a large round pancake covered in black sesame seeds. The locusts hovered in the air, circling, swooping, and rising like a living whirlwind.

Some of the older people knelt on the ridges between the fields, holding smoking sticks of incense in both hands as they faced east, and prayed for the locusts to move on. It was not easy to grow these crops, they said in their prayers. The crops were the lifeblood of the village, and everyone in the village, from youngest to oldest, depended on them. Damaidi was a poor place. If the locusts stopped here, the village would not survive. The sincerity in their eyes was genuine, as was their desperate belief that their prayers could move heaven . . . or at least shift these little devils.

"Prayers aren't going to help us now," said the children's parents, who were watching the locusts as they descended.

The children had never seen anything like this before. They stood there, staring up at the sky, transfixed.

Sunflower grabbed the corner of Nainai's jacket. She was terrified. The hum of the locusts grew louder and louder. The vibrations caused by their legs and wings rubbing against their bodies produced a sound like steel strings being plucked. When they had descended to a few yards above ground level, the whining rasp was unbearable.

Then down they poured, onto the reeds and the trees and the crops. Down they poured, like rain from a raincloud. They rained and rained, and still more clouds of locusts came, filling the sky. As the children ran about, the locusts hit their faces, making their skin sting.

When the villagers looked at the locusts hovering

above, the brilliant red of their underwings seemed to fill the sky with tiny dots of blood, tiny red flowers. But as soon as they landed, the red dots vanished. Their sandy-colored bodies disappeared on the sandy-colored earth, and the whirring rasp ceased. They got straight down to business. Once they started eating, there was no stopping them. They devoured everything in sight.

Bronze found a broom and thrashed it about in the air. But the locusts were like a fast-flowing river: as soon as he swept some away, more flowed in to fill the space. Bronze beat the air again and again. Eventually he realized that his efforts were in vain, and he threw the broom aside and dropped to the ground. He was exhausted.

Everyone headed for their own plot of land. Each family had to fend for itself, protect its own crops. Everyone was out waving brooms or clothes, shouting and screaming, doing whatever they could to drive the locusts away. But they soon gave up. The locusts kept coming, and they couldn't care less about brooms and clothes. As hundreds and thousands of locusts died, hundreds and thousands more flooded in.

People began to despair.

Excitement had turned to terror. The children were more fearful than the adults, scared that the locusts would eat the plants, then turn on them. It didn't matter how many times the adults told them that locusts don't eat people, the children didn't believe them. The locusts were crazy, and the children didn't trust them.

Bronze's family sat on a ridge overlooking their land. No one spoke. They just watched.

The locusts devoured their rapeseed plants and their wheat, as efficiently as if each insect's work had been allocated in advance. They started at the outer edges of the leaves and ate toward the middle, stripping the crops in no time at all. Their mouths were smeared with fresh green sap, and every so often they'd raise their backsides and excrete dark-green pellets that looked like tiny herbal-medicine pills.

Sunflower nestled her chin on Nainai's arm and watched quietly.

The crops grew shorter and shorter, as did the reeds and the grass. The leaves disappeared from the trees until the branches were bare, and Damaidi looked as bleak as in winter. The chemical spraying equipment that the Cadre School and the village had prepared was apparently useless. People looked up at the sky, hoping the spraying planes would appear. But they never did. It had been an empty rumor from the start.

Then, as though an instruction had been issued, the locusts spread their wings and rose into the sky, all together. The sky suddenly went black, and everything was thrown into shadow. A few hours later, a faint light began to appear around the edges of the swarm. As the locusts moved westward, the light spread across the sky until the whole of Damaidi was bathed in sunshine. And the horrific scene was exposed. Damaidi had been razed to the ground.

❀ ❀ ❀

Almost none of the villagers had reserve stocks of grain. They had counted on the food in the rice vats lasting until the wheat ripened. But there wouldn't be any wheat this year. As food supplies ran low, so did the mood of the villagers.

Worry and weakness began to show. The villagers

had to find ways of getting through. A few went to stay with relatives far away. Some of the stronger villagers left their older relatives and children at home and went to find work at the reservoir thirty miles away. One or two went into town to pick refuse off the street but didn't tell their friends and family.

The family thought long and hard. There was only one thing they could do: stay in Damaidi and do the best they could.

Since the locusts had destroyed the crops, the family kept a close eye on the rice vat. They all but counted the grains one by one into the pan. Bronze would forage when he was out grazing the buffalo. Nainai often went out on the ridges between the fields or by the river and would bring back wild plants in her basket. From morning till night, the question of food twisted itself around every thought in Baba's and Mama's minds. They went to the paddy field to look for arrowhead corms and water chestnuts that might have been missed. They blew air through last year's chaff again and again, trying to salvage every last grain of rice.

The days grew hotter and longer. The sun blazed

for hours on end, and the villagers felt they were roasting. The hairs on their skin twitched in the heat to move the air along. It seemed to go on forever. Everyone longed for the days to be shorter, for night to come sooner, so they could go to bed and not think about eating.

Across the river, the teams at the Cadre School kept changing. People came. People went. Only a few of the original group who had come with Sunflower and her father were left. Life was hard for them too, and although they didn't really have enough for themselves, a few of them arrived with a bag of rice for the family.

Mama looked at the precious rice. Tears rolled down her face. "Say thank you to your aunties and uncles, Sunflower," she said quickly.

Sunflower did as she was told.

The group looked at Mama and said, "We're the ones who are grateful—to you and your family."

Soon after that, they returned to the city. The villagers heard that everyone at the Cadre School would be leaving.

Sometimes Sunflower would stand by the river and

gaze over at the Cadre School. The roof tiles had once been so red, so bright and new. It had once been so busy with activity. Now the tiles looked old, and the place seemed almost lifeless. Wild grass was creeping in on all sides. The Cadre School seemed to grow farther and farther away from her.

Eventually, the last people moved out of the Cadre School and the place was left silent and abandoned amid the endless reeds. By the time the last city people left, the family had completely run out of food. There was not a single grain of rice in the rice vat. And they were not the only family in Damaidi that was coming to the end of the road.

Everyone said the emergency supply boat would arrive any day. But there was never any sign of it. Most probably the locusts had ravaged such a vast area that it was affecting the distribution of supplies, and Damaidi would have to hold out a while longer. Every so often, the villagers would go to the river and look into the distance. It was a river of hope, the clear water flowing merrily in the sunshine as it always had.

One day, Bronze and Sunflower set out with the buffalo toward the reeds. Bronze walked along, leading the buffalo and balancing a spade across his shoulders. Sunflower sat on the buffalo with a basket on her back. They were going to go into the reeds and dig up a basket of tender, sweet reed roots. Bronze knew that the deeper they went into the reeds, the sweeter the roots would be. In the sun and rain, they had already grown new leaves; it was hard to believe that a plague of locusts had swept through and stripped them only a few weeks before.

From the buffalo's back, Sunflower saw the swaying reeds rising and falling like waves on the sea and, here and there, pools of water shimmering silver in the sunlight. Above the pools, she saw birds in the sky: wild ducks and cranes and birds she couldn't name.

She was hungry.

"Are we nearly there?" she asked Bronze.

He nodded. He was hungry too. He'd been hungry for a long time, so hungry that his head felt heavy and his feet felt light, and the images before his eyes kept shifting. But he wanted to keep going. He wanted her to taste the best reed roots, the ones that oozed sweet juice the moment you bit into them.

Sunflower looked around. Damaidi was already

disappearing into the distance. They were surrounded by reeds. She felt scared.

Eventually Bronze brought the buffalo to a stop. He helped Sunflower down, and they started to dig. The reeds here were quite different from those at the edges: they had thicker stalks and wider leaves.

"These reeds have the best roots," Bronze told Sunflower, and as soon as his spade sank into the earth, they heard it cut crisply through the roots below. He worked the spade a few more times in the earth until a small pit appeared, with a tender white root in the middle. Sunflower had never tasted reed roots before, and she couldn't wait.

Quickly Bronze cut a piece of root, washed it in the river, and gave it to her.

She bit into it. Cool, sweet liquid ran into her mouth. She closed her eyes.

Bronze smiled. She took another couple of bites, then held the root up to his mouth. He shook his head. She held it there stubbornly and gave him no choice. Bronze opened his mouth. When that cool liquid slipped down his throat and into his hungry belly, like Sunflower he closed his eyes. With the sun shining on his eyelids, the world took on a warm, soft orange hue.

They spent the rest of their time digging up roots, chewing as they worked. Every so often, they would glance at each other, their newfound happiness like fresh water running into a dry pond bed, like energy returning to a weak body, a joy that breathed warmth into tired limbs. They bobbed their heads from side to side as they chewed, eating as noisily as they could and enjoying every mouthful. Their white teeth glistened in the sun.

One for you. One for me. One for me. One for you. It was the most delicious food on earth, and the pleasure was all theirs. They ate their fill and felt almost drunk. They kept digging; they wanted to take a basketful of roots home so Nainai, Baba, and Mama could eat to their hearts' content too.

They gave the slightly older roots to the buffalo. It chomped away, leaking juice from the side of its mouth and swinging its tail from side to side. Then it looked up at the sky and gave a long bellow of contentment that made the reed leaves tremble and rustle. Sunflower trailed after Bronze, gathering the roots as he dug them out and putting them in the basket.

When the basket was almost full, some wild ducks flew overhead and landed not far away. Suddenly an idea came to Bronze and he dropped the spade.

"Wouldn't it be amazing if we could catch one of those ducks?" he gestured to Sunflower, then parted the leaves and headed off to where the ducks had landed.

After a few steps, he stopped and looked back.

"Stay there," he told Sunflower. "I won't be long. Stay there and keep an eye on the reed roots. Don't move from that spot!"

She nodded. "Don't be long."

He nodded back, turned around, then disappeared into the reeds.

"Bronze, don't be long!" she shouted after him before sitting down next to the basket on a patch of reeds that Bronze had flattened before he ran off. The buffalo, its belly full, was lying on its side on the ground, pulling its lips this way and that, although there was nothing in its mouth. Sunflower laughed at the sight.

Bronze moved carefully through the reeds. He was so excited by the thought of catching a wild duck! The family hadn't eaten meat for ages now.

He caught a glimpse of a pool. He inched forward and quietly pushed the reeds apart until he could see the ducks. There were two ducks and a drake on the water, their beaks tucked under their wings, resting. Perhaps they'd traveled a long way, looking for food, and were tired.

Bronze focused all his attention on the drake, and for a while he forgot completely about Sunflower and the buffalo. The ducks were without a care in the world, and as he watched them, lost in his own world, time slipped away. He crouched in the reeds, working out a plan. If he could find a stone, he could hurl it and knock one of them out. But there were only reeds here and nothing else. He thought again. If only he had a big net or a hunting rifle. If only he'd been underwater before they landed.

Those ducks are so fat! thought Bronze, imagining a pan full of fresh duck soup. Saliva drooled from the corner of his mouth and dropped into the grass. He wiped his mouth and smiled at the thought.

Meanwhile, Sunflower was beginning to get restless. She stood up and looked in the direction that Bronze had gone. The sky had changed. The sun, which had been dancing over the reeds, was now obscured by a dark cloud. The reeds had been green. They were now black. As the wind blew in, the reeds began to sway, and the swaying became more and more vigorous.

"Where is he?" she asked the buffalo.

The buffalo seemed troubled.

In the reeds there is a mysterious black bird that wails when it's about to rain. It sounds like a child crying in the cruel north wind and sends a shiver down the spines of all who hear it, as though someone were running a cold hairy hand up and down your back. Sunflower heard it and began to tremble.

"Bronze, where are you? Why are you taking so long?"

The bird cried again. It was flying toward her.

Eventually, she couldn't stand it any longer and set off to look for Bronze. She took a few steps, then looked back and told the buffalo, "Stay here and wait for us. You mustn't eat the roots in the basket; they're for Nainai, Baba, and Mama. Be good."

The buffalo looked at her and flapped its big hairy ears.

And off she ran, calling out Bronze's name.

The wind grew stronger. The reeds swished louder, and it seemed as though there were a monster chasing after her. She thought she could hear heavy breathing. "Bronze! Bronze! Where are you?" she shouted at the top of her voice. There was no sign of him anywhere.

Bronze suddenly remembered Sunflower and the buffalo, and a cold shiver ran through him. He turned and hurried back to find them. The black cloud rolling across the sky took him by surprise.

The ducks were surprised too. They flapped their wings and took to the sky, leaving a trail of waves behind them.

Bronze glanced up at them. He didn't care about the ducks anymore. He was worried about Sunflower and the buffalo. Panting all the way, he ran back to where he had left them.

When he got there, dripping with sweat, he found

only the buffalo and the basket of roots. He stretched out his arms and spun around and around, trying to find her. But all he could see were reeds . . . and more and more reeds. He looked at the buffalo. The buffalo looked back at him. Sunflower must have gone looking for him, he thought. He ran like crazy. The reeds crashed and slapped as he passed, until he was back at the duck pool. But there was no sign of Sunflower. He wanted to scream and shout, but no sound came out. He turned and ran back.

The buffalo was already on its feet, looking restless. Bronze charged into the reeds again, running as fast as he could. The reeds snagged his clothes and scratched his face, legs, and arms, dragging lines across his skin.

As he ran, all he could think about was Sunflower. Sunflower sitting on the stone slab beneath the old tree; Sunflower reading and writing by the lantern lights he had made for her; Sunflower teaching him to write in the earth with a stick; Sunflower running and leaping along the ridge between the fields with her schoolbag on her back; Sunflower laughing; Sunflower crying.

Then he stepped on a piece of reed stubble. It

pierced almost all the way through his foot. Pain surged through him, so intense that he broke into a cold sweat. His body was weak from living on wild vegetables. He'd used up his energy running. Everything went black. He staggered and fell.

He came to when it started to rain, and cold threads of water trickled over him. He scrambled to his feet. As he looked up, a whip of blue lightning slashed through the sky. It left a momentary scar, then faded. Then there was a crash of thunder so loud it seemed the sky would split and the ground would crack.

The rain was pouring down now. Bronze struggled on, dragging his bleeding foot.

Sunflower had lost all sense of direction. She was no longer running, but walking slowly, sobbing and calling out her brother's name. "Bronze! Bronze!"

She trembled at every bolt of lightning and shuddered at every crash of thunder. Rain swept her hair across her face. Her clothes were soaked and clung to her body, now pitifully thin.

She didn't know how big the reed marsh was. She just knew that Bronze and the buffalo were waiting for her, and that at home Nainai, Baba, and Mama were waiting for all three of them. She couldn't stop. She had to keep walking until she reached the edge of the marsh.

She had no idea that she was walking deeper and deeper into the vast reed marsh, that the marsh was swallowing her up.

Bronze returned to where they had been digging. This time the buffalo was gone too, and there was just the basket of roots. He collapsed, exhausted. Roaring thunder rolled across the sky, and a mist of rain covered the earth.

Back in Damaidi, Nainai, Baba, and Mama were walking around, calling out their children's names. Nainai was out with her stick, her silvery hair glistening wet. She looked as thin as an old willow tree, swaying by the river. The wind and the rain muffled her elderly voice.

She saw Gayu on the river in his bark rain cape, punting his little boat, driving his ducks home.

"Have you seen our Bronze and Sunflower?" Nainai asked.

Gayu couldn't hear her. He tried to keep the boat still so he could listen, but the ducks were chasing after raindrops and swimming too far out, and he had to leave Nainai and go after them.

When Bronze woke again, the rain seemed to be easing a little. He struggled to sit up. He watched the reeds bowing and rising until his eyes glazed over. He was losing hope. If he couldn't find Sunflower, then he couldn't go home. Rain slid from his shiny black hair onto his face. The world in front of him blurred. He let his head hang. It felt as heavy as a millstone. His chin pressed into his chest.

In his dream, he saw Sunflower floating in front of him, his sister Sunflower, a sunflower growing in the field.

Was that the buffalo he could hear?

Bronze looked up, heard another cry, and realized it came from nearby. He got unsteadily to his feet. Then he followed the sounds. He saw the buffalo running toward him, the reeds parting to let it through like water parting around a boat. And there was Sunflower, riding on its back!

As Bronze fell to his knees, a spray of water splashed up.

When the rain stopped and the sky cleared, Bronze

limped out of the reed marsh, leading the buffalo. Sunflower sat on its back, carrying the basket of roots. The rain had washed them as clean as ivory.

The grain relief boat had set out on its journey of several hundred miles, but after a long period without rain, the river was low, and the boat could only move slowly. With every day that passed, the villagers tightened their belts even more.

Bronze and Sunflower were getting very thin. Their eyes, which had been large to start with, were now bulging. Their teeth looked very white in their gaunt faces and glistened with hunger. It was the same with the adults.

The children now walked instead of running and leaping. They had no energy. If the adults saw them running and jumping, they'd tell them not to. "Don't jump about—you need to save your energy!"

Of course, it was more about saving food.

The life seemed to be draining out of Damaidi. The villagers looked sick. When they talked, they sounded like invalids. When they walked, they reeled from side to side. But the weather was good, and there was sunshine every day. Plants and trees were thriving; there was green everywhere. Birds were flying in the sky, calling and singing all day long. But the villagers didn't have the heart to appreciate any of this. They didn't have the strength. The children went to school as usual, and read their books as usual, but the beautiful rise and fall of their voices as they read out loud got weaker and weaker until they were no longer capable of reading aloud; their thin bellies weren't up to it. People were worried. They were sweating with anxiety. When the hunger was at its worst, they thought about gnawing on stones. Everyone in the village, young and old, was in low spirits.

The family kept going and put on brave faces. No one said they were hungry. Even when they went without food at night, none of them would complain. They kept the house and themselves cleaner than ever. Bronze and Sunflower never left the house without clean faces and clean clothes. Nainai still went to the riverside to wash her hands and face in fresh, cold water as she had always done. She never had a strand of silver hair out of place or a spot of dirt on her clothes.

But now, when she walked about in the sunshine, her loose clothes flapped in the breeze like wings.

Bronze and Sunflower were good at foraging for food. In the wide open fields, in the countless rivers and streams that ran through the reed lands, there was always something they could eat. Bronze was good at remembering the places where he had found food before. When he took Sunflower along, they almost always found some tasty surprise.

One day, Bronze was steering a large wooden boat toward the bay in the river. He'd remembered a big stretch of reeds by the bay, and within it a small pool where wild water chestnuts grew. He took Sunflower with him, thinking they could eat some as they picked, then take some back for Nainai, Baba, and Mama. This time, however, they found nothing: the water chestnut plants were there, but someone had already pulled the corms from the mud.

They steered the boat back toward home. Bronze needed to rest, so he lay down under the awning.

Sunflower lay down beside him. In the light breeze, the boat slowly started to drift. They could hear the water slapping against the bottom. It was a clear and soothing sound, like a musical instrument being plucked. White clouds drifted in the sky.

"Just like cotton candy," said Sunflower.

The white clouds kept shifting shape.

"That one's like a steamed bun," she added.

Bronze traced the outline with his finger.

"That's not a steamed bun—it's an apple."

"No, it's a pear."

"There's a sheep."

"A herd of sheep."

"I wish Baba would kill a sheep."

"The biggest, fattest sheep."

"I want three bowls of mutton broth."

"I'll have four."

"I'll have five."

"I'll add a spoonful of chili."

"I'll add a handful of coriander."

"Come on, drink up, don't let it get cold."

"Let's drink it all up!"

"Let's drink it all up!"

And with that, they started to gulp down the imaginary soup, swallowing noisily. When they were finished, they smacked their lips and licked around their mouths with their tongues.

"Finished," said Sunflower.

"Have an apple."

"No, I'll have a pear; they're juicier."

"I want an apple first, and then a pear."

"I want two apples, then two pears."

"You'll burst!"

"Then I'll walk on the ridges between the fields. Do you remember the time I ate too many water chestnuts and you took me to walk on the ridges, and we walked until it was dark, and when I went home I ate another one?"

The clouds in the sky were forever changing shape. Bronze and Sunflower saw fields of yellow corn, golden waves rolling across paddy fields, a towering persimmon tree, a chicken, a goose, a fish, a vast pan of bubbling soy milk, an enormous watermelon, a huge cantaloupe . . .

Their feast was so delicious, their conversation so

delightful. They ate and ate to their hearts' content, and happily drifted off.

One day, when Sunflower came home from school, she had just stepped inside when everything went black, her legs turned to jelly, and she collapsed on the floor.

Nainai hurried over.

"What's wrong, precious?" she asked as she helped her granddaughter up. Sunflower had hit her cheek on the door frame, and she was bleeding. Mama carried her to bed. When she saw how pale Sunflower was, Mama went to the kitchen and quickly boiled up some rice soup. Luckily, she had just borrowed a cup of rice from a neighbor.

When Bronze came back from grazing the buffalo, he took a fishing net and, without saying a word to anyone, went off by himself to the reed marsh. He found the pool, but there was nothing floating on the surface, just the reflection of the sky.

The ducks are gone, he thought. He was disappointed, but he sat down behind the reeds and told himself to wait patiently. They're probably out looking for food; they're bound to be back soon. He broke off a couple of reed leaves and folded them into two little boats. He glanced up at the sky to see if it was going to rain, then stepped out of the reeds, placed the boats on the water, and hurried back to his hiding place. When he pushed the reeds apart, he could see his boats moving along the river in the breeze.

An hour or so passed, but there was still no sign of any wild ducks.

"Please come back. Please come back," Bronze prayed.

At about midday, he was thrilled to see a large flock appear in the sky. But they didn't land; they just kept flying. He sighed, picked up the net, and prepared to move on.

Then more ducks appeared. Bronze followed their every move. They looked familiar. Yes, they were the ones he had seen the day Sunflower got lost! They circled in the air, then began their descent. Wild ducks are clumsy creatures, with heavy bodies and short wings. They landed on the water with the grace of a dozen bricks. *Splat! Splat! Splat!*

They made a quick check of their surroundings, and once they were satisfied, they relaxed and began to swim about. They flapped their wings and quacked a bit, using their flat beaks to splash up water to wash their feathers and to *glug-glug-glug* it down their throats.

The drake was big and fat. His head was dark purple that shimmered like soft satin. The females swam nearby, each one doing as she pleased. There was a beautiful little duck that seemed to be the drake's favorite, and every time she swam off, he would follow her. They would preen each other, combing their beaks through the other's feathers and dashing their beaks in the water as though they were trying to say something. After a while, the drake flapped his wings and climbed onto her back. But he was so heavy that her body was pushed underwater, only her head remaining above the surface. It looked a little strange, but she didn't put up any resistance, just stayed like that, half in, half out of the water, until eventually he slipped off. The pair spent some time shaking out their wings, looking pleased with themselves. Then the drake flapped his wings and flew off.

Bronze was worried that the other ducks would follow him, but they continued floating around, doing what ducks do. The drake circled above the pool, then landed back on the water with a splash. Little drops of water caught the light as they rolled down his back.

Bronze grabbed his net and waited for his moment. The only way he could catch a duck was to wait until they were all playing underwater or diving for shrimp and snails, then cast his net over the water and wait for them to resurface. One or two were bound to get caught, especially if they poked their heads through the netting.

But the ducks showed no interest in diving underwater. While they were floating about, Bronze's legs began to go numb, his head felt a bit fuzzy, and things were going black before his eyes. He couldn't hold out any longer and lay down for a rest.

After a while, Bronze's strength was restored. The ducks' energy seemed to have been restored too, and they were beginning to swim around and explore.

Two of the younger ones started a game, one teasing, the other chasing. When the chaser got too close, the teaser went head-down and bottom-up, paddled its orange feet in the air, then disappeared altogether. The chaser swam around in a circle, then vanished underwater too. The others gradually joined in the fun until the pool was busy with ducks popping up and plunging down.

Bronze was on tenterhooks. He held the net tightly. His hands were slippery with sweat, and his legs were trembling. He told himself to stop, but his legs wouldn't listen and the shuddering continued. When his legs trembled, his whole body shook. And when his body shook, the reeds shook too, making a rustling sound. He closed his eyes. It took a lot of effort, but gradually he brought his legs under control.

Suddenly the water went completely still. All the ducks were underwater. This was Bronze's moment. He was almost certain to catch a few. But he hesitated, and by the time he was ready to cast the net, the ducks were already popping up again. He wished he'd been faster. Now he'd have to wait for another chance.

Two hours passed before the next opportunity

came. All the ducks were underwater except for one, which was floating on the surface. Bronze used no subtlety at all. He charged out of the reeds, spun around, and cast his net. It opened out like a flower in the sky and skim-landed on the water. The startled duck quacked and flew. It seemed as though the other ducks had heard the alarm, and they began to appear at the surface. Not one of them came up inside the net. They flapped their wings as hard as they could and flew off. Bronze watched them, his hopes dashed.

The water under the net was as still as could be. Clouds in the sky floated across the surface. Bronze's head hung low as he walked into the water to gather his net. Then he noticed two lines of bubbles rising below it. As the bubbles became bigger and bigger, the net seemed to move and rise up from the surface. Bronze's heart pounded like a wooden mallet inside his chest. The water began to break into waves, and it was clear that some living thing was struggling for its life. Bronze went over to see what it was.

It was a wild duck. Its head and wings caught in the net, it was using all its strength to break free. Bronze recognized it as the drake he'd been watching earlier. When the bird saw the sky, he beat his wings furiously, raising the net as he did so.

Bronze threw himself forward and tried to push the net back underwater. He pressed forward with all his body weight. He could feel the drake struggling. He felt terrible, but he kept the net pressed down until the water went completely still.

The other ducks hadn't gone far. They were circling above and crying out.

When Bronze hauled the net in, the drake was dead. He was a handsome creature. His eyes were like shiny black beans, his beak caught the light like a translucent horn. There were sleek feathers around his neck, his plumage was rich, and his golden feet were clean and shiny. Bronze looked at him and felt so sad. The other ducks eventually flew off. Bronze hauled the net over his shoulder and ran from the marsh.

As he passed along the river, people saw him and asked, "Hey, boy, what's in your net?"

He opened it proudly and let them see his fat wild duck. He gave them a big grin, then turned and sped home like a tornado.

It was late afternoon when Bronze arrived home. The house was empty. Nainai was out digging wild vegetables, Sunflower was at school, and Mama and Baba were still out working in the fields. Bronze took the duck out of the net, felt its weight in his hands, and took a good look at it. He decided to give them a surprise. He plucked the feathers, wrapped them in a lotus leaf (they could sell them later), and pushed the bundle under the bottom of the haystack. Then he took a knife, a chopping board, and an earthenware bowl to the riverside, cut open the duck, cleaned out its insides, chopped it up, and put the pieces in the bowl.

Back at the house, he tipped the pieces of duck into a pan, half-filled the pan with water, and lit a fire in the stove. He wanted to have a delicious duck soup ready for his family when they came home.

The first person to arrive home was Sunflower. The village children had been developing a very keen sense of smell recently, and she had picked up the mouthwatering aroma from a long way away. Was it coming from their kitchen? She looked up, and sure enough, there was smoke rising from their chimney.

She sniffed the air, then ran home as fast as she could, into the kitchen, where she found Bronze by the stove, his cheeks bright red from the heat.

"What are you making?" she asked. "It smells wonderful." As she lifted the lid of the pan, a cloud of white steam escaped, blurring everything before her eyes. It was a while before she could see the pan clearly again. The soup bubbled away, and the delicious smell filled their nostrils.

Bronze handed her a bowl of soup. "Here, take this. I caught a duck. It's still cooking, but have some broth first."

"Really?" Sunflower's eyes lit up.

"Go on." He blew on the broth to cool it.

She held the bowl with both hands and breathed in the wonderful aroma. "I'll wait till Nainai and the others come home."

"Go on—there's plenty more."

"Are you sure?"

"Go on!"

She took a tiny sip and pushed out her tongue. "Oh, oh, oh, it's wonderful!"

She glanced at Bronze, and without caring how hot

it was, she held the bowl to her lips. Bronze stood quietly and watched her. She'd grown so thin. As she swallowed one mouthful after another, he silently willed her to finish up so he could fetch her another bowlful!

And as he watched, his eyes seemed to mist over, perhaps because of the hot air rising from the pan, perhaps because of the tears that were welling up.

At lunchtime the next day, Gayu and his father turned up at the house. Gayu's father wore a long face, and it was clear in Gayu's hateful eyes that he had come to pick a fight. Bronze's father invited them to come and sit inside.

"Is there a problem?" he asked.

Neither Gayu nor his father answered. Gayu's arms were folded across his chest. His head was twisted to one side, and his lips were pursed.

"Has our Bronze been fighting with you?" Baba asked Gayu.

"Hmpf," Gayu snorted.

"Is there a problem?" Baba asked again.

"Are you saying you don't know why we're here?" said Gayu's father.

Gayu glanced at Bronze and Sunflower, who were writing out their characters, and repeated what his father had just said. "Are you saying you don't know why we're here?"

Baba rubbed his hands together. "If there's a problem, then tell me!"

Gayu's father narrowed his eyes. "You really don't know?"

"We really don't know," said Baba.

"How was the duck?" Gayu's father asked coldly.

Gayu jumped out from behind his father. "Yes, how was the duck?" he said, looking at Bronze and Sunflower.

Baba smiled. "Oh, you mean the wild duck?"

"Wild duck?" said Gayu's father, curling his lip.

"Yes, it was a wild duck," said Baba.

Gayu's father smiled a crooked smile. Gayu saw his father smile, and he smiled too, another crooked smile.

"So, what brings you here?" asked Baba.

"Isn't it obvious?" asked Gayu's father.

"Isn't it obvious?" Gayu chimed in, shooting a sideways glance at Bronze and Sunflower.

"No, it's not." Baba was beginning to get annoyed.

"Well, it should be obvious to your son," said Gayu's father.

"It's obvious to your son," said Gayu, pointing at Bronze.

Baba stepped forward. He pointed his finger at Gayu's father. "If you have something to say, then say it, and if not"—Baba pointed to the door—"then get out."

Nainai and Mama came over. Gayu's father looked at them and shook his finger.

"If there's a problem, then tell us," said Nainai coldly.

"One of our ducks is missing," said Gayu's father.

"One of our ducks is missing," repeated Gayu, leaping into the air.

"A drake," said Gayu's father.

"A drake," said Gayu.

"And what's that got to do with us?" asked Mama.

"You might well ask!" said Gayu's father. "If it had nothing to do with you, do you think we'd be here?"

"Say what you've come here to say," said Baba, grabbing Gayu's father by the collar with one hand and pointing a finger in his face.

When Gayu saw this, he ran out to the road and shouted, "There's a fight! There's a fight!" There were a lot of people out on the road at that time, and they all came running over.

Gayu's father struggled to break free. "One of our ducks is missing," he said loudly so the crowd could hear.

But Baba was much stronger than Gayu's father. He dragged him outside by the collar. "If one of your ducks is missing, then go and look for it!"

Gayu's father dug his heels in and yelled, "Someone in your family stole it! And you ate it!"

"WHAT did you just say?" Baba challenged. By now, Gayu's father had drawn quite an audience.

"People saw what happened. Your Bronze caught our duck in his fishing net."

Mama was furious. "We did not steal their duck!"

she told the crowd. She hauled Bronze over and asked him in front of everyone, "Did you steal their duck?" Bronze shook his head.

Sunflower was standing behind him. She shook her head too.

"Bronze did not steal your duck!" Mama declared.

Suddenly Gayu leaped forward, holding the lotus-leaf bundle that had been tucked under the haystack. He tossed it to the ground, and the leaf unrolled to reveal the duck feathers. The crowd was silent. The breeze blew a few of the feathers into the air and up toward the sky.

Nainai dragged Bronze to the front of the crowd. "You need to tell all these people what happened."

Bronze broke into a sweat. He tried to explain using hand gestures. But the crowd didn't understand.

"He says it was a wild duck," explained Nainai. Bronze continued.

"He says he caught it in the reeds. He says he caught it in his net. . . . He waited in the reeds for hours, then caught it in his net."

Bronze darted through the crowd to fetch the net.

He held it up with both hands and invited everyone to take a look.

Someone in the crowd said, "You can tell by the feathers whether it's a wild duck or a farm duck."

Some of the villagers crouched down to inspect the feathers. The rest kept quiet, waiting for the verdict.

But the villagers inspecting the feathers couldn't tell. All they could say was "They're feathers from a drake."

"And the one we are missing is a drake!" shouted Gayu.

"The people who saw the duck in Bronze's net said it was a drake," Gayu's father added.

"It's not so easy to catch a wild duck in a net," someone muttered at the back of the crowd.

"Well, if you say you caught that duck with a net, let's see you catch another one!" Gayu's father struggled to break free from Baba's grip. "If you wanted a duck so badly, why didn't you just ask?" he said with a snort. "Oh, of course, you can't."

When Nainai heard Gayu's father talking like this, she slipped one hand around Bronze's hand and the other around Gayu's, and stepped up to face him.

"Can you hear what you're saying? How can you talk like this in front of the children, including your own son? You should be ashamed of yourself."

Gayu's father pulled himself up as tall as he could, straining his neck and opening out his chest. "*I* should be ashamed? I'm not the one who's stolen a duck!"

He had barely finished what he was saying when Baba raised a fist and punched him in the face. The moment he let go of Gayu's father's collar, the other man fell backward and landed hard on his bottom.

Gayu's father took a moment or two to come to his senses and get up again. Then he leaped into the air with a massive roar and hurled himself at Baba.

"First you steal a duck, then you steal a punch!"

Baba was ready for a fight, but the crowd rushed in to separate them.

"Stop it. Don't fight." There was mayhem in front of the house.

Mama cuffed the back of Bronze's head. "Look where greed gets you!" Then she grabbed Sunflower's hand. "Let's go inside."

But Bronze wouldn't move. Mama had to push him in, then she closed the door behind him.

The crowd was split, one half supporting Bronze's family, the other half supporting Gayu's.

Nainai was shaking. Someone took her arm and said, "Don't get angry! Everyone in the village knows you are a good family. And we all know what Gayu's father is like. There's no reasoning with him."

Others were comforting Mama. She wiped her tears on the corner of her jacket. "He tramples all over people. It's not right. Yes, we're poor, but we're not thieves or cheats."

"We know," said the women, trying to calm her, "we know."

Others were urging Baba to keep calm.

Gayu and his father were dragged away. People told them, "You see it from up here; they see it from down there. Don't make a big fuss about it. What's one duck, when you've got so many?"

"I could give them a duck, I could give them ten ducks, but they can't go around stealing!"

"Maybe you'd better stop saying it was stolen. Did you see it? Do you have any proof?"

"You saw the pile of duck feathers! Are you saying they didn't look like a drake's?"

Some of them had seen Gayu's drake and thought there was a similarity, but they didn't say anything.

At that moment, a gust of wind blew the nice neat pile of feathers up into the air. They were so light that they went wherever the wind blew them.

When Gayu's father saw them, he stamped his feet and roared at Bronze's family, "That was our drake!"

Eventually the crowd dispersed and the family was on its own. No one said a word.

Every now and then Baba glared at Bronze out of the corner of his eye.

Bronze had done nothing wrong, but the look on Baba's face made him feel as though he'd committed a crime. He was wary of provoking him any further. Sunflower didn't dare look at Baba either and followed Bronze wherever he went. Occasionally she stole a glance at Baba, but when he looked back at her, she would begin to shake and quickly look away or hide behind Nainai or Mama.

Baba's face was dark and heavy. He didn't utter another word, but it was clear that this was the calm before the storm. Like the bird that knows when bad weather is on its way and hurries to find a tree, Bronze sought a refuge. Maybe his tree was Nainai and Mama. But if the storm came with full force, that particular tree would not necessarily be able to protect him.

He didn't know what to do.

Sunflower was even more worried. If Bronze had done something wrong, it was all because of her. She wanted to tell him to run away and lie low for a while.

Baba could see that the villagers had started to look at his family in a different light, and he was shaken to the core. No one in this family—no one—had ever stolen anything, not so much as a cucumber from a vegetable plot. No family in the village cared more about their reputation than his did.

Once Baba had been walking past a persimmon tree when one of the persimmons had fallen off. He'd picked it up off the ground, put it on the wall, and shouted across to the owner, "One of your persimmons just fell from the tree. I've put it on your wall."

"Oh, take it. Eat it!" came a voice from the other side.

But Baba had refused, saying, "I can't do that. But I'll call at your house sometime and eat some with you."

This was how Nainai had brought him up.

But now, Gayu's family had accused them of stealing a duck! And the entire village had come to watch. What was worse, the matter had not been resolved. Baba had to get to the bottom of it. He needed to know: was it a wild duck or a farm duck?

Later that day, Bronze went out in search of Nainai, Mama, and Sunflower. He thought they were in the vegetable garden at the front of the house, but they were collecting firewood around the back. Without making a sound, Baba followed him outside. He saw a stick on the ground, picked it up, and held it behind his back.

Somehow Bronze sensed that Baba was following him. He wished he'd stayed inside. Baba was quickening his pace. Bronze could have run for his life, but he didn't. He stopped. He didn't have the strength to run. And he didn't want to. He turned around to face Baba.

Baba was out of breath and almost out of his mind with rage. As he came closer, brandishing his stick in the air, Bronze fell to his knees.

"I want the truth. Was it a wild duck or their duck?"

Baba slammed the stick on the ground, shooting up clouds of dust. Bronze didn't answer. Two lines of tears rolled down his thin face.

"The truth! A wild duck or their duck!" He slapped the stick across Bronze's backside.

Bronze fell forward onto the ground.

Sunflower was struck by a sudden anxiety. She dropped what she was doing, left Nainai and Mama, and ran inside. When she saw that Baba and Bronze weren't there, she flew outside, shouting, "Bronze! Bronze!"

Nainai and Mama heard her shouts and followed her.

Sunflower saw Baba, and then she saw Bronze lying on the ground. She ran over as fast as she could, cradled his head in her hands, and used all her strength to help him to his feet.

"Baba . . . Baba . . ." She looked at him, her eyes filled with tears.

"Get away," he said, "or you'll be next."

Sunflower hugged Bronze tightly. Just then Nainai and Mama arrived. Nainai was shaking. She flew at Baba. "Come on! Hit me! Hit me! Come on, what's the matter with you? Hit me! Beat me till I die! I'm old! I've had enough!"

Nainai used her hard, wizened hands to wipe the tears and dirt and bits of grass from Bronze's face. "I know it was a wild duck!"

Then she looked at Baba. "Not once has this child ever told a lie. Not once. And you beat him. And you would have kept beating him. Shame on you!"

Bronze shook uncontrollably in Nainai's arms.

Early the next morning, Bronze went to sit by the river. The water had been calling him since the moment he woke up. He didn't know what his mind was up to, but fortunately his legs seemed to know what they were doing.

The summer sun glowed red and yellow. Its reflection shimmered on the water. The crops on either side of the river were growing and ripening, and at the same time they were tormenting the hungry villagers, who couldn't wait for the crops to become food.

By now Bronze was used to feeling hungry. As he sat by the river, he tore off a few blades of young grass, put them in his mouth, and chewed slowly. It was a bitter taste, but there was also a sweetness to it. A few magpies flew across to the other side of the river, then back, and then to the other side again, where they headed for the Cadre School. Bronze looked at the Cadre School's red-tiled roofs. They would soon be swallowed up by the reeds, which were growing like crazy.

A weaver-girl grasshopper on a reed leaf was singing a pure and lonely song, the sound of the insect rubbing its wings together. It was a clear, quiet sound amid the buzz and hum of summer.

Bronze sat cross-legged, looking at the river as though waiting for something to appear.

The villagers saw him there, looked at him for a moment, then walked on. They had never been able to figure him out. There was something about Bronze. He was different from the other children somehow; they couldn't put their finger on it.

Bronze sat there on the riverbank till midday. Sunflower came to tell him it was lunchtime, but he wouldn't leave, and she had to go home without him. Mama put two vegetable dumplings in a bowl and asked Sunflower to take them to him. Bronze ate the dumplings while she watched, then he headed into the reeds, where she heard pee spattering in the water. Then he sat down again in the same place. Sunflower couldn't stay with him; she had to go to school.

As the villagers dozed in the early afternoon, something appeared on the river in the east. Bronze watched as the black dot approached. It seemed to be a duck, swimming closer. Bronze wasn't the least bit excited; he wasn't even curious. It was as though he'd been sitting here all this time waiting for it.

The duck was heading straight for Damaidi. Every now and then it would stop and look in the water for something to eat. But it knew where it was going, and as soon as it had eaten, it would swim on. It swam closer. It was a drake, a handsome drake. Bronze did not take his eyes off it. The duck seemed to be aware of his attention and began to swim a bit hesitantly.

Bronze recognized it as the duck that had gone missing from Gayu's flock. He had no idea where it had been or how it came to be swimming all by itself on the river. This duck had some nerve!

The day the drake had gone missing, Gayu had met another flock of ducks while he was driving his flock home. The two flocks were heading in different directions, and for a while they became one enormous group of ducks, some facing east and some facing west. Gayu didn't worry; he knew the ducks would eventually sort themselves out and rejoin their own flock.

Sure enough, that's what happened.

This particular drake, however, had taken a fancy to one of the females in the other flock, and followed that flock home. It was a dark and gloomy day, and Gayu didn't notice that he was a drake short, and the owner of the other flock didn't notice that he had an extra drake.

Gayu's drake spent the night with the other flock, wandered around with the ducks all day, and then spent a second night in their pen. It was a big flock, and the owner still hadn't noticed the newcomer. But some of the other drakes had. They tried to scare him off and make him leave, but he kept brazenly pestering the females, until the drakes could stand it no more. They surrounded him, attacked him with their flat beaks, and drove him out of the flock. A little worse for wear, Gayu's drake remembered his original flock and started swimming back toward Damaidi.

As the drake drew closer, Bronze stood up. He saw that his feathers were similar in color to those of the wild duck. He followed him from the bank. Just as he was about to reach the village, Bronze leaped into the water. The drake flapped his wings and surged forward, quacking.

Bronze didn't come to the surface immediately but kept his head underwater. When he appeared, he was only a few yards from the drake. He swam over, and the drake flapped his wings and moved away. The chase went on for a long time. Bronze didn't have much strength and kept slipping into the water. Then he'd resurface and go after the drake again. The village children saw that something was happening and came to watch from the bank.

Bronze slid underwater again. When he looked

up at the sky, he saw the sun melting in the water, turning it gold. He slipped down, and soon his feet were touching the weeds at the bottom. When he felt them curling around his feet, he yanked his legs up in shock and started to float to the top. He kept looking up at the melting sun, and when he rose a little higher, he saw a pair of bright yellow drake's feet paddling away. He positioned himself, then reached out his hand and grabbed the duck's legs.

The drake flapped his wings like crazy. Bronze rose to the surface and swam to the shore. He had enough energy to hold the duck, but not an ounce more. He lay down on the sandy shore and held the duck tight. The drake was exhausted too and didn't struggle. Bronze could hear him panting, trying to catch his breath.

A boy driving his sheep saw Sunflower as she was walking to school. "Your brother's caught Gayu's drake, the one that went missing."

Sunflower forgot she was on her way to school, turned, and ran into the village.

When Bronze recovered enough strength, he held the duck in his arms and walked along one street, then the next, then the next. He proceeded slowly all the way from one end of the village to the other, not looking at a single person he passed.

The duck seemed calm, happy to let Bronze carry him. The villagers had finished their afternoon naps and were just coming outside. Many people saw Bronze walking with the duck in his arms. He walked down one street, then another. It was a blazing-hot day, and the dogs were lying under trees with their tongues hanging out, panting.

The duck was heavy and Bronze became tired. Then Sunflower appeared. She knew exactly what Bronze was doing. He wanted to show everyone in Damaidi that he hadn't stolen Gayu's duck. Sunflower followed him everywhere, like a tail.

Bronze walked around with the duck, quietly and calmly. When people saw him, they stopped and watched. Soon, the only sounds in the village were the footsteps of Bronze and Sunflower. The villagers felt every footstep as a beat of their hearts.

An old lady came out with a ladle of cold water and blocked Bronze's way. "Child, we know you didn't steal Gayu's duck. You're a good boy. Listen to this old grandmother. You don't need to walk anymore."

She wanted him to take a drink, but he refused and continued walking. The old lady gave the ladle to Sunflower, who looked gratefully at her, took the ladle, and, holding it very carefully so as not to spill the water, followed Bronze. As she walked, the reflection of the sky and the village buildings swayed about in the water.

When Bronze had walked the length of every street in the village, he plunged his face into the water and drank every last drop. People gathered around them. Still holding the drake, Bronze walked to the river and threw him into the air. The duck flapped his wings a few times, then landed on the water.

News came that the grain boat had been looted by some villages upstream. The villagers of Damaidi had been waiting anxiously, and this was a heavy blow. They could not hold out for much longer— people were already beginning to collapse from hunger. As hope dwindled, the threat of death began to hang in the air. The villagers walked with a stoop, they were too tired to talk, and when they did speak, it sounded like the low drone of mosquitoes. They stopped doing the things they enjoyed: there was no more singing, no more performances, no more gathering to hear people read. There was no laughter, no fun. Even the arguments stopped. The villagers began to sleep, on and on as if they might sleep forever. The dogs staggered about the streets, little more than skin and bone.

The head of the village was very concerned. His belt was as tight as it could go too. He walked around the village streets, calling, "Get up! Everybody up!"

He summoned the villagers to the threshing ground at the end of the village. He had them line up and asked one of the primary schoolteachers to lead everyone in a song. They sang rousing songs about being strong and brave. The head of the village had a terrible voice, but he led by example and sang louder than anyone. Occasionally he would stop and look at the villagers. If he spotted someone who was slacking, he'd shout at them to put more effort in.

"We must be as strong as bears!" he shouted. "Straighten those backs! Keep those backs straight! We need backs as strong as tree trunks!"

And the villagers—no matter how tall or short—straightened their backs and pulled themselves up as straight as tree trunks.

The head of the village looked at the forest of people in front of him. There was a lump in his throat and tears in his eyes. "We have to keep going. Just a few more days—then we can harvest the rice."

In the heat of the sun, the starving villagers sang as loudly as they could.

"That's the spirit of Damaidi!" said the head of the village.

Damaidi had been deluged with floods, burned by fire, plagued with disease, had seen bloodshed at the hands of bandits and Japanese troops. It had been through one disaster after another, but this village in the lush reed lands had always survived. Early the next morning, wisps of smoke curled from every chimney and merged to form a sea of cloud in the sky.

That day Nainai was nowhere to be seen. They searched everywhere, but they couldn't find her. She turned up in the evening, on the dust road that ran near the end of the village. She couldn't have walked any slower and had to take a long rest after each step. Her back was bent forward, and over her shoulder was slung a small sack of rice. The whole family went to help her. She gave the sack to Baba.

"Tonight, make some rice for the children," she told Mama.

They all noticed that Nainai's shiny gold ring was missing from her finger. But no one mentioned it. Bronze and Sunflower helped Nainai home, one on each side of her.

As the sun set in the west, the sunlight cast a red glow over the fields and rivers. In the deep hours of the night, a large grain boat finally pulled up outside Damaidi.

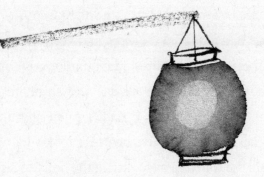

The Paper Lantern

The sickles were brought out, the rice was harvested, and the new crop was taken to the threshing ground. The air above Damaidi was filled with the fresh scent of newly cut rice. Baba was busy leading the buffalo as it pulled the stone roller that separated the rice from the chaff. Every so often he would shout out loud, and the sound would ring around the autumn fields and make people feel that the whole world was bright. It was more difficult to thresh rice than wheat, and it could take as long as seven or eight hours to process one batch. All the rice ripened at the same time, and because it tended to rain in autumn, the whole village had to join in the work and keep harvesting it, transporting it, and threshing it until it was done.

Baba led the buffalo all day and all night. It was an old animal, and as it hadn't eaten any grain all summer, just a bit of fresh grass, it took a lot of effort to pull the roller. Baba looked at the buffalo's slow gait and the loose skin on its bony buttocks. It was painful to see. But he had no choice; he had to shout at it and occasionally raise the whip and bring it down on the buffalo's body to make it go a little faster. But at the back of his mind, he was worried that the buffalo wouldn't survive the winter.

Baba himself was exhausted. He nodded off as he walked behind the roller. When he shouted, it was partly to keep the buffalo moving and partly to keep himself awake. In the middle of the night, his instructions rang out crisp and clear through the cool, fresh air.

After a few rounds with the roller, it was time to turn the rice. He banged on a gong to call the villagers to the threshing ground. As soon as they heard it, they picked up their forks and hurried over. At night, when everyone was tired, it was difficult to rouse them from their sleep, and Baba had to beat the gong for a long time until they came, yawning, to help.

When the first batch of rice had been separated, it was quickly shared out according to the number of people in each family. And that evening, everyone ate new rice.

New rice has a pale-green skin, like a luminous coating of oil, and when it is cooking, it gives off the most wonderful aroma. In the light of the moon, each villager held a big bowl of either fluffy rice or rice soup. As they thought about the hard times they had just been through, they could barely bring themselves to eat. It was such a pleasure to smell this intoxicating scent. Some of the old people dripped tears into their bowls. Everyone came outside holding a bowl of rice and walked around the streets, sharing their delight in the fragrant new rice.

After a few days of eating new rice, the pale, thin villagers had color in their cheeks and strength in their bodies.

One evening, Nainai announced that she was going to her sister's in Donghai, near the sea. She'd been thinking about it for a long time now. She was getting old, she said, and she had to go while she still could. She had only one sister.

Baba and Mama were worried, but they understood she had to go. They didn't know that Nainai had other reasons for going to Donghai. During the hard days, the family had borrowed a lot of grain, and when they paid it all back, the family would be short again. Nainai thought that if she went to stay with her sister for a while, there would be one less mouth to feed. Also, her sister lived in a well-off cotton-growing area, and at harvest time they hired lots of cotton pickers. The wages were paid in cash or cotton. Nainai had been there and picked cotton many times. She wanted to bring some back and make padded jackets and trousers for Bronze and Sunflower, in time for winter. Despite being poor and short of food, the two youngsters had shot up. Their clothes weren't worn through yet, but the children had outgrown them. Last winter it had pained her to see their bare arms and legs poking out of their sleeves and trousers.

But all Nainai said was that she wanted to visit her sister. She wanted to leave that day; there was a boat departing soon that was taking people to pack carrots in Donghai. Bronze and Sunflower went to the river to see her off. Sunflower started to cry.

"Why are you crying, child? I'm not going forever. Be a good girl at home, and I'll be back before you know it." Her silver hair rippled in the breeze.

The boat sailed off with Nainai on board.

Family life felt empty without Nainai. Within a day or two, Sunflower was asking, "Mama, when is Nainai coming back?"

"Are you missing her already? She's only been gone a couple of days."

But Mama missed her too. She worked and worked, but her mind kept wandering, thinking about Nainai.

Two weeks passed, and there was neither sight nor sound of her.

Mama began to blame Baba. "You shouldn't have let her go."

"She was determined to," said Baba. "Could you have stopped her?"

"Someone should have stopped her. She's too old to be making long journeys."

Baba was worried too. "Let's wait a few more days,

and if she doesn't come back, then I'll go and fetch her."

Two weeks later, Baba asked someone to take a letter to Donghai, asking Nainai to come home soon. The message came back that Nainai was just fine and that she'd be staying another month.

But within two weeks, the boat from Donghai had brought Nainai back. It arrived in the night, and on board were Nainai and her nephew, Baba's cousin. He carried Nainai on his back to the house and knocked on the door.

Everyone got out of bed. Baba opened the door.

"What happened?" he asked.

"Let's talk inside, shall we?" said his cousin.

They hurried inside. Nainai looked small and thin, but she was smiling and doing her best to look relaxed. Mama quickly made up her bed, and Baba lifted her off her nephew's back. His heart almost missed a beat when he held her—Nainai was as light as a piece of paper.

The family members were all hurrying around, trying to do things for her.

"It's late," said Nainai. "Go to bed, all of you. I'm fine."

Baba's cousin began to speak. "She fell ill two weeks ago. I wanted to tell you, but she wouldn't let me. She didn't want you to worry. We thought we'd wait till she was a bit better, then get in touch with you. We never thought she'd get worse. When my mother realized she was not getting better, she said I should bring her home as quickly as possible." He glanced back at Nainai. "She collapsed with exhaustion." His voice was shaky.

Baba's cousin told them all about Nainai's visit to Donghai. "When she arrived at our place, she rested for two days, then went to the cotton fields to pick cotton. No matter how hard we tried to dissuade her, she wouldn't listen. As soon as morning came, she was out in the fields. Almost all the cotton pickers are girls or young married women. She was by far the oldest person there. The cotton fields are so vast, you can't see where they end. It takes about a day to walk from one side to the other and back. We were all worried she'd taken on too much, and wanted her to stay home, but she always said she was fine. My mother told her that if she was going to keep picking cotton, she'd send her home. Nainai said she'd go home as soon as she'd earned enough cotton. Then one lunchtime she fainted in the middle of the cotton fields. Fortunately, someone saw it happen and brought her back to our home. After that, she didn't get out of bed. I tell you, I've never seen an old person like her! Even lying down, she was still fretting about going to pick cotton, saying she had to make padded jackets and trousers for Bronze and Sunflower. My mother told her not to worry, and said she could take as much as she needed from our house. But Nainai said we only had old cotton and she wanted to earn two bags of new cotton. She had asked to be paid in cotton rather than cash. She had already picked a lot, almost enough to make the new clothes. But she insisted she needed more. She kept saying it was cold in winter and she wanted to make thick padded clothes for the children. Everyone where we live got to know her. They all said they'd never met such a good-hearted old lady."

Bronze and Sunflower kept watch by Nainai's bedside. Her face seemed to have shrunk, and her hair was as white as snow. When her trembling hands reached out to touch them, they felt cold on their skin.

Nainai had brought two large sacks of cotton with her. When they opened them in the sunlight the next day, everyone was stunned at how white the cotton was. They had never seen such good cotton.

Mama took a handful and squeezed it into a tiny ball inside her fist. When she opened up her fingers again, the cotton fluffed out in her hand as though it had been inflated. She glanced at Nainai, who was lying quietly in her bed, then turned away, tears rolling down her face.

Nainai couldn't get out of bed anymore. She lay there peacefully, listening to the wind outside, to the birds singing, and to the chickens and ducks clucking and quacking.

Then one night the wind howled madly. Winter had arrived.

The family had been saving up to take Nainai into town to see a doctor.

"But I'm not ill," said Nainai. "I'm just old, and my time's coming to an end, just like a buffalo."

Nainai meant the family's buffalo. When the first snow of winter fluttered to the ground, the buffalo had collapsed, just like Nainai. There was no particular reason why. It had dropped to the ground with a great crash that sounded like a wall falling down. Baba, Mama, Bronze, and Sunflower ran out to the pen to see what had happened. The buffalo lay on the ground, looking helplessly at them. There was no groaning, not even a little moan. It struggled to raise its heavy head and looked at the family with its big, round, glassy eyes. Baba asked Mama to grind some beans quickly and give it some soy milk to drink. But when they put the bowl down beside the buffalo, it didn't move. It was as though it knew there was no point. When Nainai heard about the buffalo, she sighed. It was old, she said, but it had collapsed before its time.

"And don't worry about me," she added. "I'm fine. We'll get through winter, and then it'll be spring, and I'll be better again. Go and look after the buffalo. It's been with us so long, and it hasn't had an easy life."

The family had lots of vivid memories of the buffalo. All these years, it had never been lazy or bad tempered. In fact, it was more placid and better natured than most humans. It got on with its work, quietly followed its masters. Sometimes, when it was happy, it would look up at the sky and let out a long cry. Most of the year it lived on grass, fresh grass in spring, summer, and autumn, and hay in winter. They gave it beans and wheat as well, but only when it had to do a lot of heavy farmwork; and if it was ill, soy milk and eggs. The buffalo was happy. It flicked its tail as it grazed. It liked to have Bronze and Sunflower riding on its back, swaying from side to side as it walked. It liked to feel their round little bottoms on its back. It was always pleased to see them. If it hadn't seen one of them for a few days, the next time they met, it would stick out its warm tongue and lick the back of their hand. And they let it lick them and didn't mind the wet stickiness of its saliva.

The family often forgot it was an animal. If they had something on their mind, they would often confide in it. They were always talking to it, never giving a thought to the fact that it couldn't understand what they were saying. And when they talked, it kept chewing but pricked up its big ears.

Like Nainai, the buffalo tried to struggle on. But in the end it couldn't. It gave up and lay on the ground, unable to move. It listened to the wind, to the birds singing, to the chickens and ducks clucking and quacking.

Snowflakes were fluttering outside the buffalo pen. Bronze and Sunflower brought in armloads of rice straw and tucked it around the buffalo until only its head was showing.

Then Baba said to the buffalo, "We should have treated you better. All these years, all we've done is make you work. Plowing the fields in spring, fetching water in summer, pulling the roller in autumn, and barely letting you rest in winter. I've even used the whip on you."

The buffalo's eyes showed nothing but kindness. It was grateful to them for not turning their backs when it was covered in sores, for hanging a woven reed screen at the gate of its pen in summer to keep out the mosquitoes, for taking it out to feel the warm sunshine when it was winter . . . Throughout the year, through all four seasons, through the wind, sun, rain, and snow, it had enjoyed so many things that a buffalo seldom gets to enjoy. It had had a good life. What more could it have asked for?

But it was time to go. The buffalo looked at the family, and its only regret was that Nainai wasn't there. It thought, when spring comes next year, and Damaidi is covered in wildflowers, she'll be out of bed again. Nainai called it "the beast" but always with affection, just as she sometimes called her grandson and granddaughter "little beasts."

That night, before they went to sleep, Baba lit a paper lantern and went out in the wind and snow to check on the buffalo. Bronze and Sunflower followed him.

"I don't think the beast will make it through the night," said Baba when they were back in the house.

The next time they saw the buffalo, it lay dead on top of a large pile of golden rice straw.

The family took Nainai to the hospital in Youmadi for tests, but the doctor could find nothing wrong. He suggested they go to the county hospital for more tests. The tests at the county hospital revealed that Nainai was seriously ill, but they couldn't tell for sure what the illness was. The hospital urged the family to pay right away so she could be admitted for observation.

Baba went to the cashier's window to ask how much it would cost to admit Nainai to the hospital. The woman clicked away on her abacus and said a number.

"Oh, oh," Baba repeated, again and again. Then he went quiet. It was such a large amount, far beyond what the family could ever afford. Baba felt the weight of a mountain on his head and slipped down on his haunches. Eventually, he stood up and walked from the cashier's window all the way down the corridor to the consulting room. Nainai was lying on a bench in the corridor, and Mama was looking after her.

Baba and Mama had no choice but to take Nainai back to Damaidi.

"I don't need to see a doctor," said Nainai as she

lay in bed back at home. "I never thought the beast would go before me." She sighed.

Baba and Mama worried all day and all night. Where could they get the money? They tried to appear calm, but Nainai knew exactly what the family could and couldn't afford. She looked at Baba and Mama, who seemed to be growing older by the day, and tried to console them.

"I know my body better than anyone. I'll be better when the weather warms up again. Don't worry about me. Get on with the things you have to do.

"The money in the wooden box is for Sunflower's school fees next semester. You mustn't touch it," she kept telling them.

As Baba and Mama looked everywhere for money, Nainai lay in her bed with Bronze or Sunflower or both of them by her side. She felt the illness had brought her closer to her grandson and granddaughter. She loved having them by her side and worried about them if they weren't there. When Sunflower went to school, Nainai wanted to know how soon the school day would finish. And when the school day ended, she would listen for Sunflower's footsteps outside. If school ran late and Sunflower couldn't hurry home at the usual time, Nainai would worry and tell Bronze to go to the end of the road and see what was happening.

One day, very early in the morning when the family had just gotten up, Gayu came to the house. He had a duck in each hand: one male, one female. The family was puzzled. As soon as Gayu put the ducks on the ground, they flapped their wings and tried to escape. But their legs were tied, and after whipping up a cloud of dust and realizing they couldn't go anywhere, they lay down quietly.

Gayu was evidently embarrassed and kept tripping over his words. "My f-father told me . . . to b-bring them, these t-two d-ducks, f-for N-Nainai, s-so she c-can have s-soup. He says sh-she'll f-feel b-better after s-some d-duck s-soup. . . ."

The family was overcome with gratitude.

"I—I'll go now. . . ."

"Child!" Nainai called out.

Gayu stopped.

"Leave one. Take the other home with you," she said.

"No!" said Gayu. "My f-father s-said to b-bring t-two." And off he ran.

The family watched him hurrying into the distance, and for a long time no one spoke. Then Bronze picked up the female—she could still lay eggs—and carried her in his arms to the river and let her go.

Mama turned to Sunflower. "You need to stop dawdling and go to school. Don't you have a test today?"

Sunflower said something in reply, but Mama had already gone to feed the pig. For the past few days, Sunflower had been trying to find the courage to tell the family that she didn't want to go to school anymore. There were lots of children in Damaidi who didn't go to school because their families couldn't afford it. Sunflower had been at school for four years now, and they were one of the poorest families in the village. She was the only one who did nothing to earn her keep, and what was more, she was the only one who needed any money spent on her. She was a burden. When she saw Baba and Mama worrying about money, she felt dreadful. She had done well at school, partly because she was smart and partly because she knew she had to. But how could she keep going when Nainai was ill and they needed money so she could go to the hospital? She was sure leaving school was the right thing, but she knew they'd be angry when she told them.

She had devised a plan, a plan that made her feel excited just thinking about it. The idea had come to her on her way home from school, and it was such a shock that she'd looked all around her to check that no one had seen anything. It was like a restless bird in a cage and kept flying about in her mind, crashing into her thoughts, chirping and squawking. She held her hand to her mouth as though it might leap out at any moment. She couldn't let anyone see it, especially not the family. Before she stepped inside the house, she had to calm the little bird and keep it quiet. But it didn't want to stay locked up in a cage; it wanted to fly out, to soar in the sky. She put her fingers to her cheeks. Although it was bitterly cold in the winter wind, her face was burning. She walked around for a while, waiting for the little bird to settle and her cheeks to cool down.

For the next week, the little bird sang in its cage every moment of every day. Then the day came when she would put her plan into action. She would fail all her exams! The little bird was calm and quiet, just as birds are calm when they find a forest at dusk and know they won't be disturbed.

She looked out over the fields. The schoolchildren lived in different places, and as they came to school from different directions, walking along the bare ridges between the bare fields, their brightly colored clothes breathed life into the bleak winter landscape. She wouldn't be one of them for much longer.

She felt a little sad.

She loved learning, and she loved going to school. All the children together: young, old, tall, short, clean, dirty, naughty, good, clever, slow, all gathering in one place, making all that noise. When the bell rang, they'd dart off to their classrooms like startled fish, leaving behind a quiet pool of water calmly reflecting the clouds in the sky. And, a few hours later, they'd burst out of the classrooms, whipping up dust in front of the school.

Sunflower ran around in the dust of the school-yard. All the girls liked her. They played keepy-uppy with the shuttlecock, and hopscotch, and all kinds of games. The girls had plenty of arguments, but they rarely argued with Sunflower. She wasn't any good at arguing anyway. Whatever they were doing, they wanted her to join in.

"Sunflower, come and play with us!".

"Sunflower, come and play with us!"

The girls always had something to talk about. They talked on the way to school, in the classroom, any little corner would do, even in the bathroom—especially in the bathroom. And the boys would eavesdrop, except they couldn't hear clearly. As soon as the girls thought someone was listening, they'd stop and listen too, but only for a while, and then they'd start talking again.

In the summer the children took their afternoon nap at the school. They could lie on the desks or the stools. Sunflower thought it was great fun to see so many people in the same place supposedly sleeping, all being quiet. But nobody wanted to sleep, so they talked with their hands and eyes, and whispered to each other. At last when the bell rang, they breathed a sigh of relief and leaped to their feet. No one would have slept at all.

On cold winter days, they played squeeze. They'd line up by the wall and push in from the sides, squashing the children in the middle. They would struggle to stay in line, but eventually they'd be squeezed out. Then they'd run to the end of the line and join in the squeezing. All the squashing and squeezing soon warmed them up.

Sunflower thought about the familiar smell of lots of children packed into a little classroom and the warm, slightly sour smell of children's sweat.

She loved the characters and numbers. They were magical. She loved it when everyone read aloud together, and especially when her teacher stood up and read. Her voice wasn't loud, but it sounded pure and clean, as though it had been washed in fresh water. She brought out the rhythm; she knew where to pause and how to vary her voice, to rise and fall. She transported them to a far distant place, like the call of insects in the moonlight, lulling them into a sleepy state. They would cradle their chins in their hands, and when she finished, they wouldn't remember what she had read.

Sometimes they'd be so entranced, they wouldn't even realize she'd finished. They'd only wake up when the teacher said, "Now let's all read it aloud together."

Sunflower would soon be leaving all this behind.

The Chinese test was in the morning, and the math test was in the afternoon. The questions were very straightforward, and she made a complete mess of them. Afterward she seemed very relaxed. In the evening she sat with Nainai and even sang a few of the songs that Nainai had taught her.

"Did she find a happy rice ball, or something?" Baba asked Mama.

Sunflower kept singing, one song after another. She sang even when she went outside. It had been snowing before supper, and the trees, buildings, and fields were covered in a thick layer of white. The moon was thin but large, and cast its light over the land. As Sunflower looked around her, it felt like daytime. It was light enough that when she looked up, she could see crows perching in the trees. In the distance, she saw the school, its tall flagpole now a thin gray line in the sky. From now on, she'd only be able to look at it from a distance. At last she could stop adding to the burdens of the family. She could work with Bronze and help to get things done. She wanted to earn money so that Nainai could go to the hospital. She felt she had grown up.

Two days later, school let out for the winter vacation. The children went home with their test results in one hand and their little stools in the other. Almost all of them knew about Sunflower's results. They were shocked. They couldn't understand it. All the usual noise and laughter of the walk home was missing. Sunflower walked home with some of her best friends. When they parted, the girls stood there for a while.

"Come and play sometime." Sunflower waved to them, then headed home. All the way, she was holding back her tears. The girls stood there, watching her go.

Later that day, Sunflower's teachers arrived at the house and told Baba and Mama about her results.

"Ah, no wonder she *ummed* and *ahhed* when I asked to see them," said Baba. He was angry and ready to beat her, although he'd never laid a finger on Sunflower before. Mama was so shocked that she had to sit down, one buttock on the tiny stool.

Meanwhile, Sunflower had gone with Bronze to the paddy fields to break the ice and catch fish. To breathe fresh air, the fish blew on the ice to make tiny holes. If you looked across the ice and could see white bubbles just below the surface, you could smash the ice with a hammer and stun the fish below. Then, all you had to do was break a bit more ice, put your hand into the water, and pull them out. There were already quite a few fish in Sunflower's basket. Her test results were in her pocket. She'd been wanting to show them to Bronze, but she wasn't brave enough. She waited until he'd caught another really big fish, then pulled out the piece of paper and gave it to him.

When Bronze saw the results, the hammer dropped from his hand, narrowly missing his foot.

The piece of paper flapped in the wind. Then—perhaps Bronze's hand was numb with cold, or his mind was elsewhere—the wind blew it across the ice. The folded paper looked like a white butterfly flying over blue ice.

Bronze ran after it. He slipped and rolled but finally managed to get it. Then he staggered back. He shook the piece of paper in front of her face, so hard that you could hear it flapping.

Sunflower bowed her head. She didn't dare look him in the eye.

"You did this on purpose!" he accused her, gesturing with his hands.

She shook her head.

"You did it on purpose! On purpose!" He punched the air with his fists.

Sunflower had never seen him so angry. She was scared. What if he hit her? She raised her hands to her head to protect herself. Bronze kicked the basket of fish over. The fish were still alive and started leaping about in the dry grass on the field ridge and spilling over onto the sunlit ice. He grabbed the hammer, spun around and around like a whirlwind, then let go. The hammer hurled through the air and hit the frozen surface with a thundering crack, shooting a white streak of lightning through the ice. With the results paper gripped tightly in one hand and Sunflower's arm in the other, Bronze marched her home.

When they were almost there, he let go of her.

"You can't tell them," he gestured. "If they find out, they'll kill you." He glanced back over his shoulder, then dragged her off in the opposite direction. They stopped in some woodland.

"You have to go to school!" said Bronze.

"I don't want to."

"You do."

"I don't."

"You're only saying that because Nainai's ill."

Sunflower lowered her head and started to cry. Bronze moved closer and stood beside her, looking beyond the woodland at the fields covered in snow. He was close to tears too. They hung around until darkness fell and they had to go home.

Baba and Mama were waiting for them.

"Where are your test results?" asked Baba.

Sunflower looked at Bronze, then down at her feet.

Baba raised his voice. "I'm asking you to give me your test results."

"Your father's talking to you. What's wrong with your ears?" Clearly Mama was not going to take her side.

Sunflower looked at Bronze again.

Bronze took the piece of paper out of his pocket and handed it to Baba with trepidation, as though they were his results, not Sunflower's.

Without looking at the results, Baba ripped the paper into pieces and threw them at her. Some of them fluttered to the ground, and quite a few landed in her hair.

"On your knees!" Baba roared.

"On your knees!" Mama repeated.

Sunflower knelt down.

Bronze wanted to go and help her up, but Baba shot him a fierce look warning him to stand aside.

Nainai's elderly voice carried in from the other room. "Let her speak! Let's hear what she has to say for herself."

It was the first time Nainai had been angry with her. Sunflower had never imagined that the whole family would react so strongly to whether or not she went to school. She was terrified.

Baba, Mama, and Nainai had never forgotten what happened by the old tree all those years ago. From the moment they'd brought her home, they had resolved not only to take care of her, but to bring her up with a future to look forward to. None of them had ever said this out loud, but they all knew that each felt the same way. Over the past few years, they had put one thing above all else: that Sunflower should go to school. They would smash their wok and sell the metal for scrap; they would beg for rice with a gourd ladle if that was the only way Sunflower could go to school. They believed Sunflower's blood father was still there in Damaidi, that his soul was wandering in the sunflower fields and among the crops. No one could explain it, but they felt linked to Sunflower and her father by fate, in the same way that her father had felt linked to Bronze that day. There are some things in this world that can never be explained.

Sunflower was terrified. She was kneeling on the ground, shaking. Apparently, the teachers had made it clear that she could either leave school or stay back a year. Although they acknowledged that these results were not a true reflection of her ability, there were a number of students who had not made the grade, and the school would be requiring the same decision from their families. If they allowed Sunflower to retake the test as her parents requested, then all the other parents would ask for retakes as well. Baba and Mama couldn't understand why Sunflower had done so badly. The teachers couldn't either. All they could think was that Sunflower had not worked hard enough, or that her mind had wandered, or that she'd made careless mistakes.

Nainai, Baba, and Mama were stunned when Bronze told them the real reason. Sunflower hung her head low and sobbed quietly. Mama went over and pulled her to her feet.

"You silly girl. How could you be so silly?" And as she hugged her tightly, two lines of hot tears fell onto Sunflower's hair.

"I want Nainai to see the doctor," Sunflower said, sobbing in Mama's arms.

"Sunflower, Sunflower . . ." Nainai called from her bed.

As light snowflakes fluttered in the air outside, Bronze and Sunflower helped Nainai get out of bed. She not only got out of bed, she also walked out of the house, and, with Bronze and Sunflower helping her along, she hobbled all the way down the road to the school. The villagers stood to one side to let her pass. The fine snow swirled in the sky like tiny white dust mites. Nainai hadn't seen the sun for a long time, and her face was very pale. Her padded jacket and padded trousers seemed enormous, flapping about on her thin little frame.

Eventually the three of them arrived at the schoolhouse. The school head and the teachers hurried outside to meet them. Nainai gripped the head teacher's hand. "Please let my granddaughter take the test again." She explained what had happened.

When they heard that Sunflower had failed deliberately, and that she had done it to help Nainai, they were shocked.

"Please let her take the test again," Nainai implored the head teacher. She tried to kneel in the snow.

"Nainai, Nainai," the head teacher repeated again and again, hurrying to hold her steady. "Yes, yes. Of course she may retake the test. Of course she may."

That was the last time Nainai appeared in the village.

Baba and Mama had been trying to scrape together the money to take Nainai to the hospital. When she could barely walk anymore, they carried her on their backs. She was getting weaker and weaker. She wasn't in any pain, but she was getting thinner by the day. She was barely eating now. In time, it became an effort even to raise her eyelids, and she was sleeping most of the time. Her breathing was softer than that of a baby. She lay in her bed, barely moving. Bronze and Sunflower couldn't stand seeing her like this. Baba and Mama rushed around all day, visiting relatives and neighbors, going into the village and the town, to wherever they thought they might be able to borrow money or apply for support to get medical treatment.

Nainai said what she always said. "I'm not ill. I'm just old. There's no point rushing around like this."

Every day, come rain or shine, Bronze went into town to sell reed shoes. Sunflower felt useless; she was the only one who wasn't doing anything to help. All day long, she thought about how she could earn some money to help Nainai go to the hospital. She wasn't a little girl anymore; she should be sharing some of the load, some of the worry. But where could she get money?

She suddenly remembered a conversation she had overheard while doing her homework at Cuihuan's. It had gone something like this:

For many years, people from the area had been hiring boats in Youmadi and going to Jiangnan to pick white ginkgo nuts, which they could then sell. Jiangnan was filled with mile after mile of ginkgo trees, and although the people of Jiangnan picked the nuts, they didn't have enough hands to pick all of them, so there were always plenty left on the trees. If you collected just the ones that were on the ground, you could still gather a lot. Hardly anyone in Damaidi grew ginkgo nuts, but lots of people liked to eat them or take them for their health. The children liked to dye them different colors and stuff them in their pockets or keep them in a box, partly because they were pretty and partly to play games with.

So, toward the end of every year, people often traveled to Jiangnan to pick ginkgo nuts. The people of Jiangnan weren't too bothered about getting a good price because the nuts would be left to rot on the trees otherwise. Sometimes they'd strike a deal: for every 100 *jin* that was picked, the owner would receive a tenth, maybe as much as a fifth. That way, both sides stood to gain. It was business, but it was friendly. Adults and teenagers went to pick the ginkgo nuts, teenagers always with an adult.

For a few days, Sunflower thought about nothing else. Like her brother, once she had an idea in her head, she couldn't get rid of it, no matter what. She did not care about anything else until she'd seen it through. Even if the idea was a mistake, she still had to do it.

One morning, soon after Bronze set out with his reed shoes on his back, Sunflower also set out for Youmadi. She went straight to the river, where all the boats were moored, and went from boat to boat asking if anyone was going to pick ginkgo nuts in Jiangnan. Eventually someone pointed to a big boat. "You see that one over there? It's filling up fast. I think I heard people saying they were going to Jiangnan to pick ginkgo nuts."

Sunflower ran to the boat. She could see that there were already lots of people on board, mostly women, but also some children, including two or three girls who were about her age, chatting and giggling. She could hear that they were going to Jiangnan to pick ginkgo nuts, that they were from the villages around Youmadi, and that someone was negotiating the price of hiring the boat with the owner. It didn't seem to be going very smoothly. The owner was complaining that the money wasn't enough, and the other man didn't want to pay any more. The boat owner wouldn't agree but said, "We can wait a bit longer, and if a few more people come, then you can pay a bit extra, can't you?"

Slowly, things began to settle down on board. Everyone was looking toward the riverbank, hoping that more people would come along. It was a big boat and could easily take another ten to twenty people.

Sunflower's plan had been to come and look at boats today and travel another day. She hadn't made any preparations; she had no money and no bag to collect ginkgo nuts. But now that she was here, she wanted to get on board and go to Jiangnan. Today!

Listening to the people on the boat, she heard that the ginkgo picking started in late autumn and early winter, and that they'd probably be the last group going there this season. She thought about Nainai, tucked in bed and barely moving. Her heart was racing. This boat would be leaving today, and it could set off at any moment.

Sunflower hadn't said anything about her idea at home; she knew they'd never let her go. She had planned to leave a note for Bronze before she set out, telling him she was going away without saying where. But she hadn't written it yet. She ran to the riverbank and asked a woman in a shop for a piece of rough paper, the kind they used to wrap rock salt and rock sugar, and borrowed a pen. Then she leaned against the counter and wrote a note to Bronze:

Bronze,

I'm going away. There's something very, very important that I have to do. I'll be back in a few days. Tell Nainai, Baba, and Mama not to worry about me. I can look after myself. In a few more days, Nainai can go to the hospital.

We'll have enough money. Don't stay out too late
today — don't wait till you've sold all the shoes
before you go home.

Your sister,
Sunflower

She was so excited and so pleased with herself. She was going to earn a fortune! She took the note and rushed to the riverside. Another six or seven people were boarding the boat. She knew it would be leaving soon. How could she get the letter to Bronze? She was getting anxious.

Then a boy appeared, selling paper windmills. She ran up to him. "Please could you give this letter to the boy who sells reed shoes?" she asked. "He's my brother. He's called Bronze."

He looked at her, puzzled.

"Please could you give it to him?"

He nodded and took the letter.

When she turned around, she saw the men pulling the gangplank onto the boat.

"Wait!" she yelled, and ran as fast as she could. The

boat was just beginning to pull away from the bank. Sunflower stretched her hands out in front of her. The people on board thought she must be the child of one of the passengers, accidentally left behind. Two of the men reached over the front of the boat until their hands met Sunflower's. They gave her a big pull and lifted her on board.

The boat had to be turned to face the right direction, then the sail went up, and off they went, proudly, majestically, down the river.

The boy selling paper windmills walked on along the riverbank. He stopped and sold one to a little girl, and when he set off again, a boy selling reed shoes came into view. Assuming that he must be the one that Sunflower had mentioned, he went up to him, handed him the note, and said, "Your sister asked me to give this to you."

The boy took the note and looked puzzled.

Two girls asked the windmill seller how much the windmills cost, and his mind turned back to business. The girls walked away—perhaps they thought the windmills were too expensive or were only looking. The boy went after them, wanting a sale, and all thought of Sunflower's letter vanished into thin air.

It wasn't until much later that the boy selling reed shoes opened the piece of paper and started to read it. He didn't quite know what to make of it. He read it a few times, then laughed and put it back in his pocket. Then he moved off to sell his shoes somewhere else.

Bronze returned home very late that day. As soon as he walked in the door, Nainai called from the other room, "Have you seen Sunflower?"

Bronze ran in and gestured with his hands that he hadn't seen her.

"Quickly, go and find her. Your baba and mama are out looking for her. It's so late. The child should have been home ages ago."

Bronze ran outside. Baba and Mama had looked everywhere and were on their way home.

"Have you seen Sunflower?" Mama called from the

distance. Bronze shook his head. "Sunflower, come home! It's suppertime," she called out.

She shouted again and again, but there was no answer.

The sky was so dark.

Baba, Mama, and Bronze looked everywhere. Their voices rang out in the dark. "Have you seen our Sunflower?"

The answer was always the same.

Bronze went home, lit a paper lantern, and went out to the sunflower fields. In the winter, there was nothing but dead sunflower stalks, leaning awkwardly this way and that. He walked around the fields with his paper lantern and then went back to the village.

Baba and Mama were still out in the street, asking if people had seen Sunflower. And the answer was still the same.

None of them felt like eating that night, and they kept searching.

Nainai was lying in bed. She lacked the strength to do anything. She lay there worrying, all by herself.

Lots of people came to help look for Sunflower.

They split up, then regrouped. There were all kinds of suggestions.

"Could she have gone to her other grandmother's?"

But someone had already checked there.

"Could she have gone to Miss Jin's?" Miss Jin was a teacher who lived outside the village and had a soft spot for Sunflower.

"Good idea. Could someone go and see?"

A big man called Daguo volunteered to go.

"Thank you, Daguo," said Baba.

"No need for thanks," said Daguo as he set off, clomping along the road.

"Let's think. Where else could she have gone?"

They thought of a few more places, and people went to look. You could hear the pounding of their footsteps on the roads.

Those who weren't searching went back to the house and waited for news. Bronze stayed out, searching the fields, the riverside, and the schoolyard with his paper lantern. He'd been standing selling shoes all day in Youmadi and hadn't eaten, and he could feel his legs trembling. But he kept walking, tears glistening in his eyes.

It was almost dawn by the time the search groups reported back to the house. Sunflower was nowhere to be found. They were all worn out and needed to go home to sleep. But the family couldn't sleep; their minds were racing and every noise startled them.

A new day dawned. Slowly, they began to pick up a lead. First, Cuihuan told them something important. She said Sunflower had told her two days earlier that she wanted to go and earn some money, a lot of money, so that Nainai could go to the hospital. As Nainai, Baba, and Mama heard this, tears rolled down their faces.

"That silly girl. How could she be so silly?" wailed Mama. How did Sunflower even know of anywhere she could earn money?

Then there was another lead. The day she disappeared, someone had seen her in Youmadi. Mama stayed home to look after Nainai while Baba and Bronze went to look for her there. They asked lots of people, and some said they'd seen her but didn't know where she had gone. When night fell, Bronze and Baba went home.

In the night, Bronze suddenly woke up. The wind

was blowing outside and the branches were creaking and groaning. If Sunflower was on her way home right now, she'd be terrified out there all on her own. Quietly, he got out of bed and took the paper lantern. He went into the kitchen, found a match, lit the candle in the lantern, and set off again for Youmadi. If that was where she'd disappeared, that was probably where she'd return.

That wintry night, the paper lantern moved through the fields as if it were the soul of night itself. Bronze didn't walk fast. He was half walking, half waiting. He reached Youmadi in the early hours of the morning. As he walked with his lantern down the long street, his footsteps on the stone slabs were the only sound. He went to the bridge and looked out over the vast river. He saw the boats moored along the banks. If Sunflower had taken a boat, she would come back by boat. If the boat came back during the day, that was fine; she could walk home by herself. But if she came back at night, she'd be scared. How would she get back to Damaidi on her own? Bronze changed the candle in the paper lantern and kept watch on the bridge. After that, he went to Youmadi every night.

In the town, a man got up in the night to go to the toilet and spotted the paper lantern on the bridge. He saw it again the next night, and the next. He thought it was odd but didn't think too much about it. Then one night he went to the bridge and found Bronze holding his lantern.

"Who are you waiting for?" he asked. Bronze didn't answer. He couldn't answer. The man went a bit closer and recognized him as the mute who sold reed shoes.

Word spread, until almost everyone in Youmadi knew the story—that the mute boy Bronze had a sister called Sunflower who'd wanted to earn money so her grandmother could go to the hospital and had set out from Youmadi, but nobody knew where she'd gone, and that was why Bronze was waiting with his lantern on the bridge every night.

The boy who sold paper windmills wasn't from Youmadi, and the next time he came to town, he heard the story and was reminded of the little girl who had asked him to pass a letter to her brother who sold reed shoes.

"I know where she went," he said, and told them his story.

"What happened to the letter?" someone asked.

"I must've given it to the wrong person. To another boy who was selling reed shoes."

They were about to set off and look for the other boy when he came walking down the road.

"That's him!" said the windmill boy. "Do you still have the letter I gave you? It wasn't meant for you. I was supposed to give it to somebody else."

By chance the boy had kept the letter—perhaps he was intrigued by it, or thought it might be important—and was able to pull it out of his pocket. One of the adults read it and quickly told Bronze what it said.

Bronze took the letter. When he recognized Sunflower's handwriting, tears streamed down his face. Some adults followed up the new lead and traced it to the big boat that had gone to Jiangnan. Sunflower must have gone with them to pick ginkgo nuts. The family was so relieved to hear this news and began the anxious wait for her return. Baba wanted to go to Jiangnan and look for her, but they managed to dissuade him. Jiangnan was so big—how would he find her? Instead, they arranged that Baba and Bronze would keep watch in Youmadi: Baba during the day and Bronze at night. The paper lantern lit up the road, and the river, and the hearts of the people of Youmadi.

The big boat was on its way back to Youmadi. It had been a long trip, and Sunflower had missed her family so much. She thought about them all the time.

When the people on the boat had realized she was on her own without an adult to look after her, they had been shocked. They wanted the owner to pull into the shore and send her home. But she clung to the mast with tears streaming down her face and refused to budge. When they asked why she was going to pick ginkgo nuts, she told them she wanted to earn money so Nainai could go to the hospital. They were moved. They also laughed at her. "There's not much money in it. You'll barely make enough for one tablet of herbal medicine."

But she didn't believe them. She was determined to go and pick as many nuts as she could.

"Does your family know where you are?" they asked.

"My brother knows."

Seeing how upset she was, someone stepped in and said, "OK, let her come with us. At least her family knows where she is."

Sunflower calmed down and let go of the mast.

The people on the boat loved this little girl and were happy to look after her. She hadn't brought any food or bedding, so when they ate, they shared their food with her. And when they went to bed, the women let her sleep under their covers. They tucked her in tightly, worried that she might slip out and get cold. As the boat rocked and the water slip-slapped, Sunflower slept snugly. When the women woke in the night, they would check that her arms and legs weren't sticking out. When she rolled over onto her side, she would wrap her arm around one of their necks and snuggle up. And the women would whisper, "Isn't she sweet!"

Sunflower hadn't brought a bag for collecting ginkgo nuts either, so they gave her one. They shared everything with her. The only things she could share with them were the songs that Nainai had taught her. In the evenings, when the cabin was filled with people lying down to sleep and the wind and water rocked the boat like a cradle, the sound of Sunflower singing filled the cold and lonely night with warmth and joy. They were glad that they had let her stay on the boat.

When they reached Jiangnan, they hurried anxiously from one place to the next. It was late in the season, and there weren't many ginkgo nuts left, either on the trees or on the ground. They had to keep moving. Sunflower went with them. When she lagged behind, one of the women or another girl would stop and wait for her to catch up. One by one, she collected ginkgo nuts, each a tiny bit of hope. The adults tried to help her and pointed out places where there were lots.

"Sunflower, look over here!" they'd say. She was slow at first, but after a couple of days, her eyes were sharp and her hands were fast, and the adults were saying, "Hey, Sunflower, leave some for us!"

Sunflower wasn't trying to outdo them. She blushed and slowed down until the women laughed. "Don't be so silly! Hurry up and pick as many as you can! There's plenty for all of us."

On the way back to Youmadi, the big boat stopped

at every town, and they took their ginkgo nuts to sell at the market. The women all knew how to haggle with the buyers and helped Sunflower get a good price.

"Look at these beautiful ginkgo nuts!" they would say, pulling a big handful out of Sunflower's bag. They put more effort into selling Sunflower's ginkgos than their own and haggled over every *jin*. As soon as Sunflower had some money, one of them said, "Let me look after your money so you don't lose it, child." And Sunflower took the money out of her pocket and put it in the woman's hand.

"You really trust me with all your money?" The woman laughed.

Sunflower nodded.

The boat sailed on through night and day. One night, when she was half-asleep, Sunflower heard someone outside the cabin say, "We're just about to join the big river. We'll be back in Youmadi in a few hours."

Sunflower couldn't sleep anymore. Her eyes were open wide in the dark as she thought about Nainai, Baba, Mama, and Bronze. How long had she been away? She couldn't remember, but it felt such a long time. She was worried about Nainai. She hoped she might be a bit better.

For a moment, she wondered if Nainai might have died, and tears rolled from the corners of her eyes. Then she told herself to be strong. How could you think such a thing? Come on, you'll see her very soon. She wanted to show Nainai how much money she'd earned! How capable she was! She wished the boat could move faster.

But after a while she dozed off, and when the women woke her, the boat was pulling in at Youmadi. It was still dark. She was half-asleep and all thumbs, so they helped her to get dressed. They put her money safely in her pocket and fastened it tightly with a pin.

Then, clutching the small bag of ginkgo nuts she had kept for the family, she wove her way through the cabin. The cold wind blowing up from the river sent a shiver down her spine and made sure she was wide awake. She looked straight ahead of her and saw the paper lantern on the bridge. She thought she must be dreaming. She rubbed her eyes and looked again. It really was a paper lantern, giving off an orange glow.

"That's my family's lantern," she told the women, pointing toward the bridge.

One of the women came and felt her forehead. "You're talking nonsense, and you don't even have a temperature."

She pointed again. "It is! It's my family's paper lantern!"

"BRONZE!" Sunflower shouted, her clear, crisp voice ringing through the still night. The paper lantern seemed to move a little. "BRONZE!" she shouted, even louder this time.

A bird in a tree by the river flapped its wings and flew off. Then everyone on the boat saw the lantern on the bridge begin to sway furiously and fly toward the pier.

Bronze had heard Sunflower.

"That's my brother! My brother!" Sunflower told the women. Everyone on board knew about Bronze, that he was mute and that he was the most wonderful brother to Sunflower.

She waved to everyone on the boat with genuine emotion, and with help from an adult, leaped onto the pier with her bag of ginkgos. Bronze and Sunflower

ran toward each other. When they met in the middle
of the pier, they stopped and looked at each other.
Everyone on board was watching. Eventually, Bronze
took Sunflower's hand and off they walked. After a few
steps, Sunflower turned and looked back, then waved
again to all the people on the boat. Bronze waved
too. Then, hand in hand, they disappeared into the
darkness. As the lantern bobbed about in the night,
the women and girls on the boat dabbed at their eyes.

It was getting light by the time Bronze and Sunflower
reached Damaidi. As usual, Mama was up early,
making breakfast. She happened to glance up the
road in front of the house and noticed two children
in the distance.

They're up early, she thought, not imagining they
might be Bronze and Sunflower. She took one step
into the kitchen, then stepped right out again. She
looked back at the road. Suddenly, her arms were
flapping like a tree full of leaves in the wind. "The
children!" she shrieked with excitement.

"What's the matter?" asked Baba.

"Quick! Get up!"

Baba got up and went outside.

"Look! On the road!"

The sun was rising behind the children. Mama saw Bronze with a thin, dark little girl, filthy from head to toe but full of life. Mama ran toward them. As soon as Sunflower saw her, she let go of Bronze's hand and ran toward her.

"Mama!" Sunflower flung open her arms. Mama leaned forward and wrapped her arms around Sunflower. As she held her tight, her tears spilled down the back of Sunflower's jacket. Sunflower proudly patted her front pocket. "Mama, I've earned lots of money!"

"I know, I know," said Mama.

"How's Nainai?"

"Nainai's waiting for you. She's been waiting for you every day." Mama took her hand and led her inside. Sunflower ran straight to Nainai's room.

"Nainai!" she said. She was by her bedside in a couple of steps. "Nainai!" She knelt down.

Nainai was not even taking sips of water now. She had been holding on, waiting for Sunflower to come back. She opened her eyes ever so slightly and, summoning all her energy, smiled at Sunflower.

Sunflower undid her jacket, removed the pin, and took two large handfuls of coins out of her pocket.

"Nainai, look how much money I've earned!" She still didn't understand how little the coins were worth.

Nainai wanted to reach out her hand to stroke Sunflower's face, but she was too weak.

The next day, Nainai left them.

Before she went, she motioned to Mama to remove her bracelet. She'd already requested this when she was still able to talk. She wanted Sunflower to have it. "Give it to her when she gets married." Nainai had made Mama promise over and over again.

Nainai was buried at dusk. When the adults began to disperse from the graveside, Bronze and Sunflower stayed behind. No matter how hard the adults tried to persuade them, they would not come home. They sat on the dry grass in front of Nainai's grave in the dark and leaned against each other. Bronze held the paper lantern. The light shone on the fresh earth, and on the wind-dried tear tracks on their faces.

The Big Haystack

Sunflower was now in her fifth year at school. Some news had been hanging over Damaidi like a black cloud since the early autumn: the city people wanted Sunflower to go back to the city. Exactly where this news had come from, the villagers weren't too sure, but they believed it was true. As the news circulated, and the villagers added imagination to the facts, the whole thing seemed to become more and more concrete until it felt very real indeed. Only the family hadn't heard the news. When the villagers talked about it, they checked over their shoulders that they weren't within earshot. If they happened to be talking about it when one of the family came along, they'd quickly change the subject. "It's so cold today!" or "Isn't it warm!" They didn't want the family to hear the awful news.

The family sensed from the expressions on the villagers' faces that they were talking about something that concerned them, but none of them came close to guessing what it might be.

It was Sunflower who felt the most left out. She could sense from Cuihuan and the other girls, from the look in their eyes, that they were hiding something—and that it concerned her. They were always off chattering in a corner, glancing across at her, and as soon as they saw her coming, they'd say in a loud voice, "Sunflower, come and play hopscotch!" or "Sunflower, come and play drop-the-handkerchief!" They'd always been good to her, but now they were being nicer than ever.

One day she slipped and grazed her knee. Cuihuan and some other girls crowded around, offering to help, asking if it hurt. When school finished for the day, they took turns giving her a piggyback home. It was as though they were all trying to be kind before it was too late. The teachers were especially nice to her, and the villagers were all very friendly when they saw her.

Then, one day, Sunflower heard the news. She was playing hide-and-seek in the village with Cuihuan and the other girls, and she had burrowed into a haystack to hide in the straw. Cuihuan and two other girls came looking for her, but they couldn't find her. They met at the bottom of the haystack, walked around it without finding Sunflower, then stopped.

"Where can she be hiding?"

"Where can she be?"

"I wonder how much longer we'll be able to play with Sunflower."

"I heard the adults saying that someone from the city will be coming to get her soon."

"If Bronze won't let her go and she refuses, there's not much they can do about it."

"The adults say it's not that simple. They think the city people won't go to the family. They'll go straight to the head of the village, and they'll bring the authorities with them."

"Do you know when they're coming?"

"I heard my father saying they'll just turn up one day."

After a while, the girls walked off, chattering away. Sunflower had heard everything. She waited until Cuihuan and the other girls were far away, and pulled herself out of the haystack. She went straight home.

Mama noticed her anxious look and asked, "What's the matter with you?"

She smiled at Mama. "It's nothing."

She sat on the wooden threshold, stunned by what she had heard. At suppertime, she was miles away. The person sitting eating her food looked like Sunflower but didn't behave like Sunflower at all. The family kept looking at her. After supper, she'd usually hang around Bronze and make him take her to the threshing ground at the end of the village, where the children gathered in the evening to run around and let off steam. But that day, after supper, she took herself off to the other side of the yard and sat on a woven-grass prayer cushion under the tree, looking quietly up at the moon and stars in the sky.

It was an autumn evening, and the sky was clear. The stars were pale yellow, and the moon was a pale blue. The sky seemed so high and so vast, much lighter than in spring, summer, and winter. Sunflower rested her chin in her hands and stared up. She didn't know what to do.

The family let her be, but they were all puzzled.

Soon after that, Bronze heard the news. He rushed home so fast, he tripped along the way. As soon as he saw Baba and Mama he hurried to tell them what he had heard. Now they understood why the villagers had been looking at them so strangely.

"Is it true?" asked Bronze.

Baba and Mama could barely believe it themselves.

"Sunflower can't go!" gestured Bronze.

"She won't go," they said firmly, trying to comfort him.

"I won't let her go," gestured Bronze.

"We won't let her go," said Baba and Mama.

Baba went to see the head of the village and asked him point-blank if the rumor was true.

"Yes, it's true," said the head of the village.

Baba felt faint, as though he'd been hit on the head with a hammer.

The head of the village explained, "The people

in the city want to take her away, but they can't just come and do it. They have to talk to you and your family first."

"We don't want to talk," said Baba. "Tell them no one's taking her anywhere." He felt quite weak.

"That's exactly what I said," the head of the village agreed. "Don't worry about it for now."

"When the time comes, you'll have to back me up," said Baba.

"Of course," said the head of the village. "And remember, they can't just turn up and take her away. That would be unreasonable."

"Unreasonable!" said Baba.

"Unreasonable!" said the head of the village.

If it was so unreasonable, then what were they worrying about?

Baba went home. "We don't need to worry about them coming," he told Mama. "We're not going to let them take her."

"That's right!" said Mama. "I won't let anyone take her away!"

Their words were loud and clear, but the matter weighed heavy in their hearts and grew heavier with the passing of time. Baba and Mama would lie awake at night, unable to sleep. When they finally did drop off, they'd wake again with a start, and their minds would churn over and over. Mama would get out of bed, take the oil lamp over to Sunflower's bed, and look at her in the lamplight. Sometimes Sunflower would wake too, but would close her eyes when she saw Mama coming over. Mama would watch her for a long time, sometimes stroking her daughter's face gently. Her hands were rough and hard, but Sunflower loved them.

There was another pair of eyes looking around in the dark. Bronze could not sleep either. He was on tenterhooks, convinced that someone would turn up one day and snatch Sunflower off the road. He'd started following her to school, albeit keeping a good distance behind her. And he'd be at the school gate waiting to pick her up. Sunflower didn't let on to Baba, Mama, and Bronze that she knew about being taken to the city. And they didn't let on to her that they knew.

Then, one day, a little white boat stopped at the pier in Damaidi. Someone must have seen it and spread the word—that the city people had come to take Sunflower away. Quick as a flash, one of the villagers went to tell the family. As soon as Baba heard the news, he ran to the river to see for himself. When he saw the little white boat, he turned around and ran straight home.

He found Bronze. "Quickly, go to the school, get Sunflower, and hide with her somewhere. And don't come out until I've talked some sense into these people!"

Bronze ran all the way to school without stopping for breath. He charged into the classroom and pulled Sunflower outside. She didn't ask for an explanation, just followed him deep into the reeds.

"They've come to take you to the city," gestured Bronze.

Sunflower nodded.

"You knew?"

Sunflower nodded again.

They sat side by side at the edge of a pool deep in the reeds, listening anxiously to the sounds on the other side of the marsh.

At about midday, they heard Mama calling them

for lunch. Cuihuan and the other girls were calling Sunflower too. It was a signal that it was safe to come out. But Bronze and Sunflower didn't dare move. Bronze made the first attempt, but Sunflower held his hand and refused to go, scared that someone would grab her as soon as she appeared. Bronze had to reassure her. Only when he insisted that it was safe would she let him lead her by the hand out of the reeds. As soon as she saw Mama, she flew straight into her arms and burst into tears.

"There's nothing to worry about. Nothing to worry about," said Mama, patting her gently on the back.

It had been a false alarm. The white boat belonged to the county government, and the official in charge was making a local inspection. He'd been in the area, noticed the large village in the reeds, and stopped to take a look. Nothing more than that.

Gradually, the autumn wind quieted. It grew colder by the day. The leaves on the trees withered and fell to the ground. When the last line of swallows flew across the cold, clear sky, Damaidi was already a dull matte brown. When the wind blew, the dry branches and the dead leaves were swept together with a swishing and a rustling. The family slowly began to relax and unwind. The days flowed by, as the river flowed on and on toward the east, in sunlight and in moonlight. After about a month, autumn had run its course, and winter arrived.

On what seemed like a very ordinary day, five people from the city turned up unexpectedly in Damaidi, accompanied by an official from the authorities. When they arrived, they went straight to the village committee. The head of the village was there.

They told him why they had come.

"It's difficult," said the head of the village.

"It has to be done," said the official.

No one from the city really understood what had happened. This little girl had been left in Damaidi all these years, apparently forgotten about, until one day, someone suddenly started worrying about her. Somehow it had developed into a major project, to bring her back to the city. The mayor himself had said, "We must bring that child back!"

This particular mayor had held the position before. The first time, he'd been demoted and sent to a remote place to do physical labor. Now he'd returned to the city and to his former position. On an inspection of his city, he'd seen the bronze sunflowers in the main square, glistening and gleaming in the sunshine, sacred and full of life. They'd been standing there proudly when he was mayor all those years ago. They were so evocative and stirred such feeling in him that he began to wonder about the artist who made them. The people around him said that the artist had died; he'd been sent to a Cadre School and had drowned in the river at Damaidi. The mayor heard the news with tears in his eyes and grief in his heart. So many things had been turned upside down in just a few years.

Later, the mayor discovered by chance that the artist's daughter had been brought up in Damaidi. He raised a question about the matter at a meeting and asked for the relevant department to bring her back to the city as soon as possible.

Some people suggested it might be difficult.

"The situation was very unusual. It's not entirely clear how official the arrangement was."

"Whatever the situation was then, I want you to bring her back," said the mayor. He looked at Damaidi on the map. "That poor child. Just think how we have let her father down."

He personally made sure that a considerable sum of money was allocated as a trust fund for Sunflower, and oversaw the arrangements being made for her return to the city, her education, and her future.

Meanwhile, a cloud of uncertainty hung over Damaidi. Village life continued: the roosters still crowed, the dogs still barked, the children still played, but there was tension in the air.

The time had come. The city people were here, and they were talking to the head of the village.

"We can agree to whatever conditions they ask for. They've looked after this child for so many years, and it can't have been easy."

"Have you any idea what they've been through to raise her?" The village head paused. "I can say she should go, but I can't guarantee that it'll happen."

The official took him to one side. "There's no alternative. It has to be done. Everyone can understand that they won't want to let the child go. It's difficult enough to part with a dog, let alone a child. Go and talk to them. Tell them how city people think and what city people do. And stress that this is all for the child's benefit!"

"OK, I'll go and talk to them."

So the head of the village went to see the family. "Someone from the city wants to see you," he told them.

As soon as Baba and Mama heard this, they told Bronze to take Sunflower, who was playing outside, and go and hide.

"There's no need to hide," said the head of the village. "He's come to talk, not to snatch her away. Remember where we are. This is Damaidi! Do you think the people of Damaidi would stand back and let someone snatch away one of our children?" He turned to Bronze. "Go and play with Sunflower. There's nothing to worry about."

The head of the village sat down. He got straight to the point. "The situation's not going to change. I can't see that they'll let her stay."

Mama began to cry. She ran after Sunflower, who clung to her tightly. "Mama, I won't go!"

A crowd began to gather. The scene brought tears to their eyes.

"No one's taking her anywhere!" said Mama.

The head of the village sighed and went outside. As he walked down the road, he told the people he met, "They want to take Sunflower away! They're at the village committee office!"

Soon, the whole village knew. They ran to the committee office. A large crowd surrounded the office, several people deep, packed so tightly together that even water could not have seeped through.

The official pushed open the window. "What's going on?" he asked the head of the village.

"I don't know," said the head of the village. "What's going on out there?"

At first the crowd was quiet, but after a while they began to speak and then to shout. "You can't just take her away!"

"She's one of us!"

"Do they know what this family has done to raise her? Do they know that they gave her their only mosquito net in summer and burned bulrushes so the smoke would keep the mosquitoes away?"

"Do they know that her *nainai* used to fan the air with a reed fan every night in summer until she was cool enough to sleep?"

"Since the day she stepped through their door, we've all thought of her as one of their family."

"They've had a hard time, but no matter how hard it's been, they've never made it hard for her."

"She's such a thoughtful girl. We've never known such a thoughtful girl."

"That family is so close. You can't split them up."

A few people made their way into the office. The head of the village ordered them out, but they just stood there, refusing to move, looking coldly at the city people. When the city people saw how many there were standing outside, they were shaken, unnerved.

"We haven't come to snatch the child away," they told the head of the village.

"I know," he said.

Then, one of the young men who had pushed his way inside shouted, "You can't just take children away!"

And the crowd outside shouted, "You can't just take children away!"

The head of the village went to the door. "Why are you shouting?" he asked. "These people have come to discuss the situation. Can't you see that? They didn't go directly to the family but came to ask me to talk to them first."

The same young man went up to the city people. "We'd like you to leave."

"That's no way to talk to our visitors. Please show some respect." The head of the village went back inside, sucking on his teeth. "You can see how hard this is going to be."

There was not much the city people could say after that.

"Perhaps we should go now," they said to the official who'd come with them. "When we're back in the city, we'll make a report and take it from there."

The official glanced at the crowd outside. "We've done all we can today," he said, then turned to the head of the village. "But this isn't the end of the matter, I can tell you!"

The head of the village nodded.

"Tell them to disperse," said the official.

The head of the village came outside again. "That's enough. Go away. They're leaving, and they're not taking Sunflower."

And with that, he led the line of visitors out of the office. The villagers politely stepped aside and let them pass.

After New Year's, when the weather suddenly turned warm and the wind began to howl again, the head of the village was called to see his superior.

"There's no room for discussion," said his superior. "You need to get on with it." They could wait a couple of days, he explained, or a couple of weeks, but it was just a matter of time. The instruction had come from the highest level, and it had to be carried out.

The mayor had made it his mission to demonstrate that his city had a conscience and a sense of responsibility. He wanted everyone to know that this little girl who had been left behind in the poor, remote countryside was at last coming back to her home city. But, he promised over and over again, it was to be done properly; the girl's parents were to understand that she would still be their daughter, and that in wanting her to come back to the city, he was thinking foremost of her future. It would also be a way of honoring her blood father. The mayor believed that the girl's parents would understand. He wrote personally to the head of the village on behalf of the entire city to pay their respects to the people of Damaidi and to the girl's parents.

The head of the village went to see the family again and read the letter to Baba and Mama. Baba said nothing. Mama was clearly upset.

"They have a point," said the head of the village. "It would be good for Sunflower. Think about it. What kind of life would she have if she stayed here in Damaidi? And what kind of life would she have if she went to the city? Two completely different lives! Everyone knows how painful it would be for you if she went. Everyone knows that. These past few years we've had disasters and hard times. Fortunately she was part of your family. Otherwise . . . Oh, it's hard to think about. We've all seen how you went without so that you could provide for Sunflower. When her *nainai* was alive"—at this point the head of the village had to wipe his eyes—"she treated her with such love and such care, always putting her first. . . ."

The head of the village sat down on a stool and kept talking. Baba hadn't said a word. Mama hadn't stopped weeping. Bronze and Sunflower hadn't appeared.

"Where are the two children?" the head of the village asked.

"I don't know," said Mama.

"Maybe they're hiding," said the head of the village.

Bronze and Sunflower really were hiding. It was Sunflower's idea. This time they didn't hide in the reeds. "There are snakes," Mama had told them. "You can't stay there too long."

So they hid on a big boat with an awning and let it drift about on the river. Only one person knew where they were hiding, and that was Gayu. He was out punting his little duck boat when he went past the big boat and noticed Bronze and Sunflower on board.

"Don't worry," he said, "I won't say anything." Bronze and Sunflower believed him. "Do you want me to tell your parents?" he asked. Bronze nodded.

"Tell them that we're hiding, but don't tell them where," said Sunflower.

"OK." Gayu punted his little boat and moved his ducks along the water.

Quietly he passed the message on to Mama. When he saw how worried she looked, he said, "Don't worry. I'll look out for them."

All the villagers, young and old, showed their loyalty. From then on, Gayu drove his ducks near, but not too near, the big boat.

"Your mama says you're to keep hidden and not come out."

Mama had said no such thing—it was Gayu himself who was saying this. At mealtimes, he would bring them food that Mama had prepared for them. He'd carry it in a basket, quietly put it on his duck boat, and quietly deliver it to the big boat.

The city people came again, five or six of them, this time on the white boat of the next administrative level up, and with them were another half-dozen people from the highest level of authority. The villagers recognized two of them as the women who had brought Sunflower to Damaidi all those years ago and sat with her under the big old tree. They had changed and looked a lot older now. When they saw the head of the village, they clasped their hands around his to show their respect. They tried to say something, but the words caught in their throats, and their eyes were blurry with tears.

The head of the village took them to see the Cadre School on the other side of the river, and as the two women stood in the overgrown wilderness, it brought back painful memories. Eventually they raised the matter of Sunflower's return to the city.

"We're discussing it right now," said the head of the village. "I seem to be making some headway with the girl's parents. But we need to take it slowly. You can all help to persuade them. You know, their feelings for her are so strong."

The two women wanted to see Sunflower. The head of the village said, "When they heard that you wanted to take her away, she persuaded her brother they should go and hide." Then he laughed. "Those two little devils could be anywhere."

"We could look for them," suggested the women.

"We've looked everywhere," said the head of the village. "Never mind. Let them hide for a while."

The next time Gayu saw Bronze and Sunflower he said, "Some people have come from the city. For goodness' sake, stay where you are."

Bronze and Sunflower nodded.

"There's nothing to be scared of. Just stay on the boat," said Gayu, then punted his little boat off after his ducks.

The head of the village took the two city women to Sunflower's house. As soon as Baba and Mama saw them, they froze for a moment, then jumped up from their stools.

"Sister! Brother!" cried the two women, reaching out with both hands. One of them clasped Baba's hands; the other clasped Mama's. In the years since they had last seen them, Baba and Mama had aged a lot. The women were shocked to see their dark, dull skin and their almost skeletal frames, and held their hands tightly, reluctant to let go.

"I'll leave you to talk," said the head of the village.

One of the aunties wore glasses now, and it was she who did most of the talking.

"So many years have passed. We've often thought about coming to see Sunflower and her family. But we couldn't bear the thought of troubling you.

"We'd ask how she was getting on here. We knew she had a good life. We discussed coming back, but none of us wanted to alarm her, or you."

Gradually the conversation turned to taking Sunflower back to the city. There were tears in Mama's eyes.

The woman described all the arrangements that had been made: which school Sunflower would go to (the best school in the city), who she would live with (the one with the glasses, who had a daughter about the same age as Sunflower), when she could come back to Damaidi to see them (she would spend the winter and summer school vacations there), and so on. It was clear that the people in the city had put a lot of thought and consideration into this.

"She will always be your daughter," she said.

"If you miss her, you can go and stay in the city

too," said the other one. "The mayor has told the city committee's guesthouse that you can stay there whenever you wish."

"We know this will be hard for you. I would feel the same way."

"And clearly the child herself doesn't want to go."

Mama let out a cry. Both women put an arm around her shoulder.

"Sister, sister!" they said, and they cried too.

Villagers had been arriving to see what was happening. They stood both inside and outside the house. "We only want what's best for the child," the older woman told them. "Nothing else."

The villagers were less belligerent than before. They were beginning to come around to the city people's way of thinking.

That night the two women stayed with the family. The next day, the head of the village came back.

"Any news?" he asked.

"Our sister has agreed," one of them replied.

"And the others?" he asked.

"Our brother has agreed too," said the other.

"Good, good, good!" said the head of the village.

"It's in the child's best interests. Damaidi's a poor place, and we don't want to let her down."

"If she's the considerate child you say she is, then she'll never forget the kindness she's known in Damaidi," said the auntie.

"You cannot imagine how considerate she is. Everyone loves her. These good people will be heart-broken when she goes!" said the head of the village, pointing to Baba and Mama.

The two women were nodding in agreement.

"And then there's her mute brother. . . ." The head of the village was touching his nose, trying to hold in the tears. "What will he do without her?"

Mama burst out sobbing.

"Don't cry, don't cry," said the head of the village. "It's not as though she's not coming back. Wherever she goes, she'll still be your daughter. Please stop crying. When the child sets out for the city, you mustn't cry. Think about it. She'll have a good future ahead of her. You should be happy for her!" he said, dabbing the corner of his eye.

Mama nodded. The head of the village passed a cigarette to Baba and lit it for him.

Baba took a long drag, then asked, "When do you want to leave?"

"There's no hurry," said the women.

"Where did you moor the boat?" he asked.

"The head of the county and the mayor have agreed that the boat can wait here as long as we need," said one of the women.

"In that case," said the head of the village, "tell the children to come home and spend some time together as a family."

"But I don't know where they are," said Mama.

"I do," said the head of the village.

He'd been watching the big boat floating on the river.

The head of the village took Mama to the river.

"Sunflower!" she called out. There was no answer. "Sunflower!" she shouted again. There was still no answer. "You can come out. It's safe," said Mama.

Only then did Bronze and Sunflower open the cabin door and show their faces. She told them to come home.

Mama began to collect Sunflower's things. She kept herself busy, saying what needed to be said, doing what needed to be done.

Mostly, the two children stood or sat to one side, watching. They didn't know what to do. They stopped hiding. There didn't seem to be any point now. Mama said nothing as she began packing up Sunflower's things. She'd be busy doing this and that, and then she'd suddenly stop and look blank.

Mama opened up her trunk and from the bottom of it took the jade bracelet that Nainai had given her for Sunflower. She looked at it and remembered the gold ring and jade earrings that Nainai used to wear.

"Apart from her clothes Nainai didn't keep anything for herself." She sighed, then wrapped the jade bracelet carefully in a piece of cloth and put it in a little wicker basket, which was already full of Sunflower's things.

That evening Mama and Sunflower slept side by side.

"If you're homesick, you can come back. They've already said that all you have to do is tell them you want to come home, and someone will bring you.

When you get there, you have to study hard. Don't think about Damaidi. It'll still be here; it's not going to fly away. And don't worry about us—we'll be just fine. And if we miss you, then we'll come and see you. Be happy that you're going, because if you're happy, then Baba, Bronze, and I will be happy too. You'll have to write to us, and I'll tell Bronze to write back to you. Your aunties will be good to you. That year, when they were sitting with you under the old tree, I could see they had kind faces and kind hearts. You must do what they say. When you go to bed, try and tuck your arms under the cover. You'll have to wash your own feet before you go to bed; you can't ask your auntie to do it. You're a big girl now; you have to wash your own feet. From now on, you'll have to look after yourself. Don't walk around with your head in the clouds all the time. There are cars in the city, and they're dangerous. It's not like around here, where if you don't look where you're going, the worst you'll end up with is a mouthful of mud. And don't get all excited like you do with Bronze, Cuihuan, and the girls. You'll have to see what your new friends are like first. . . ."

Mama's instructions flowed on and on, just like the river.

During Sunflower's last days in Damaidi, the villagers often saw a paper lantern bobbing about in the fields at night, stopping for a while in the sunflower fields and in front of Nainai's grave.

The head of the village came by. "Are you going to let her go?" he asked.

Baba nodded. Mama was more cautious. "I'm scared that when the time comes, Bronze won't let her go," she said.

"Haven't you discussed this with him already?"

"Yes," said Mama, "but you know Bronze — he's not like other children. If he has a wild notion in his head, no one can hold him back."

The head of the village said, "Try to keep him away."

When the day came, Mama told Bronze, "Go to Grandma's house and fetch the shoe patterns. I'd like to make another pair of shoes for Sunflower."

"Now?" asked Bronze.

"Yes, now," said Mama.

Bronze nodded and went to Grandma's. Meanwhile,

the head of the village was hurrying the city people along. "It's time to be going," he told them.

The white boat had been moored at the pier since it arrived. The engine started up, and the boat moved along the river, closer to Sunflower's house. While Baba took her things on board, Sunflower stood on the bank, clutching Mama's hand. The entire village seemed to be standing at the riverside.

"Time's moving on," said the head of the village.

Mama nudged Sunflower, never expecting that she would throw her arms around her waist and wail, "I'm not going! I'm not going!"

Many of the villagers had to look away. Cuihuan, Gayu, and the other children started to cry. Mama pushed Sunflower forward. The head of the village gave a big sigh, went over to Sunflower, picked her up, turned around, and headed toward the boat. Sunflower flailed her arms in the air, screaming, "MAMA! BABA! BRONZE!" She kept screaming for Bronze, but he wasn't there. Mama turned her head away.

The head of the village carried her aboard the boat

and delivered her to the aunties. Sunflower struggled, but the women held her tight and said over and over again, "Be good, Sunflower! Be good! If you get homesick, we'll bring you back. This will always be your home. And your brother and baba and mama can come to see you in the city!"

Gradually, Sunflower became calmer, though she was still sobbing.

"It's time to go!" said the head of the village. The engine started up again. A plume of black smoke sputtered out of the stern and onto the water. Sunflower opened the wicker basket, took out the jade bracelet, and ran to the bow of the boat.

"Mama!" she shouted.

Mama came to the pier. Sunflower handed her the bracelet.

"I'll keep it safe for you," said Mama.

"Where's Bronze?"

"I told him to go to Grandma's. If he were here, he'd never let you go."

Tears streamed down Sunflower's face.

"It's time to leave now," shouted the head of the village. As he pushed the boat off with his foot, Mama and Sunflower were separated. The aunties came out of the cabin and stood with Sunflower at the prow, each holding one of Sunflower's hands.

The boat turned around. It paused for a moment, then, churning up spray, it dipped its stern into the water, raised its bow, and sped off, leaving Damaidi behind.

Anxious that Sunflower didn't have much time left, Bronze had run all the way to Grandma's and then all the way back. He arrived as the boat was heading downstream, a white dot no bigger than a dove on the horizon. He didn't cry or make a fuss; he just went numb.

From then on, he left the house early each morning and went to sit on top of a big haystack by the river. Some of the haystacks near the river were as high as mountains, as high as three-story city buildings. There was a white poplar near the haystack, and every morning Bronze would climb it and clamber onto the haystack. Then he sat completely still, facing the east. From here he could follow the river far into the distance. He could see the point where the white boat had disappeared from view.

No matter how bad the weather, Bronze spent all day, every day on the haystack. He was even seen there at night sometimes.

The villagers soon discovered where he was. At first, they came — both adults and children — to see him on the haystack, but as the days went by they tailed off until only the occasional visitor passed by.

"He's still up there," they'd say, out loud to whoever was there or silently to themselves.

One day, the rain came down in such torrents that it was almost impossible to see anything. The villagers heard Mama calling Bronze. They could hear the tears in her voice as she walked through the curtain of rain, and their hearts went out to her. But Bronze ignored his mother. The rain had smoothed down his hair, as it smoothed down the hay. His hair clung to his head, almost covering his eyes. As the water ran down from his brow, he blinked, forcing his eyes open again and holding them open wide as he stared down the river as far as he could, at the rain and at the vastness of the water.

When the rain stopped, people looked up at the haystack. Bronze was still there, but he seemed to have shrunk.

By midday, the low autumn sun was dazzling. The leaves on the plants were drooping or starting to curl. The buffaloes walked on the dust road near the end of the village and made their plaintive bellowing noises. Ducks hid in the shade of trees, their flat beaks open, their chests rising and falling. Villagers hurried across the open threshing ground, eager to get out of the baking heat. And still, Bronze sat on the haystack.

"The sun'll kill him up there," said one of the older people.

Mama would have fallen to her knees and begged him to come down if only it would have made any difference. They could all see how thin he was getting, as lean as a monkey.

As Bronze stared ahead, the sunlight spiraled like a whirlpool and the river glowed with golden heat.

The villages, trees, and windmills, and the people on the roads and on the boats, all seemed to be an illusion, both real and unreal. It was as if he were seeing things through a curtain of rain, as if their forms were always changing. Sweat dripped off his chin into the hay. He saw everything as gold, then black, then red, then all the colors of the rainbow.

Bronze felt the haystack begin to move, and then gradually to sway, until it was swaying like a boat on the river. At some stage he must have turned around: he was no longer looking at the river but at the fields. The fields were underwater, even the sky seemed to be in the water.

Bronze looked straight ahead. He rubbed his eyes. They stung from the sweat. He rubbed them again.

She seemed to be running as if through a screen of rain toward his haystack. But she was completely silent—in a silent, fluid world. He staggered to his feet on top of the haystack. It was clearly her, running through the rain toward him. He ran to meet her.

Bronze lay on the ground, completely still, completely quiet. When he came around, he leaned against the haystack for support and slowly pulled himself up.

There she was, running through the screen of haze, waving to him.

He opened his mouth, summoned all the strength in his body, and shouted, "SUNFLOWER!"

Tears were flooding down his face.

Gayu was out with his ducks. When he heard Bronze shout, he was astonished.

Bronze shouted again, "SUNFLOWER!"

The sound wasn't perfectly clear, but it had definitely come out of Bronze's mouth. Gayu left the ducks and ran to Bronze's house, and as he ran he shouted out so all the villagers could hear, "Bronze can speak! He can speak!"

Bronze ran like crazy from the haystack to the fields.

Sunshine spilled over the boundless fields of sunflowers, filled with thousands and thousands of stems whose big round heads were turning, just as they should, to face the golden body of heaven as it rolled across the sky.

Historical Note

Bronze and Sunflower is set in rural China in the late 1960s and early 1970s, during a time known as the Cultural Revolution, when the political situation in the cities was very tense. The Chinese authorities sent huge numbers of professional people (known as "cadres") from the cities to labor camps (known as "cadre schools") in remote rural areas. These were educated people who had worked in government offices, universities, and schools. Many had never been to the countryside before and found living there extremely hard. Like Sunflower's father, they spent all day doing physical labor and then had to attend political meetings in the evening. It was exhausting. Children like Sunflower who went to the cadre schools with their parents were often left to play by themselves.

Farming the land and looking after the animals was backbreaking work for the villagers who had always lived in the countryside. Natural disasters such as plagues of locusts could be life threatening or ruinous, especially for poor families like Bronze's. The villagers and the cadres came from very different backgrounds. They didn't always understand one another, but they had to get along as well as they could.

In the early 1970s, as the Cultural Revolution had run its course, the cadre schools were closed, and the city people returned to the cities.

Author's Note

In the 1990s, a friend told me stories about her childhood. Her father worked in one of the government ministries and was sent to a cadre school in the countryside. When she went to stay with him, he couldn't spend time with her because he had to work on the land. She got bored and went to play with the children in the village across the river. As she was talking, the endless reed marshes of my own childhood drifted into my mind. There'd been a cadre school hidden in the reeds. I knew what life was like at a cadre school, so I thought this might be a good setting for a book.

For a long time it was just an idea. Then one day I started wondering what it would be like for a little girl to move from the city to a small village in the middle of nowhere and to make friends with the village children. And I thought if two children from very different worlds could become close friends, that would make a special story, with the contrast of city life and country life in the background. So, more than a decade after that conversation with my friend, I had what I needed: the setting, the characters, and the plot. But the different parts of the story weren't coming together—they were like islands in the sea, and I didn't feel ready to start writing, so I put it to one side.

A few years later, the night before Chinese New Year, I thought I should get on with writing this book. After all, I already had plenty of good material for the story. But I still couldn't put pen to paper; I felt something was missing. Then, at about half past five the next morning—I remember it so clearly—I was lying in bed when all of a sudden four Chinese characters appeared in front of me: 青铜葵花 . . . Bronze and Sunflower. It just happened; just like that. And when I saw them, everything fell into place. The boy was named Bronze; the girl was named Sunflower. I saw fields of sunflowers reaching into the distance, then Sunflower's father appeared—an artist, a sculptor who'd spent a lifetime creating sunflowers in bronze.

At last, my story had a soul. It seeped into all the material I had prepared and brought it alive. And I realized that this was what I had been waiting for.

Discussion Questions

1. This novel has many themes, including family, poverty, loyalty, and community. How do these themes interact?

2. Based on what Sunflower thinks, says, and does, how would you describe her? What is important to her? What are her strengths? How does she change over the course of the story? What about Bronze?

3. What are the key relationships in the novel? How do they change over the course of the story?

4. Why do you think the villagers were so reluctant to take Sunflower in? Why do you think Bronze's family decided to take her in?

5. The setting is very important to the novel, including the location and time. What do the villagers eat, what do their houses look like, and what do they do for work? How does this shape their lives?

Hans Christian Andersen Award winner Cao Wenxuan
offers a family saga during a time of upheaval in the
reimagined rural China of the Cultural Revolution.

Dragonfly Eyes

Cao Wenxuan

translated from the Chinese by **Helen Wang**

1960s Shanghai is a hard place to grow
up, especially for Ah-Mei since she doesn't
look like the rest of her family. But Ah-Mei
and her French grandmother, Nainai, share
a tender bond—even when they have
nothing else.

CAO WENXUAN is a professor of Chinese literature at Peking University and one of China's most important writers for children. He has won several of China's most prestigious awards for children's literature and is the 2016 recipient of the international Hans Christian Andersen Award. Many of his books have become bestsellers in China, and his work has been translated into French, Russian, Japanese, and Korean. *Bronze and Sunflower* is his first full-length book to be translated into and published in English.

HELEN WANG studied Chinese at the University of London's School of Oriental and African Studies and is now a curator at the British Museum. She has been translating from Chinese into English for more than twenty years. She lives in London.